Henrietta Dorothy Everett (January 1851–September 16, 1923) was born in Kent, England to John and Julia Huskisson. At 18, she married a solicitor, Isaac Edward Everett (1845-1904). She began her writing career in 1896 at the age of 44. Between that time and 1920, she published 22 books under the pen name Theo Douglas. Beyond these basic contours, very little is known about her life. She enjoyed popular success in her time and was an influential figure in the early days of science fiction and fantasy writing, cited in H.P. Lovecraft's extended 1927 essay "Supernatural Horror in Literature." Many of the esoteric themes found in *One or Two* were repeated throughout Everett's body of work, especially interrogations of material embodiment and the location of the eternal soul. These works include *Iras: A Mystery* (1896), the story of a doomed love affair between an Egyptologist and a beautiful mummy, and *Nemo* (1900), in which the protagonist's soul is entrapped in an automaton.

Madeline Porsella is a cofounder and editor of Mandylion Press. In her spare time, she is pursuing a PhD in History of Art at Yale University.

MY
MANDYLION
BOOK

H.D. Everett
Introduction by Madeline Porsella

Mandylion Press
New York

Originally published in 1907 by Brown Langham & Co., Ltd.

Mandylion Press
c/o Mabel Taylor
PO Box 84
Cold Spring, New York 10516

Copyright © Mandylion Press, 2025
Introduction copyright © Madeline Porsella, 2025

ISBN 979-8-9886061-3-0

All rights reserved. No part of this book may be reproduced in any form by any electronic or mechanical means (including photocopying, recording, or information storage and retrieval) without written permission from Mandylion Press.

Printed and bound in Lithuania.

Available through ARTBOOK
D.A.P. 75 Broad Street, Suite 630 New York, NY 10004
www.artbook.com.

Designed by Emily Wissemann.

Front and Back Cover Images: Plates from Baron von Schrenck Notzing, *Phenomena of Materialisation: A Contribution to the Investigation of Mediumistic Teleplastics*, translated by E. E. Fournier d'Albe. London: K. Paul, Trench, Trubner, E. P. Dutton, 1923.

Jacket Flap Image: Plate showing Tubercular Lung from Vol. 1 of *The Journal of Roentgenology*. Iowa City, Iowa: Western Roentgen Society, 1918.

www.mandylionpress.com
@mandylionpress

One or Two

A Romance

Punctuation Personified: or, Pointing Made Easy
(London: John Harris, 1824).

Punctuation (and Editorial) Note

"Yikes,—punctuation in the nineteenth century; why so complicated!?—We should do something about it!'" Mandylion Press publishes novels that, on a good day, languish on the dusty shelves of libraries. Our goal is to pluck these literary gems out of obscurity and share them with a wide community of readers. To that end, we strive to make our books as legible as possible. We strategically excise unnecessary punctuation and hyphenation and make minor adjustments to spelling and style to ensure a seamless reading experience.

CONTENTS

CHAPTER					PAGE
	INTRODUCTION				
I.	SCHOOL FRIENDS	-	-	-	1
II.	CATCHING AT A STRAW	-	-	-	11
III.	SALVADOR	-	-	-	22
IV.	THE EXPERIMENT BEGINS		-	-	34
V.	THE FOURTH VIGIL	-	-	-	48
VI.	SWORN TO SILENCE	-	-	-	57
VII.	THE BELL RINGS	-	-	-	67
VIII.	DIFFICULT QUESTIONS	-	-	-	77
IX.	HOSTESS AND GUEST	-	-	-	89
X.	LADY SARAH	-	-	-	100
XI.	THE DOCTOR IS CALLED IN		-	-	112
XII.	A CONFIDENCE TO MAXWORTHY		-	124
XIII.	IN THE ROSE GARDEN	-	-	-	141
XIV.	TWO WIVES	-	-	-	155
XV.	THE LOST RING	-	-	-	169
XVI.	A LATE CONFESSION	-	-	-	181
XVII.	"WENN DU DAS HERZ HAST—"		-	193
	GLOSSARY				211

Introduction

Is it possible to interest the reader in a heroine who is a victim to adipose tissue?—A fat man is not so hopeless.... But a fat woman is beyond the pale of sympathy. Her aspirations must of necessity be ridiculous, her very woes become comic, and all because of that fifty or sixty pounds of unnecessary flesh. The fat woman of fiction may serve as a devoted nurse or a passably good cook, but she is completely out of place in any situation tender or tragical: no average novel-devourer could be moved to drop a tear over her woe.

I suppose, given my larger intellectual project of insisting that the present day is simply an amplification and acceleration of problems born in the nineteenth century, that the quote above shouldn't surprise me. Or rather, I shouldn't be surprised that this quote could describe the current media landscape and ongoing conversations about body image and positivity. The assumption that the fat woman's weight is not just a problem but *the* problem, is itself indicative of a worldview that remains largely unchallenged today. There cannot be a fat female protagonist whose singular problem is not that she is fat.

In Henrietta Dorothy Everett's metaphysical melodrama, *One or Two*, Frances Bethune née Wayland is plagued by the weight she has gained since returning to England from India where her husband, Colonel Bethune, remains, serving in the British colonial army. When Colonel Bethune is unexpectedly dispatched home to England, Frances frantically searches for a quick fix to her woes. Realizing that no modern medicine is strong enough to return her to the slim girl she once was, Frances recruits Ursula Adams, a girlhood friend with whom she has been recently reacquainted at a séance, to summon supernatural help. The two women call on the spirit realm to reduce Frances's size. But meddling with unknown forces proves risky. Rather than dissipating, Frances's unwanted bulk transforms into a double, a manifestation of her soul divided. This doppelganger takes the form of a younger version of Frances, called Fancy after a childhood nickname. Fancy, a lovesick girl of eighteen, believes it is the eve of her engagement to Colonel Bethune a decade prior. While Fancy embodies the sweet, naive, hopeful soul of the young lover, Frances is left hollowed out, thin but empty—heartless, vain and cruel.

Everett began her career publishing under the pen name Theo Douglas, but after her identity was revealed in 1910 she started publishing under the name Mrs. H. D. Everett. Her father was a first lieutenant in the Royal Marines, her husband a solicitor. Little else is known about the prolific writer. About her 1920 collection of ghost stories, H. P. Lovecraft wrote, "Mrs. H. D. Everett, though adhering to very old and conventional models, occasionally reaches singular heights of spiritual terror." Esoteric subject matter is a through line in her work, beginning with *Iras: A Mystery* (1896)—the story of a doomed love affair between an Egyptologist and a beautiful mummy, and *Nemo* (1900)—in which the protagonist's soul is trapped in an automaton. In both of these stories, as in *One or Two*,

Everett grappled with the problem of embodiment and the precise location of the immortal soul.

The premise of *One or Two*—namely that all of Frances Bethune's problems would be solved if she weighed 125 pounds—is one that most women I know can relate to. The perfect partner, social life, and career all seem to hang in the balance. In the novel, Frances's transformation is her undoing, not her salvation. Though the book's ending seems to reinforce the idea that Colonel Bethune could only love the younger, prettier version of Frances Wayland, it is her personality that he prefers, not her physicality. He is never given the opportunity to love his wife in a larger body. Instead, Frances banishes her adorable traits—her romanticism, her naivete—in her monomaniacal pursuit of thinness. Ursula even speculates that the romantic Colonel would have greeted his changed wife "without reproach or recrimination," ready to love her as he had before, regardless of her appearance. Meanwhile, "Frances was meeting it after her manner, with all this despair about the measure of her waist, and her register upon the scales. Perhaps neither woman was wholly in the right, the one in losing sight of the ideal, and the other of the practical." Here is the story's true tragedy: Frances Bethune's mortal wound is self-inflicted, founded on an assumption about the conditions of her husband's love. Her desperation to be thin originates within herself. She is blind to all else, denying herself the possibility of a happy ending.

Without regard to the consequences, Frances was willing to do anything, even summon spirits, in pursuit of the slender figure she enjoyed in her youth. I too have been obsessed with disappearing in this manner for as long as I can remember. When I was younger, I became a historian of the diets of famous women—famous thin women, though the two descriptions are essentially synonymous—reciting them to myself in nightly devotions, counting off calories like rosary beads. Jackie O. limited herself to a single baked potato with sour cream and a dollop of beluga caviar daily, while Wallis Simpson survived on scotch and soda, and Gwyneth Paltrow on baby food. I learned to be bulimic. With 127 pounds as my North Star, I navigated through early adulthood believing that once I arrived at that number I would be free to focus on other things—love, career, intellectual fulfillment, "any situation tender or tragical." It wasn't until college, when I met a boy who was obsessed with the diets of famous philosophers, that I realized that people ate for reasons other than thinness. He told me that Kant followed the guidelines Michael Pollan would recommend three hundred years later: "Eat food, not too much, mostly plants"; Nietzsche avoided alcohol and German food, preferring oil to butter; and Schopenhauer advocated vegetarianism. My classmate was interested, he explained, in how diet affects the mind. Like Frances, it had not occurred to me that my obsession with thinness could have a negative impact upon my intellect or my soul. I had never considered, in my years of obsession, what else I would be losing if I lost weight.

In purely scientific terms, weight loss is a side effect of metabolic function: when the body requires energy in excess of calories ingested, fat stores are drawn into the blood, muscle, and lungs, where they are broken down for use. When broken down, fat is converted into carbon dioxide which is then exhaled. Yet in a culture that privileges thinness, this simple process takes on an almost religious significance. There is a metaphysical quality to weight loss: what was once a solid part of the physical body evaporates into thin air, leaving no trace.

When Ursula discovers Fancy, the young girl made up of Frances's discarded weight, she is unnerved to find that "when she touched it with a reluctant finger, it was warm and soft with the warmth of living flesh." Expecting dissipation, Ursula and Frances are shocked and dismayed by the stubborn persistence of Frances's unwanted mass. The pathos of Everett's era is on full display here. Spiritualism, a religious belief system that animates the action of *One or Two*, took hold of the popular imagination in the nineteenth century. The religion originated in 1848, when three girls from a remote town in upstate New York began hearing—or producing—disembodied knocking sounds around their family home. The Fox Sisters, as they came to be known, drew national attention for hosting well-attended public séances in Rochester and New York City. In these demonstrations, the sisters communicated with the dead via a spirit proxy whom they called Mr. Splitfoot. Arthur Conan Doyle, a devoted Spiritualist, wrote that the Fox Sisters intercepted spirit messages on topics as diverse as "the state of railway stocks or the issue of love affairs."

Over the second half of the nineteenth century, Spiritualist practice was formalized. Spiritualists believed that after death, an individual's immortal soul remained intact in a suprasensory realm. Séances provided settings in which imperceptible spirit realms were made accessible to highly sensitive people (usually women) known as mediums. Ironically, these extraordinary events often occurred in commonplace settings, such as the drawing rooms of *One or Two*, led by lower class women like the seamstress Mrs. Warden. In addition to Spiritualism's popularity, Everett was writing during a period marked by scientific and technological disruptions to how the material world was known. Germ theory, electric light, X-rays, telegraphs, and telephones all demonstrated the very real impact of invisible phenomena on observable reality. These discoveries also opened formerly skeptical minds to the possibilities of other extrasensory forces, like those purportedly at work in Spiritualist séances. When presented with irrefutable proof of immaterial worlds that existed beyond their perception, scientists and occultists alike sought new ways to understand the unstable nature of a world they had previously accepted as solid. When Ursula Adams is confronted with Fancy Wayland's soft pink flesh, she is horrified because "materialised shapes were said to be evanescent." For the characters in *One or Two*, it is not dissipation that is surprising, it is the persistent existence of matter in the face of these suprasensory forces. In Ursula's previous experience with Spiritualist materialisations, they "had melted into air."

This dissipation of the physical body in the late 1890s, during which *One or Two* is set, is exemplified by the widespread popularity of X-ray images. In 1895, the German physicist Wilhelm Röntgen (1845–1923) accidentally discovered the X-ray while experimenting with a cathode ray tube. His arresting images of skeletal hands, the result of exposing photographic plates with X-rays instead of light, captured the popular imagination; X-ray booths were set-up in department stores and cinemas. Not only did the appearance of the X-ray call subjective sensual experience into question, it upended assumptions about the very nature of the material world. Previously impenetrable, flesh fell away under Röntgen's rays. Spiritualist texts frequently used the X-ray to rationalize the existence of clairvoyance and telepathic communications. For Spiritualists who sought scientific explanations for the phenomena seen at séances, Röntgen's discovery seemed to confirm long-standing occult beliefs about a "real" world, a realm of higher being, beyond the limited powers of human perception. These unlikely bedfellows—science and occultism—are personified in *One or Two* by the spirit medium Mrs. Warden and the rational Dr. Maxworthy. Before Ursula and Frances conduct their slenderizing séance, Ursula recounts Mrs. Warden's pseudoscientific description of the pliability of her weight:

> She is a large thick-set person, if you remember, but she told us she could be slender if she chose. The extra substance about her body is all used—drawn out of her—when the spirits materialize; and then they put it back to serve for another time.... She said if we could only see her while the process is going on, she would appear quite small.

Dr. Maxworthy later accepts this explanation of Frances's sudden weight loss. While Mrs. Warden's Spiritualism and Maxworthy's scientific rationality may seem incompatible today, the line between science and the occult was more permeable at the time Everett was writing. *One or Two* demonstrates how the two categories were themselves in flux. In private, Maxworthy applies his rational thought to more esoteric subject matter, treatises "on Double Consciousness and the Suspensions of Trance," which he publishes "under a pseudonym, so as not to scare away his patients."

In 1848, the same year the Fox Sisters first encountered Mr. Splitfoot, Karl Marx published his *Communist Manifesto*. The obvious Marxist metaphor to draw through an analysis of *One or Two* would be that of the fatted bourgeoisie, personified in Frances Bethune, creating the tools of its own destruction through an endless appetite for disruption and accumulation. Bethune's collaborator is lean working-class Ursula, whose economic precarity leads her to compromise her religious and moral values for the few dollars that would be the "butter to the very dry bread of small means." However, addressing a discontented Europe in the midst of sweeping revolutions, Marx describes not only ongoing class struggles, but also the subtler and more nefarious reconfiguration of material conditions that occurred as free-market capitalism replaced centuries-old hierarchies of production. Value was increasingly determined not by use or skill, but by a never-ending process of circulation and abstraction. In place of the stability propagated through previous generations of Europeans by monarchies and guilds, industrial capitalism had installed a regime of "everlasting uncertainty and agitation." Employing the same metaphor that Everett would later use to describe Spiritualist phenomena, Marx famously condensed the period's myriad changes: "All that is solid melts into air."

One or Two is set nearly fifty years after both Marx and the Fox Sisters had—in their own ways—augured the coming era's obsession with the immaterial. Everett grapples with persistent metaphysical questions about the weight of material reality in a world that, with each new innovation, slipped further and further away. In this age of technological disruption, it is significant that women contacting the spirit realm were called "mediums." At the time, the word was being adopted to describe new modes of communication. In the eighteenth century, "medium" was widely used to mean "environment," the medium humans occupied was ether or air, while that of fish was water. With the invention of the telegraph in the 1830s, the definition of "medium" narrowed: what had once referred to any organism's environment now referred to the intraspecies correspondence of humans. Spirit mediums imitated the action of the telegraph insofar as they facilitated the rapid exchange of information by collapsing distances previously thought insurmountable. The mass adoption of the telegraph was soon followed by photography and the invention of telephones, mediums that further allowed people to communicate with each other without the necessity of being present face to face. Media theorist John Durham Peters has argued that "in photography or cinema, in sound recording or telephone, effigies of personal identity only loosely tethered to the body could circulate in a new spirit world." In this new world, the best physical bodies could do was "catch up with the phantasms" that preceded them.

In *One or Two*'s pendant publication, *The Morgesons* (1862) by Elizabeth Stoddard, the act of two girls looking at each other becomes a proto-photographic medium. Everett represents this exchange, instead, as a kind of haunting—each woman pursuing an image of herself through her relationship to the other. Today, this pursuit has been heightened to absurd extremes, realizing early photography theorist Oliver Wendell Holmes's prediction that "form is henceforth divorced from matter." Women mistreat their real bodies to create images for circulation—phantasms they will perpetually pursue, yet never reach. In the world of accelerated image consumption we inhabit, Mandylion Press believes that mooring images to words and words to images restores us to the world of the real. To that end, we have included a Visual Glossary at the end of this book, creating constellations of images in the hopes that our stories won't move through this new spirit world unaccompanied.

Everett leaves it to the reader to decide, at the book's end, whether Frances's is a story worth telling. We must answer her with a resounding "yes." But we are not interested in rehashing the same old discussions about women's bodies and thinness. Everett's novel is valuable because it allows us to probe the moral and metaphysical questions that accompany extreme weight loss. While Everett is telling a classic Victorian morality tale—in which goodness is

xix

equivalent to beauty and wickedness manifests ugliness—she also grapples with upheavals in how the material world was understood in the second half of the nineteenth century. The novel's fundamental questions are not about morality but matter, and what it means to be both a body and the spirit that animates it.

— *Madeline Porsella*
New Haven, Connecticut

Sources

Doyle, Arthur Conan. *The History of Spiritualism (Vols. 1 and 2)*. London: Cassell & Co., 1926.

Holmes, Oliver Wendell. "The Stereoscope and the Stereograph." In *Classic Essays on Photography*, ed. Alan Trachtenberg. New Haven, Connecticut: Leete's Island Books, 1980.

Lovecraft, H.P. "Supernatural Horror in Literature." *The Recluse* (August, 1927).

Marx, Karl and Friedrich Engels. *The Communist Manifesto* (1848). Chicago: Charles H. Kerr & Co., 1906.

Peters, John Durham. *The Marvelous Clouds: Toward a Philosophy of Elemental Media*. London: The University of Chicago Press, 2015.

ONE OR TWO

𝔄 Romance

BY
THEO DOUGLAS

AUTHOR OF
"Miss Caroline," "A Golden Trust," etc.

BROWN LANGHAM & CO., LTD.,
78 New Bond Street, London, W.

1907

I.
SCHOOL FRIENDS

It is the amiable few, and not the irascible many, who are patient when interrupted; though the urchin scholar may hail any disturbance which breaks in on his detested lessons, and perhaps the devotee does not quarrel with a summons calling him away from that dismal business of the self-inflicted scourge. Ursula Adams drew her dark brows together in the pucker of a frown, as she laid down her graving-tool, and took the dainty envelope her landlady held out, a fold of apron protecting it from the impact of a blackened finger and thumb.

"Yes, ma'am, just come from The Mount, and the messenger seemed in a hurry. He said as how Mrs. Bethune had told him to take back word."

The good woman fell back a step or two, and folded her hands complacently. The situation afforded her a certain satisfaction. Her cottage lodgings were cheap and small, such as suit with narrow purses; and it pleased her to have a real born lady in them, if only for once, on intimate terms with Mrs. Bethune of The Mount, which was the great house of the neighbourhood. She felt her own importance exalted when liveried servants called at her door, and sometimes a carriage and pair stopped the way in the green lane below, and Mrs. Bethune waited there for Mrs. Adams. For Mrs. Bethune was accustomed always to be driven, even the short distance between the great house and the cottage. Though still quite a young woman, walking had become irksome to her by reason of a certain misfortune—an ill that flesh is heir to, and more especially indolent flesh.

Meanwhile Mrs. Adams opened her letter, ruthlessly breaking through the delicate initial which distinguished the envelope. That impatient knitting of the brow continued as she read, though the contents were brief.

"Tell the messenger to say yes. I will be there in half an hour." She glanced back at the open page, a single page of writing. "And, Mrs. Minter," in a suaver tone, as one mindful of compensations— "you can keep the cold mutton over for tomorrow. I shall stay to lunch with Mrs. Bethune."

The landlady withdrew, and Ursula Adams proceeded to cover the block on which she had been working, and fit back her tools into the case. "Another three hours," she was saying fretfully, in that internal colloquy which becomes a habit of solitude, "and I could have had it ready to send in. Never mind, I must make up time when I get back, and I have still a day to spare." The work was important to her, for it meant butter to the very dry bread of small means; but the summons had importance also, from another point of view. For Mrs. Adams was the chosen friend and confidante of her rich neighbour at The Mount, and sundry indirect advantages accrued from that association, though no salary was offered or received for a serious tax upon her time. The friendship dated back to their mutual schooldays, now remote by the passage of a decade. But it suffered interruption, as such friendships will, when the two girls drifted apart and into the altered interests of marriage, and had only of late been renewed through an accidental encounter.

It had been a close friendship once—ardent and almost loverlike, as the attachment of very young girls is apt to be, one for another; clinging and adoring on the side of Frances, admiring and protecting on that of Ursula; the weaker nature, slight and sweet, imposing the weight of its own helplessness upon the strong, after a fashion not uncommon. And it was the ashes of this flame which Ursula raked together with a stick or two of circumstance, to serve in these later days to warm her hands by—as she was apt to think cynically to herself. For the solitary young widow had a vein of bitterness in her nature; sorrow and sordid struggle combined to harden her. She was accustomed to regard the world as her oyster, which she with sword would open—or any less magniloquent tool which came handy, and would not soil her fingers. For as to soil she was wont to be fastidious, whether typical or actual. Just at this time it served her purpose to attach herself to Frances Bethune; and so, in spite of some self-contempt, she lingered on at Saltringham till a better opening should induce her to strike the pole of her tent, and wander forth like an Arab nomad into pastures new.

Her work put aside, she turned back to the letter, checking the impulse to tear it through till she had glanced again over the brief message it contained. "Dearest Ursula," it began. "I am in the *greatest* trouble," —with many dashes under the adjective. "I have had unexpected news—such news!—and I don't know what to do. Come at once and advise me. My hand shakes so, I can hardly write. Your utterly distracted—FRANCES."

The dainty initial F. which marked the envelope, headed this sheet also in curves and tendrils. It stood for many fond names, as well as for the commonplace Frances. Ursula remembered how a doting father used to shower them upon her when she still was Frances Wayland. She was his Fay, his Fairy, his Fanchette, but more commonly and enduringly his Fancy. Which did Colonel Bethune call her by in these later days of marriage, queried the widow. But that did not come within her knowledge. Colonel Bethune, far away in India, was known to Ursula only by hearsay, in school-girl times as the Paladin with whom Frances was desperately in love—latterly as the distant husband who had become of little account in her altered life.

The letter was torn across by this time, and tossed into the waste-basket, and Ursula was hurriedly arraying herself in the cottage chamber overhead—a small bare place, where the roof sloped inconveniently low on either side, and the wretched square of mirror in the dormer window shut out more than half the light. But, wretched as it was, Mrs. Adams surveyed herself in it with some satisfaction as she fastened her plain black gown, and clasped the belt about her slender waist. She still wore black for the husband whose death had left her a widow ere she ceased to be a bride—black, or those soft half-tones of grey and touches of violet which are pretty in themselves, and becoming to an emergent mourner. She could not wear anything livelier, she was used to say, because of poor Keith—though Keith had now been more than six years dead, and even when he was alive, poor fellow, had never inspired her with a grand passion, such as Frances once entertained for Colonel Bethune.

Yes, there was a distinct satisfaction in her face as she contemplated her own trim figure. Here at least the advantage was on her side, and not on Frances Bethune's, though Frances was the rich woman and she the poor one. Frances was her junior by two important years, the years from twenty-eight to thirty. Frances could within reasonable limits indulge her every caprice; and yet she would have given it all, and perhaps the husband in India into the bargain, for that same slenderness of shape which the elder woman had successfully preserved.

Is it possible to interest the reader in a heroine who is a victim to adipose tissue?—A fat man is not so hopeless. Readers by the hundred thousand have thrilled over the villainies, have delighted in the daring, of a certain Count Fosco, perhaps the fattest serious character in Victorian fiction. But a fat woman is beyond the pale of sympathy. Her aspirations must of necessity be ridiculous, her very woes become comic, and all because of that fifty or sixty pounds of unnecessary flesh. The fat woman of fiction may serve as a devoted nurse or a passably good cook, but she is completely out of place in any situation tender or tragical: no average novel-devourer could be moved to drop a tear over her woe.

And yet it is precisely this woe of Frances Bethune's with which the reader is asked to sympathise. If the lady of The Mount had followed the fashions of ordinary human- ity, and remained shapely and commonplace, a certain extraordinary hazard and perilous perplexity would never have come about, and there would have been no story worth relating. As it is, the question of worth hangs in the balance, and must be measured at the end of the tale, and not at the beginning.

Though Mrs. Adams was well contented with her own reflection in the cottage glass, she did not waste time in regarding it. The short distance was soon traversed between her country lodging, and a side gate which admitted her to the policies of The Mount. She was at a loss to conjecture what had prompted the urgency of the summons, but her knowledge of Frances did not lead her to apprehend any serious emergency. It was altogether in her friend's character to suffer from these transient despairs, and fling herself, a helpless weight, upon the firm support of somebody else's common-sense. Ursula expected easily to succeed in drying the facile tears, if tears indeed were flowing. The woe of the superabundant tissue was a woe of long-standing; and nothing else was wrong when they parted only yesterday. There seemed no quarter of the serene horizon which could suddenly develop any cloud.

The gate clicked to behind her, and presently by a turn of the path and the descent of some rocky steps, Mrs. Adams emerged from the cover of plantation upon a rustic bridge crossing a miniature ravine. This ravine made a chief feature in the picturesque surroundings of The Mount. A swift brown stream, broken into foam by a succession of falls, flowed far below; and on the left, from this point of vantage, the eye wandered over woods already spreading the delicate greens of spring, to a blue horizon line—so blue and so clearly defined that it could only be the sea. Ursula loved this view and all in haste as she was, she paused for a moment to gaze. Among the many things which she in her indigence was minded to envy Frances, perhaps she most keenly envied her the possession of her beautiful home.

She remembered well how sharply the beauty and the luxury had struck a note of contrast years before, when the poor pupil-teacher came for the first time to spend her holidays with her friend and schoolmate, Mr. Wayland's petted daughter. Three or four such visits were paid to The Mount before Frances took wing into the gay world; and a later and more memorable one came about before the tide of circumstance swept them utterly apart. Frances fell ill—mainly because that doting father had set his will against the lover she desired; and in her trouble she cried out for Ursula, and Ursula was summoned. Frances, or Fancy as they called her, was dying of a broken heart—so she thought, and so those about her began to believe—and all because Mr. Wayland could not endure the thought of separation from his darling, and had sent away the soldier-lover, Major Bethune. By some odd association of idea, the fresh appeal of the morning's letter recalled that other long-past emergency. As she hastened to The Mount, she thought of her hurried journey and arrival there ten years ago, and once more by the magic of remembrance saw Fancy tossing about in fever, her golden hair cropped short about her pretty head, and heard the cry of her distress. She could not live without Charles Bethune; she was dying because her father had been cruel. Ursula did her best to mediate, but Mr. Wayland was already alarmed and penitent. The engagement was allowed, but by the time Frances was able to rise from her sick bed, and the lover to return on leave of absence, Ursula had gone back to her employer, who was on the eve of removal abroad.

This proved the point of division, though not forecasted in the parting. Frances was not to marry till she had completed her twenty-first year—so much the father still stipulated; and then Ursula should be bidden to the gayest of gay weddings at The Mount. But when the marriage came about there could be no bidding of guests; the season was one of mourning, and the wedding was hurried over privately on account of Mr. Wayland's recent death. It was whispered there had been no accident, but that Mr. Wayland had met with serious losses in business, and had died by his own hand.

Whether this were true or false, it is certain that his affairs were left in great disorder. Instead of inheriting a colossal fortune, Frances had for her portion only The Mount, and an income counted by hundreds instead of the former thousands. Major Bethune held himself absolved from the undertaking to give up his profession; he married Frances and took her to India, and from this time forward the few letters exchanged with her friend grew ever colder and shorter, and finally ceased altogether. And then—not at once, but after a hardworking interval came the one brief romance of Ursula's own life.

So much for retrospect—a necessary sketch of past foundation, on which the present was built up. Ursula only knew that Frances fell ill during her last year in India; the climate was supposed not to suit her and she came back to live at The Mount, with an elderly relative as companion, till her husband's regiment was ordered home. She knew also that Frances bore the separation with equanimity; for the years had wrought their changes, and she no longer cried out in despair with fate, that life was not life to her unless passed at the side of Charles Bethune—an alteration to the full as significant as that which transformed the fairy figure into a shapeless bulk, though not so immediately obvious to the sense and eye.

II   The Mount was a big rambling house of no architectural pretension; sundry additions had been built on to it, and it covered an extravagant amount of ground. It was low and spacious—the comfortable space of wide passages and broad shallow staircases, as well as airy rooms. The hall door stood open to the spring sunshine, the hall itself was deserted, but a voice called over the balustrade of the upper gallery.

"Ursula, is that you? Come up here at once, to the boudoir."

The voice was imperative, and at the top of the stairs Mrs. Adams was met by a short figure in a tea-gown—intended for flowing ease, but filled out unduly by the excessive bulk within. Mrs. Bethune's face, naturally a pretty one, was red and pale with weeping, and the hands that closed on Ursula's burnt hotly, as if with fever.

"You have come at last! Oh, I have wanted you, ever since the post came in; but at first I could not collect myself enough to write, even to you. I hoped something would tell you I was in trouble and would draw you here."

They were alone in the boudoir by now, and the door was shut. A luxurious place, with a bow-window looking towards the sea, and so recessed and indrawn with curtains that it formed a room within a room. There was a couch heaped with cushions in manifest disarray and thrust half behind them, some crumpled papers. Ursula's first glance noted these, but Mrs. Bethune drew her on to the window-seat. Then she began to cry again, and the explanation halted.

"The trouble came by post? Well, I am here now, Frances," in some impatience at the falling tears, with her as rare an expression as with the other they were facile. "Tell me what is the matter."

Mrs. Bethune made an attempt to dry her eyes with a drenched and ineffectual handkerchief, but her voice was still choked and barely audible. "It is about Charles," she said.

Ursula looked again at the crumpled letter on the distant sofa. "You have heard that he is ill? Is that it?—Not—" The woman who was a widow conjectured at once the worst news that could be sent, but she caught back the impulsive question and altered it. "Not in danger?"

"No, not now." The wife wept again. "He has been ill, very ill, but it isn't that. He says he is much better."

"He has written to you himself?"

Mrs. Bethune nodded with her face hidden.

"Then the worst is over, and you must be thankful. Of course—" rather uncertainly, as one might step along a dark road, for the direction of her assumption led into the unknown. "Of course, it is a trial to you to hear he has been ill, far away from you like that, and perhaps with only strangers about him." A faintly interrogative pause, which was not broken by reply. "Was it an accident?"

"No. More horrid than any accident. Cholera. But he says he is getting strong."

There was a minute of shocked silence. Ursula had perhaps a clearer notion than the wife, of what a cholera visitation might be. And yet something in Mrs. Bethune's manner made her doubt whether this acute distress had really been called forth by the husband's past danger, and she waited for the fuller information which would certainly follow now Frances had found her voice.

"He writes—I forget the date, but some time at the beginning of this month—May."

Another pause, and a fresh sob. "Yes?" said Ursula. She must let Frances tell the story in her own way, and her way seldom went direct to the point, but she grew vaguely uneasy, wondering what was behind. When her friend began again, it was on a fresh tack.

"You know—when I came home from India, the regiment had four years to stay out. Very nearly four—three years and ten months."

"Yes."

"And Charles was bound to stay with it."

Ursula muttered something, again tentatively. "Such a long separation was a great trial."

"That is two years and a half ago. I thought there would be all this year and nearly all next, before there was the least prospect of seeing him again."

"Well?"

Mrs. Bethune dropped her handkerchief and looked Ursula full in the face.

"This illness of his has made all the difference. He is not fit to stay in command, and he has been invalided. He is ordered home at once. Ursula, what shall I do? He will be here in sixteen days."

II.
CATCHING AT A STRAW

Ursula looked back at her friend, and in that first amaze could find nothing to say to her. Was the trouble told at last, and could it be that the absent husband was about to return? Was this changed woman in tears and distress, really identical with the Frances Wayland of long ago, who had wept and wasted to a shadow because forbidden to give her love-plight to Charles Bethune?

It was essential she should understand; unless the situation was made plain, she could give neither help nor counsel. She took the hot hands in hers, and looked into the puffed, pallid face and the red eyes. "Frances, be reasonable," she said, almost with asperity, almost as if they were once again the girl-friends of long ago; she could hardly help giving her a little shake for emphasis. "Why does this make you unhappy? Has anything gone wrong between you?—If I heard that Keith was coming back—!"—she caught her breath there, and could not continue. "Can you really mean you are in trouble because Colonel Bethune is ordered home?"

Mrs. Bethune did not resent the enquiry, nor directly answer it. She rose and stood before her questioner, the

11

shapeless figure in the wide gown which still was over-strait, and made a despairing demonstration with the hands she had drawn out of Ursula's. "Look at me," she said. "Look what I have become. He does not know."

Ursula did look, some shocked comprehension beginning to dawn on her. The change which had passed upon the girl she remembered was great indeed, and Frances Wayland's nearest friends might be forgiven if they passed her by unrecognised as Frances Bethune. There is no disguise so potent as adipose tissue, if only it is deposited in sufficient quantity—a point clearly demonstrated in a certain famous trial which is a memory of our youth. Mrs. Bethune was not so hugely fat as the Claimant; but in her the slender girl, small-boned and delicate featured, was covered and burdened, body and limbs alike, till resemblance to her former self had well-nigh disappeared. There was still a certain comeliness in the puffed face when not disfigured by weeping; her cheek was soft in texture and bright in hue, her eyes were still deeply blue, her fair hair abundant. But such comeliness as remained was not the comeliness of Frances Wayland, who had once been light as a fairy, rare and delicate as the unfolding of a flower. Ursula repeated in amazement, "He does not know?"

"No. I didn't tell him; what was the use? And Mrs. Romer never wrote to him; I took care of that. I was not going to be spied upon and reported, though he had sent me home to her. I just wrote my duty letters—as seldom as I could with decency, and said as little. And now he is coming back, and I am like this!"

"Frances, you will write to him now. He must be told."

"I can't write to him, even if I would. He says when I get his letter he will be already on the way. And he doesn't want to be met. He is coming straight here."

"Cannot you send to meet him, even if you do not go? Oh, why didn't you tell him earlier?"

ONE OR TWO

"Think what a horrid thing it was to tell. And I did not want to lose my influence. It was the one thing left that gave me power over him—my good looks, and the admiration I used to get. That was why he mewed me up with Mrs. Romer. And I thought I had plenty of time to get better in. There was more than a year; and I have been to doctors and am taking remedies—the Rasselas remedies, as you know. *13* And I am trying to diet as well. But what will that do for me, in sixteen days?"

"Let Mrs. Romer meet him. If he has confidence in her, she will be the right person."

"Now Ursula, you are foolish. Don't you know she is at Buxton, and cannot move with her gout; and how could I send her careering about the country—in a bath-chair! *14* For Heaven's sake think of something else. Is there nothing *15* that can be done?"

"Were you quite slender when you left India? You had been ill there, hadn't you? Was not that the reason why you came away?"

"Quite, quite slender. Plumper perhaps than when I married, but only what improved me, not"—with a gesture of disgust—"like this. Yes, I was ill in India; I had a bad accident, a fall out riding. I was stunned, concussion of the brain, and I was not properly conscious for weeks and weeks. My head sometimes aches from it now, and my memory isn't what it used to be. But that was not why I came home."

She paused abruptly and bit her lip, as if the impulse of the moment had carried her too far; then went on with a sort of angry hardihood.

"I don't mind telling you. You will understand the whole thing better if you know. Romantic attachments are all very well, but a time comes when people tire of—honey, and all that. It was after my accident: Charles was different, and perhaps I was different too. I cared more about

13

being admired, and it pleased me when I found out I had a new sort of power over him—that I could make him jealous. There was a Mr. Prendergast—there were dozens of them, but he was the chief. There was never any real wrong—oh, never. But they said I had been compromised, and Charles was frantic. Oh, he was so angry. I know I was imprudent, that I went too far. I don't know what he did to that wretched man. I never asked. But he said I must go home. It was only a pretence about my health."

Frances's tears were dry, her voice had grown steady; the matter seemed after all less vital than the other trouble of her altered appearance. She went on, not waiting for comment.

"I think Charles was sorry after, when it occurred to him he had been hard on me—that I might not be having an over pleasant time, shut up here with Mrs. Romer. He wanted to exchange—and then to get leave and come back to me, but I would not have it. He had sent me away for four years, and for four years I said we should remain apart. I had been needlessly insulted, and I would not give in—not a hair's breadth; I would stand to the barrier he had set up. Besides, by that time this horrible change in me had begun."

She made the same gesture of distaste with those expressive hands, and positively shuddered.

"Imagine after all that, and when he is at last properly penitent, for him to discover what I have become; that there is nothing left in me for him to admire, or for anybody else to covet. Ursula, I can't face it. I had rather die."

"Frances, you must not talk so. It is a change—of course, and it is hard to bear. But if he really loves you? And, as he wanted to make up the quarrel, he must love you still."

"Love—! I don't know about that. He writes as if he did—sometimes, and sometimes he is bitter and angry. He has sent me presents; the last one just before I went to London, when I met you. I put it away because I hated to look at it. I will show it you, and then you can judge how I felt when it came."

She pulled open the drawer of the cabinet which stood in the recess, and took out a belt of native gold-work, pierced medallions studded with big dull turquoises, linked together and to a jewelled clasp. "He said he could not go far wrong, for he knew the size of my waist."

The brief length of it would have amply girded her as Frances Wayland, but it would need doubling to belt the waist of her present gown. She held it up significantly to Ursula, and then shut it away out of sight.

"I cannot even wear my wedding-ring. It hurt my finger, so I had to get a new one—to save appearances, you know. And even that is over tight for me now, as you see. But, talking of letters, look at the one I had this morning. Take it—read it through."

The crumpled tear-blistered sheets were those Ursula had seen on the sofa. Frances thrust them in her hand, and turned away, as if to leave her free to read. She looked doubtfully down the page.

"Are you sure you want me to see this? It seems quite a private letter, intended only for you."

"Yes—Yes, I wish you to read it," Frances persisted. "I have no secrets—I don't care for anything he says," ignoring the tears still wet, which had fallen freely on the paper. "Read it, and then you will know, once for all, what a strait I am in."

So urged, Ursula did read. Of Charles Bethune she knew nothing but by hearsay. In former times the girl Fancy's raptures about her lover, now the wife's chilling account of quarrel and division—a division which had come about as the consequence of her own folly. But scant as was her knowledge of the writer, his letter touched her profoundly. On his own illness and agony he touched lightly, as if fearing to cause distress; the mention of it was mainly to explain why he disobeyed her in returning. "I am bound to come back, as the doctor sends me," he wrote. "I must see you, Frances: and then it shall be for you to say how long my penance must continue. I would fain to come home to my wife. If I was careless of my treasure, if a misconception made me over harsh, I have repented; surely you know that by now. You were so young I should have watched over you—shielded you from the danger to which your own innocence exposed you. We both of us made mistakes—or shall I blot that out as unwritten, and own, stiff-necked brute that I am, that the mistakes were only mine? But we will put all that behind us, never to be thought of again. Let us begin afresh from the beginning, and you will find me wiser; I could not be more truly your lover. Let us go back to the old times. Let it be the girl I wooed that I shall meet again in the garden of The Mount, once more among the roses, as on that June day of long ago. Put on your white dress, my darling, and come to the gate as you came then, and all shall be forgotten and forgiven at the touch of your first kiss. When I shut my eyes now I can see her, my Fancy who loved me; I can feel her arms about my neck. All my pain will have lightly bought the hastening of that moment, when again your lips meet mine."

There was more to follow. Calculations of route and time, Port Said and Brindisi and Calais, the day he might be expected, and almost the hour. She was not to meet him on landing. Though he had no expectation she would wish it, that he forbade. He would seek her at The Mount, he would find her among the roses—it was the idea which ran through all the letter, and then it should be the Fancy Wayland of old that he would hold in a lover's embrace. It was the cry of a man who had suffered sharply and long, in mind and body both; a cry which came out from the depths of his heart, and to which, Ursula thought as she read, the heart of a woman who once had loved him, must assuredly respond.

"Oh," she said, almost with indignation, "need you be afraid? He does love you, Frances; can you doubt it after this? Let him only be told, and he will be sorry—he will pity you for the misfortune of it. He will not be alienated."

Frances, commonly so indolent, was walking up and down the room in restless impatience, as if inaction had become intolerable. She stopped and struck her hands together with sudden passion.

"You think so! Well, it shows how little you know—of men, or of the world. He loves a memory, not me. Oh yes, I remember you have married as well, but it was not for long, and I daresay your husband was always your lover. It is all very well for Charles to romance; but now I am no longer what he admires—what he knows others will admire. I could not hold him. Not for a day—not for an hour. Ursula," taking the other by her shoulders, "what can I do? I will not go through the farce of meeting him here. I have not the courage. It would be easier to kill myself than to endure it. I must go away. You must help me to go away and to be lost, if you cannot find me a remedy. Is there any remedy? Think! Think as if the position were your own. I am double the size I used to be. I should make two of the girl who waited for him in the garden. And then to read that letter! It is ridiculous; it is terrible."

Ursula looked back at her in almost equal distress. The situation had its tragic side, for Charles Bethune as well as for his wife, but this Frances seemed only capable of taking in what touched herself. She had been cruel in the long deception: to vanish without explanation would be cruel and cowardly both. And then all at once, under the piercing scrutiny of the desperate woman before her, her face changed.

"Ursula, what is it? You have thought of something. I see

it in your eyes."

It is not always well to have a countenance so transparent that it reveals the motions of the mind; or so Mrs. Adams thought. She was manifestly unwilling to speak, but Frances clung about her and would not be gainsayed.

"It was nothing that could be of use. It was only something I remembered—that came into my mind I don't know how. Let us think seriously of what you are to do. You must not go away."

"I will not consider till you have told me. You are poor—you want money—you have to work. Oh, I know about it, though you keep it all so dark. I will make it worth your while to help me—"

"Frances, if I could help you, I should not need to be bribed."

"Tell me what your thought was. It can do me no harm to hear it. Nothing can make me worse or more unhappy than I am."

Mrs. Adams had risen, shaking off the imperious pressure of those clinging hands. She stood looking out of the window as she spoke, her eyes doubtful and troubled, yielding reluctantly. She was annoyed with herself and the inopportune memory—of a suggestion made months before by a person she despised, and which in the present crisis must be void of application.

"You remember how we met, quite by accident—in London at Miss Sedgeley's, and why we were invited to her house?"

"Of course. She had gone crazy about spiritualism, and wanted to introduce a medium who was supposed to be a wonderworker. I thought it might turn out to be fun—real diabolism. But the only good I got out of it was that I met you."

"I don't know if you had any faith in what went on?"

"Not I. That Mrs. Warden was quite a common sort of

woman, who dropped her H's, and did sewing. Why do you ask?"

"Because what I thought of—what I have to tell you—was something she said about you when the sitting was over. You left early, if you remember—the carriage came for you, but I was staying the night with Miss Sedgeley. So I had a talk to Mrs. Warden at supper."

"About me?"

"I did not mention you, but she did. She was talking of herself to begin with. She is a large thick-set person, if you remember, but she told us she could be slender if she chose. The extra substance about her body is all used—drawn out of her—when the spirits materialize; and then they put it back to serve for another time. I daresay it was sheer nonsense; but she said if we could only see her while the process is going on, she would appear quite small."

"Well?"

"And then she turned to me, and said, 'That very stout young lady who went away—she is a friend of yours; a friend you have not met for many years. It is a great trouble to her that her shape is altered, and it will soon be a greater trouble still. When the greater trouble comes to pass, tell her from me that it could all be put right again, if only she would sit as we have done tonight.'"

That Mrs. Bethune was deeply impressed was plain, despite her scoff at the illiterate medium. Her whole expression altered. "When the greater trouble comes," she repeated slowly, "And now it has come indeed, as she foretold. And," reproachfully, "you did not want to tell me. All put right again! Why, for the sake of that, I would sit with dozens of mediums, and believe all their rubbish and pay their fees. Ursula, Ursula!"—in a sudden illumination of hope as wild as the previous despair, "Do you believe it? Do you think it can be true?"

"No, I don't think it can. And I blame myself for telling

you, for it is no kindness to excite false hopes. But that was the message, in her very words."

"She knew the trouble that was coming," spoken meditatively. "Is not that an assurance for the rest? At least I can be no worse off than I am now, even if I try what she advises.—I have made up my mind. I will see this woman, and sit with her."

A weak person's obstinacy is one of the least controllable of forces, Ursula, conscious of stronger intellect, accustomed to be wise for Frances, found herself suddenly powerless, carried away by the force of Mrs. Bethune's resolve. There is a saying that man is man and master of his fate; and in a lesser degree, woman may be supposed mistress of hers. But fate is sometimes like a river spread out over shallows, suffering you to wade where you will through the limpid water, but the same river and the same water will have power to whirl you to destruction where it slopes upon the rapids. Ursula had stepped unthinking unto the depths with that recollected message, and the position of the two friends was suddenly reversed. But she did not give way without a struggle.

"I was afraid you might be tempted; but I don't believe you will really do anything so unwise. You had far better have patience, and follow the doctors' treatment. Only last week you thought you were a little lighter. You know they said you might be cured, or at any rate greatly reduced, if you would live strictly by their rule."

"Yes—in the course of months, or more likely years—and Charles is coming in sixteen days! No, Ursula, I am quite resolved. And you have promised to help me."

"I said I would help you if I could, but how can I help you in this?"

"I will tell you."

The tears were dry now, and the puffed face full of purpose. Mrs. Bethune was bending over the cabinet

ONE OR TWO

where she had hidden the belt, unlocking an inner drawer. "I keep my money here," she said, "and this roll of notes came from the bank only yesterday. Count it, there should be ten of them, fifty pounds. I want you to go to London for me—at once, tonight if you can. Go to Miss Sedgeley, you know her better than I do. She will tell you how this sewing-woman is to be approached, and what is her price. I will pay anything; I do not mind the cost. Bring her here to me by the next train. I do not want to lose a day—an hour. You understand?—The money is for you. For the help you are going to give me, and for your expenses and your time. Yes, I mean it, you must take it, I will have no denial. And listen, Ursula! If we succeed; if I get rid of this—this burden—as a consequence of what you have told me, I will give you fifty more."

III.

SALVADOR

And so it came about that Ursula Adams—reluctant, disapproving, but overborne in the end by Mrs. Bethune's determination, the sudden obstinate resolve of a weak nature—departed to London on so strange an errand.

She excused herself from the night journey, but it was at a very early hour next morning that she set out from Saltringham, disturbing Mrs. Minter from her slumbers to boil the kettle and cut the cold mutton into sandwiches. Fifty pounds! Her pride revolted from the bribe, but it was a sore temptation to her poverty; and, after all, she was abetting Frances in no actual wrong doing, only in something absurd. And, as she reflected vaguely to herself, not shaping the matter in the ugly distinctness of spoken words—it was not like a thing done openly in the face of day, for the world to smile at if the world took notice, and of the affairs of each one of us, however obscure, some small section of the world is usually cognisant. Nobody need know except Miss Sedgeley, who was herself a crank, and the sempstress-medium, her protégée.

Thus Mrs. Adams consoled herself during her hurried

journey, while the train was drawing into London in the early afternoon. And when, from under the vaulted roof of the terminus, she plunged into busy streets full of the pleasure-taking throng of mid-season, the purpose she had in view seemed more than ever unreal, impossible to reconcile with any expectation of common experience.

The sunshine and the stir of the great city raised her spirits in spite of herself, solitary waif as she was, poor alike in purse and hope—the wealth, the ease, the pleasure, which swam like scum above the whirlpool, not for her. The trees were spreading into fresh green leaf in the park, flowers were abundant in the balconies, but presently the swifttrotting hansom whirled her into a stiller and less fashionable quarter, solid spacious houses fronting the square, and looking out upon a centre of common garden. She alighted at Miss Sedgeley's number, and presently a neat maidservant opened the door.

"Yes, ma'am, Miss Sedgeley is at home, but she is engaged at present. She has a meeting of ladies in the drawing-room. Will you come in and wait?"

Ursula asked when the meeting would be over. The maid thought in half an hour, so after some brief indecision, her bag was temporarily deposited in the hall, and she paid and dismissed the driver. She could not prosecute her errand till she had obtained the medium's address, and there was nothing for it but to wait Miss Sedgeley's leisure. She was shewn into a little writing-room, hardly bookish enough to deserve the name of library, but with books in abundance on shelves and tables, and a large open secretary strewn with letters and papers, which had the air of constant use. The servant offered her the *Times*, and she settled herself in the easiest chair, unfastening her cloak, prepared to abide the detention with what patience was possible.

But she found it difficult to fix her attention on the

morning's news; her eyes wandered about the little room, clean and fresh in its flat sage-greens and studied plainness, pervaded with faint fragrance from a bunch of violets newly placed in water. She became conscious of a subdued excitement in herself, not solely resulting from the whirl of her journey—memory also was busy. The last time she entered that house as Miss Sedgeley's bidden guest, it had been with a certain expectation unavowed to any other: the secret of her own bosom. If there was truth indeed in these occult dealings which Miss Sedgeley exalted as a new dispensation, might it not be that Keith, her Keith, would be able to give her some token of nearness, some sign of comfort? He had loved her and leaned upon her so entirely in the weakness of broken health, that the thought of him alone in that sphere of the departed which we call Heaven, had ever moved her with an emotion akin to pity. Surely, if possible for any to return from that far bourne, he would be ready and willing to return to her. Such had been the inducement which drew the widow; not the expectation of novelty and *diablerie* which attracted Frances Bethune.

And, as she glanced round the four walls of the little room sweet with Miss Sedgely's violets, Ursula remembered as vividly how she was disenchanted. The commonplace medium, the oppression of the darkness, the brief touches of hands made palpable, the head which floated bodiless over the table illuminated by its own light, like the medium in feature though bearded as a man, and with the same suggestion of a dinner of onions hinted by its breath. All possibly, though improbably, genuine, but empty of the close personal interest, and so not for her. The hope had never found a voice, and the pang of disappointment was equally silent; but by choice of her own she would not have returned to the locality which revived it, had she not been compelled by this business of Mrs. Bethune's.

But a kind welcome was in store for her. The half hour

had hardly expired before sounds of departure were evident in the hall, and presently the door opened, and Miss Sedgeley came in.

She was a little old lady with grey hair, almost as white as the soft cap under which it was smoothed away; very plainly dressed, and wearing a black silk apron which might have suited her housekeeper; but for all her eccentricity and old fashion, a gentlewoman, and a kindly one. "My dear," she said to Ursula, holding both her hands, "your mother's daughter is always welcome. Mary is taking your bag up to the spare bedroom, and I hope you will stay with me while you are in town. Have you travelled far? From Saltringham? That is a long journey for only one night, but you must not think of going to a hotel. And no luncheon but a sandwich in the train! You shall have something substantial right away, and a cup of tea with it, and when you are rested it will be time to tell me why you thought of the old woman, and what she can do for you."

That errand of Frances proved difficult telling face to face with those gentle eyes. Unexpectedly difficult, for Ursula had rashly taken for granted that her mother's spiritualistic friend must needs understand the situation, and be willing to cooperate.

"Yes," said Miss Sedgeley when the tea table was drawn between them, and the "something substantial" had been served on a dainty little tray at Ursula's elbow. "Yes, I recollect Mrs. Bethune, and what a pity I thought it for such a young woman to be so stout. The Whimpoles told me she took an interest, no, was inclined to be curious—(I think that was it and there is a wide difference)—about the things which interest me. That was why I asked her the evening you came here, and I remember well how you two discovered you used to be friends. So you have seen a good deal of her since, and went down to Saltringham to be near her? That would be pleasant for you both."

Ursula agreed. Yes, in a way it had been pleasant, and that oyster motive of hers need not be exposed to this dainty old gentlewoman. But the consciousness of concealment made her awkward, and the purpose of her errand to London was after all very baldly stated. Mrs. Bethune wanted Mrs. Warden's address, and to arrange to get her down to Saltringham for a series of séances. Miss Sedgeley shook her head over the last in doubt.

"I am sorry I thought your friend only curious, as her curiosity has borne fruit in a deeper interest.—But why does she not try alone, for writing, as I do, or with yourself, or some other person in close affinity, whom she can trust? Those objective phenomena are useful in their way, but they are as it were only the shell of the subject, and I would have her seek for the kernel. Mrs. Warden is very much tied. She works as a sempstress, and she has a young daughter dying of consumption. She could not take a long journey out of London."

"Mrs. Bethune is quite willing to pay for the accommodation. Mrs. Warden would be sure of a handsome fee."

"My dear! What sort of communications would your friend be likely to get through a mother who forsook her dying child for hire?"

So Ursula was forced into fuller explanation, conscious throughout of that same clumsiness, and of a certain shame. The old white-haired lady heard her first in surprised doubt—then in positive concern.

"My dear," she said again. "I have been for a great many years a spiritualist, and I have every reason to thank God for granting me this measure of His light. But, though my own experience has been a happy one, I know there are dangers on the threshold. Let him who seeks take care lest God should answer him according to the multitude of his idols.—Do you see what I mean? I would not be harsh, I would not condemn, but here the motive is altogether earthly, and for a selfish advantage."

"Not quite that," said Ursula, driven to defence. "Frances loves Colonel Bethune, and is grieved at the thought of shocking him by so great a change. It is not only her vanity."

"Well, well, my dear, you know her, and can judge her better than I. But, as your Frances loves her husband, she should have given him her confidence. Then he would have been prepared. I will send round to Mrs. Warden, and ask if she can come here to us this evening. She will come if Edith is no worse, just for a short time, as it is not far; and I daresay she will explain to us what she meant by sending such a message to Mrs. Bethune."

"Miss Sedgeley, do you think—you who are wise in these matters—that such a thing could be?"

"Nothing like it has come into my experience, that is all I can say. But, my child, where the wonders we have proved are possible, who will dare to set a limit, or say what is beyond the scope of so great a power? We know only the alphabet as yet, if indeed we know it, of this difficult science; we are as children quarrelling about the letters, and beginning to spell in the hornbook. I am not a physical medium, except for the movements of the pencil. But I have heard Mrs. Warden say that she is lighter and smaller in body when substance is drawn from her, and I have read of it in other cases. It is true that the very substance of the living body can be abstracted under certain conditions to build up a temporary form, without affecting life. And, granted the initial wonder which is greater, why should we stumble at the lesser one? That, once abstracted, it might be gradually destroyed, or held in suspense.—But you shall ask Mrs. Warden for yourself, I will try to get her in this evening, and it is settled you will stay."

The evening was far advanced before the sempstress medium made her appearance. A neighbour had promised to sit by the sick daughter for the hour or two of her absence, and for herself she was glad of the change, so she said to Miss Sedgeley. She did look tired and worn, the same plain woman of the working-class who had repelled Mrs. Bethune by her want of culture. But Miss Sedgeley did not seem to be repelled, and received her kindly as a sister, making her rest in the easiest chair while talking to Ursula, who had again to detail her errand. And here also, instead of the comprehension she expected, she was met by surprise.

The sempstress recollected sitting with Miss Sedgeley's friends, remembered Ursula, remembered the excessively stout young lady who did not seem to be interested, and who went away. But she had no recollection whatever of sending her a message, so the whole structure of the hope and the journey seemed about to collapse. "But you did say it," Ursula insisted in her amazement. "Those were your very words."

"I daresay, ma'am," Mrs. Warden answered. I don't doubt you are right. But I expect it was Salvador speaking to you, and not me at all. It is often like that; he pops in and says something with my mouth, and I'm not in the least aware."

Then to Miss Sedgeley, "The young lady doesn't know who Salvador is, but you can tell her he is just my control, and right down clever about all sorts of things—worldly matters as well as spiritual. And I see nothing for it now but to ask him to explain. He will know if there is a chance for the stout lady, and what she should do. You will let us go into the little room in front, and put out the light?"

Ursula could not repress a shudder of disinclination, but neither of the others took any notice, so the adjournment was at once arranged. It was all to come over again then, the oppression of the darkness, the sudden touches, perhaps the near presence of that unnatural face looking close into her own. She could have found it in her heart to fly to the door and take refuge in the street, but she was bound by her pledge to Frances, doubly bound by the transfer of that roll of notes. The door of the little room was locked inside, the shutters fastened to exclude any glimmer of light, and the three women sat down to a small table, Miss Sedgeley keeping a candle and matches at her elbow.

Ursula held a hand of the medium's and a hand of Miss Sedgeley's, one on either side, and the others were supposed to be similarly linked. There was an interval—whether long or brief she hardly knew, to her it seemed interminable. Then a light appeared, as if rising above the edge of the table, a light as large as an egg, and enclosed in a substance like crystal. A light bright in itself, though it did not illuminate the room.

Stay—it seemed to be lighting up something in its immediate neighbourhood, which was not either of her companions. First a hand—a large powerful hand, in which the crystal appeared to lie. Then white drapery surrounding the head and shoulders of a figure, lastly a face.

It was in profile when first she distinguished it, the face she had seen before. A man's face with a beard, and of a Jewish cast of countenance, which resembled Mrs. Warden as a brother may resemble a sister, though of a distinctly masculine type, and with a wider brow. It passed slowly before her, floating above the table. The eyes moved and the lips, but there was no audible speech. She heard Miss Sedgeley's voice bidding her question Salvador, but still she sat stupefied and tongue-tied. If at that moment all Frances's fortune had hung on the inquiry, she could not have brought herself to address this lemurian creature, a head without a body and alive with borrowed life. The bearded lips broke into a slow smile, and made another fruitless effort after speech, then the Head turned gradually from her, once more into profile, and the light vanished as if withdrawn.

SALVADOR

Following the disappearance came loud rappings on the table, giving an order through the alphabet, and Miss Sedgeley lit her candle. The medium lay back in her chair, pale as death, and with her hand still clasped in Ursula's. The Head was nowhere to be seen, nor any vestige of the voluminous white drapery, and to all appearance Mrs. Warden had not moved. "She is entranced," said her hostess in explanation. "Listen to what she says, for Salvador is going to speak to you through her."

Was this about to be a new horror? But it was less disconcerting when there was nothing visible. That is to say, nothing outstanding, but as Mrs. Warden sat up, the expression fixed upon her face was totally different to the one she wore by nature. Her voice was altered as well, with a manly depth about it perhaps not impossible to assume, though the cultivated intonation would, Ursula thought, have been beyond her. The voice took on a slightly foreign accent, and spoke with a certain emphatic deliberation which gave additional weight and dignity to the measured words.

"I, Salvador, sent the message, tell your friend, Mrs. Bethune, and I, Salvador, am persuaded that what she craves for can be done. But it will be at a cost different to the cost she counts out of her purse. A cost she cannot measure, and that I cannot certainly foretell. She need not sit with this medium, or with any other. You, Ursula Adams, will serve as her complement, for the impulse of expulsion and division is in her own sphere. You only must sit with her. You who were once her friend for love's sake, and now have been bought with a price. I can tell you how to move the lever; I can tell no more. You understand, and will remember?

"I have a further message for you to deliver and it is a message of warning.

"Let her think well before she undertakes the trial, for

once done there can be no undoing. Once withdrawn as this will be withdrawn, the substance taken from her cannot be put back, not in life and not in death, any more than can a child when born from the womb. If inert matter only is separated, all will be well, but it is possible, tell her it is possible, that life may be divided out of life. Let her look to it that she is at one in her soul, with strength to put from her the evil and hold to the good. Then the body will be strong likewise, to repel its grossness and emerge as one newborn.

"You have heard me so far. Will you warn her or approve her? Do you see her in the image I have put before you? I see her, but not bare to the soul. She is to me as one asleep, who has passed under dominion. You, whose service has been given and bought, are closer to her than I.

"I, Salvador, will tell her how to act, if she resolves upon the trial. She may discard the healing because the means are simple; because no prophet comes forth to her to strike his hand over the place and recover the leper. Naaman was granted only a message by the word of the Spirit, bidding him dip seven times in Jordan. Nevertheless at the seventh time his slough fell off him like a garment, and he arose newborn, with flesh as the flesh of a child.

"I, Salvador, will show you her Jordan. Night following night, if need be to the full measure of seven, she must sit in the house of her birth, while you sit with her and watch. For six nights maintain expectation without discouragement, but if the seventh night should also pass, and her burden remain undivided, the impulse and the power will have been spent in vain, and the hope must be foregone. I, Salvador, believe the separation will come, even to the measure of her desire.

"There is an upper room. I see it in the light of your knowledge. A room that is double, with a window curved to the front, and a window flat to the side. Close the curved window from all light, and make that portion dark and secure. Draw the silk curtains over the recess till they hang close together. She must sit alone within the curtains, and you alone in the outer part, barring the door against intrusion. You will hear her groan and sigh, but she will be as one asleep, and you must not look within. Sit after the sun has set, and while the household sleep, for the space of two hours, but you must not disturb her trance if it should be further prolonged. You must wait, were it for all the night, till she comes forth to you.—Leave the outer window uncurtained to the moon and stars! If the night is oppressive you may even open it for air.

"I see a piano there. When first your friend goes into the recess, you may make music for her, though you must not speak, soft music, to give her the assurance of your presence lest she be afraid. But as soon as her breathing becomes heavy and audible, cease, for she will then have passed beyond hearing into a deep sleep, such a sleep as came upon Adam when Eve was formed of his substance.

"You, Ursula Adams, must abide at the house on the hill from the beginning of the ordeal to the end, and from the beginning of the ordeal to the end, neither you nor Frances your friend must eat flesh food which has known life, nor defile yourselves with alcohol. When the ordeal is over give her wine, for whether in failure or success she will be weak. And Frances must enter each night having newly bathed, and having nothing upon her that is woollen, spun out of animal life, but garments of linen or cotton, ungirded, and with her feet unshod.

"I, Salvador, speak by the word of the spirit, saying to Frances Bethune: It is hers to choose the good, and put forth that which is impure. Let her see to it lest in the division her part is cast with the evil, and the lower soul abide."

The measured voice ceased; the medium sank back in her chair, and presently with a gasp and a shiver appeared to come to herself. It was once more the commonplace sempstress looking cheerfully round at them, asking if Salvador had spoken, and if he had been able to explain.— But Ursula had hardly a word to stammer in reply, so great was the confusion of her mind, and so overpowering the temporary impression. Common sense would pronounce on that oration after a while, and appraise it at a juster value; for the moment she was carried away, almost to believe.

IV.

THE EXPERIMENT BEGINS

Ursula had intended to travel back to Saltringham early on the morrow, but the morning found her prostrate with headache and unable to rise, so her hostess telegraphed to Mrs. Bethune, explaining the delay. By mid-day, however, the worst symptoms had abated, and she managed to crawl downstairs, and announce her intention of leaving by the afternoon train. Kind Miss Sedgeley protested, but finding she was really anxious to be gone, did all in her power to speed the parting guest, Ursula did not volunteer any allusion to the séance when she thanked the old lady for her hospitality, but before they parted Miss Sedgeley had a word to say.

"You would be interested in Salvador's directions. But I think if I were you, my dear, I would regard the experiment with doubt. I would be inclined to use my influence to dissuade Mrs. Bethune."

Ursula looked up with a change of countenance. "You think it is not true," she said. "You think Mrs. Warden was deceiving us?"

"No, not that—not that. I have known Emily Warden for

years, and I believe her to be absolutely truthful."

"Then how—"

"I cannot make you see the how. I do not see it certainly myself. But there are strange things in the world of spirit, and dangers on the threshold. You were bidden to warn your friend, were you not, even by Salvador? Don't omit that, Ursula my dear. If you find her bent on having her way, I would make the warning plain."

It was late at night before Ursula reached Saltringham, and walked in upon Mrs. Minter, taking her by surprise. Frances did not expect her, so there was no need to report herself at The Mount until tomorrow. She was utterly jaded, fit for nothing but bed, and the cup of tea her landlady hastened to serve to her; and she told herself it was well there should be delay—that a few more hours of reflection should intervene before she was bound to give an account of her mission.

And yet the result was a foregone conclusion, and she knew it in the innermost recesses of her heart. In the pause of respite, she stood as it were waist-deep in the river of fate, barely able to maintain her footing against the weight of the stream—that smooth rush down upon the rapids which must shortly sweep her away. Frances in the pursuit of her object would certainly be tempted, tempted by a motive she misdoubted as vanity rather than love. And if Frances had after all the wisdom to draw back, how would matters stand with herself? Would she truly endeavour to dissuade? Bought with a price! So the awful voice had spoken, echoing the reproach of her own conscience. If Mrs. Bethune changed her mind, then surely those banknotes must be returned, the whole sum, deducting only the cost of her journey. And the money was so sorely needed, would be so immediately useful—was owed to her indeed, as she strove to assure herself, by the tax Mrs. Bethune had imposed in these recent months upon her time. Forty-five

The Experiment Begins

pounds securely hers, if she only aided in this fantastic trial; and if the hoped-for result should come of it (though out of sober expectation), was she not promised fifty more? All the tenacity of her nature seemed to close on the nine banknotes still unbroken and locked away in safe keeping, it would be hard indeed to give them back, and with them all they symbolized—temporary ease in that straitness of narrow means which was wont to pinch her so cruelly hard.

She fell asleep at last and slept heavily, and between midnight and cock-crow dreamed a dream.

The dream set her among scenes near at hand and familiar. Following that path to The Mount which she was bound to traverse on the morrow. Frances had summoned her in anger, reproaching her for delay, and she was straining every nerve to obey and hasten, though hindered again and again by a grasp on her garments holding her back. A hand pulled her cloak or dragged at her skirt, and when she turned to shake it off, impatient at the detention, she caught only a glimpse of a figure vague as a shadow, vanishing like a wreath of mist against the hill. But she woke in the early dawn with her heart beating and her eyes full of tears. "Keith," she was crying in her sleep, "oh Keith, can it be you?"

The dream-portent passed unheeded. She was early at The Mount; so early that the breakfast tray and the post bag were only then going up to the lady of the house, so she was able to account with her presence for the non-arrival of a letter from town. Mrs. Bethune was eager for her story, disappointed at first, and inclined to be indignant, that she had failed to bring down the medium, and sceptical that result of any sort could accrue from the simple expedient of sitting with Ursula.

"Why, if that is all that is wanted, we have been together day after day for close upon three months, and here am

I not a bit thinner or the better for it," she objected. The breakfast was eaten by this time (it was her habit to take it in bed), and she was dressed and in the garden. A basket couch and chairs were set out of doors under the shade of a spreading cedar. There was a gentle warmth of early sunshine, while soft airs blew over to them from the sea. "Then you think it is not worth trying?" said her friend, mindful always of the money which must be given back, and yet unwilling to urge. "Certainly it seems ridiculous, and if there is really any risk—"

"Oh, risk!" said Mrs. Bethune. "I don't see how there can be risk in anything so simple. We shut ourselves up in a room for two hours, or perhaps three, and I sit behind the curtains and go to sleep. How can there be any risk in that? It will be exceedingly stupid for both of us—an absurd position, did anyone know. But if it does no good, it cannot possibly do harm.—Yes, I mean to try it. I haven't any faith, but there is just a chance for me this way, and no chance any other. That is how I look at it."

"I wish you had been with me in London. I wish you had heard all that speech just as I heard it, and what was said in warning, instead of only being told about it after."

"It might have made a difference; but," pluming herself, "you know I am not imaginative—as you are, or used to be when we were young. And it is the imagination in these cases which gets impressed, and that accounts for everything. Oh, I have read books about it, and I know!"

"But the warning was not my imagination." Ursula looked away, plucking a leaf to pieces as she talked; she felt guiltily conscious how weak were her objections, and how strong her growing relief that Frances was bent on the experiment even while she condemned it. "I should never have thought of danger, had it not been suggested to me. And Miss Sedgeley was quite of the opinion you would be wise to hesitate—wiser not to try."

The Experiment Begins

"Why does Miss Sedgeley preach what she does not practice?" Mrs. Bethune tossed her head, with its crown of still pretty golden hair. "She is always sitting with those snuffy old mediums—or sitting by herself to get a lot of stupid communications which do nobody any good. And because I want to have séances for a really useful object, she must needs be up in arms! I can tell you, Ursula, I have no patience with all that. And my mind is fully made up. We will begin tonight—No not tonight, for I had bacon for breakfast, did I not? And I daresay you had some too. I'll order vegetarian dishes—how old Choppington will stare!—for every meal all the week through; and you must leave Mrs. Minter's, and come and stay with me at The Mount. (I shall be glad to have you, for I am so low when I think of Charles coming back, that I can do nothing but sit and cry.)—And we will make the first experiment tomorrow."

It was curious how the slight nature, which yet was capable of such vehement storms, such obstinate resolve, could put aside its grief for the distraction of a new idea, and live easy and amused in the present. The experiment now bulked largely enough to fill up Frances's mental view, and postpone consideration of the crisis which had filled her, only three days before, with tragical despair. After trial and failure, it would be time enough to think of the dreaded meeting, or of avoiding it by some desperate expedient. Ursula was astonished to find her laughing lightly over her cook's surprise at the vegetarian orders, and planning with appetite how to please her own taste in the restricted diet.

"I shall tell Choppington I am trying a new remedy, and then it will get about," she said to her friend. "If any great change in me really happens—as I hope, we must be prepared to give a reason. And I mean to tell the servants to put the lights out, and fasten all the doors by nine o'clock, as I am going to bed early, and wish for no disturbance. They have a separate staircase in the kitchen wing, and we can shut them off completely from our part of the house. My bedroom is next to the boudoir; and you shall have the little white room at the end of the passage, that we may be near together if I need to call you in the night. My maid has slept there sometimes when I have been ill, but not of late. And, Ursula," striking her fat hands together with another laugh, "what a happy thing it is that Mrs. Romer is safe away at Buxton going through her cure! We could never have explained our *diablerie* to her. The ill wind which blew her that last fit of rheumatic gout, has certainly blown good to me."

So the morrow found Mrs. Adams installed as a guest at The Mount; and in the evening when the house was still and dark, and the hands of the clock pointed to half-past nine, the two women shut themselves into the boudoir. The only preparation needed was to draw the silk curtains over the recess, and unbar the side window to admit the lingering twilight to the outer portion of the room. Frances was ready attired in a white cambric wrapper covering her nightgown; she had kicked off her slippers and was barefoot. But at the last moment a shiver of nervousness overcame her, and inclined her to cling to Ursula.

"Would it make any difference, do you think, if you came in there with me instead of staying here?"

"I had better not. We know absolutely nothing of the reasons why these directions were given, and it might make all the difference, and spoil your chance. You are not afraid?"

"No-o," with hesitation, obviously the true answer would be yes. "You see it will be dark inside the curtains, and I was thinking of that head which appears with Mrs. Warden. Am I likely to see anything of that sort? I did not mind it a bit in the circle, when I had hold of somebody's hand, and when I could think it was all a trick. But I should be frightened here."

"Not at all likely." It was now Ursula's turn to be alarmed, lest at the last moment Frances should withdraw. "The object is not to show anything in drawing from you, but to dissipate the substance, and I suppose to destroy it. Nothing will happen to you but sleep; and you will know I am close to you all the while," coaxingly, as to a child. "I have opened the piano, and when once you are in the chair I will play to you—any little thing I can remember without my notes; it is too dark to see the music."

So Mrs. Bethune was persuaded, and took her place; and Ursula sat down to the piano, touching the keys softly into the dreamy melody of a cradle song; wondering the while if her playing would be audible in the servant's quarter, after the given edict that the house should be undisturbed. In the first pause Frances called out, "Go on, go on; I am not asleep." But the next time she suffered the vibration of a final chord to die away into silence, there was no voice from behind the curtains, only that sound of deepened regular breathing which Salvador had bidden her expect. She rose from the piano stool, and, moving softly, stole to a seat in the uncurtained window; and prepared to keep her vigil, looking out upon the night.

There was no absolute darkness, though the moon had not risen; she could see the garden sleeping below, the stone border of the terrace white in the summer dusk; the trees in silhouette against the sky, and above them the clear shining of the stars. Even the objects in the room could be distinguished dimly when she turned to look within but, waiting and vaguely anxious, it was a relief to gaze outward and upward to the boundless distance of the sky.

With her head resting against the pane, even from this window the sea could be glimpsed on the horizon and presently the far-off line began to shine in borrowed silver. A natural induction led her thoughts to the distant ship, far away in the coming morning of the east, and to the husband returning after painful illness, weary for home. What would he think of the reception Frances was preparing for him, could he know? Would he be willing to believe it simply love which made her wish to be young again and fair again before she met his eyes? Would a man find it easier to credit the right motive in all this, than she, Ursula, found it, who was herself a woman? Whenever she recollected the letter Frances had forced upon her, it was with a pang of sympathy so keen as to be almost pain. To her it seemed pitiful that one who loved as he had doubtless loved, and who had experienced—on Frances's own showing—grievous disappointment and disillusion, should so cling to the sweetness of an early dream, in the face of clear and bitter knowledge. That she should wait for him among the roses with the old love in her heart, ready as he was ready to take up life again from the beginning, and, without reproach or recrimination, try to make it a more perfect thing than before. Such was Charles Bethune's prayer as Ursula remembered it and understood, and Frances was meeting it after her manner, with all this despair about the measure of her waist, and her register upon the scales. Perhaps neither woman was wholly in the right, the one in losing sight of the ideal, and the other of the practical. Ursula might be mistaken also, but she could see how far and how deeply Frances was in the wrong, and how baseless was the husband's hope.

The girl of his heart! Would any emacerating process restore her as she was once, let it be never so successful? Greatly as Frances had altered in body, the alteration of mind was, so Ursula thought, far completer and more significant. If all that surplus bulk should certainly disappear, would it be possible for the worldliness, the selfishness, the vanity, the indolence, which loaded and warped her spirit, to vanish also? It would be a miracle indeed which could restore the Fancy Wayland of Ursula's earlier knowledge—the girl who loved with all the passion of her child's heart, and was ready to die of grief because denied her lover. Was this what Salvador meant about putting forth the evil, and holding to the higher nature of the soul? A reform more radical than that which touched only the grossness of the body. If so, and success turned upon moral redemption as well as physical, Frances Bethune was lost indeed; for in Ursula's opinion such a miracle could never be.

What was the time? She held her watch against the faint light of the window, and tried to see the dial; and, as if in answer to her thought, a clock struck in the hall below. Eleven; so the night was wearing on, the first ordeal was nearly at an end. How was Frances faring, she wondered, and had anything been effected in this initial trial? The regular breathing deepened, and presently was broken by an occasional groan which seemed to speak of suffering. Ursula's speculations ceased, and, during the completion of the second hour, she sat regarding the dimly distinguished curtains in growing uneasiness. The groans became more frequent; at length she felt it impossible longer to endure the suspense. She must strike a light and look within; what would become of her if Frances were to die? But she had hardly taken a step forward, when the floor at her feet was smitten with a sudden blow—a single knock, so vehement in its reminder that she shrank back and resumed her seat. It was the sole manifestation of the séance. Not many minutes after, Frances called to her in her natural voice: "Ursula, is it over? I am awake. I am coming out to you," and the unchanged solid figure appeared at the opening of the curtains.

Mrs. Bethune was tired and sleepy. Nothing had happened to her, not even dreams; she only wanted to be put to

ONE OR TWO

bed. And all the next day she was more than ever lethargic and indolent, lying among her cushions on the basket couch in the garden, or else in the boudoir, not caring to rouse herself even to talk. Visitors were admitted in the afternoon, through some mistake of her orders—friends who had driven from a distance; and when they were announced as being in the drawing-room, Frances's vexation was outspoken and unfeigned. And the carriage was already going round to the stables in expectation of a lengthened stay.

The card brought to her had three names inscribed on it: Mrs. Wyndham Lancaster—Miss Lancaster—Miss Effie Lancaster. "Oh," she said peevishly, "I cannot possibly see these people, in the midst of what is going on. You must go to them, Ursula. Say I have a headache—am ill, dead—anything you please. Stuff them with tea and cakes, and get them to go away. I had no idea they were back at Oakmarch. I thought they were still in Florence. It is really too annoying."

Ursula did not altogether relish her errand. "Are they old friends?" she said. "Tell me something of them before I go."

"Papa used to know them. Oh no, not intimately. One party a year style, when they happened to be down here. They are more Charles's friends than ours. I think there is some connection between the families."

"Then don't you think," persuasively, "that it might be better for you to see them?"

"No, no, no. They will ask all sorts of questions, they always do; and make it plain I am not cut out on their pattern, and so must be in the wrong. They can't hurt you, who are a stranger. Say anything you like that is civil, only get them to go."

So commissioned, Ursula went down, black-gowned and slim, to the large luxurious drawing-room full of colour and light, and bright with early flowers; it was Frances's wont to keep her reception-room always in readiness, seldom as it was used. Three stiff figures rose to receive her, but with a slight air of surprise, her appearance being unexpected. She made the needful apology for Frances, and they reseated themselves as stiffly in positions of vantage, the wide window behind them, and Ursula's face in full view.

They were presumably mother and daughters, but none of the three had any semblance of surviving youth. Ursula addressed herself to the most extensive bonnet, and the richest amplitude of skirt, failing other indications. The face under that bonnet was perhaps the mildest; but it was a question only of degree, where all alike were keen. She was involuntarily reminded of her one visit as spectator in a court of law, and felt herself the witness under examination by opposing counsel, suave in surface manner, but hostile of intent. The Lancaster family had set out in quest of information, and, failing Frances, they meant to make available such means as offered.

"A friend of Mrs. Bethune's? Indeed!—Very pleased to meet you. Residing with her, or only on a visit?—A short visit?—Perhaps in Mrs. Romer's absence? It does not do, of course, for such a young woman to live alone.—And so Frances is not well? We are used to speak of her as Frances, because Colonel Bethune is a connection of ours, indeed a distant cousin. Not serious, I hope? We all hope her indisposition is not of consequence?"

"No," Ursula hastened to add, "not at all serious. Nothing but a headache."

"Ah," the three bonnets vibrated in concert. "People of a lethargic temperament often suffer from headache. Our dear Frances is not very active. Does she walk much in these days? Is she in the habit of employing herself actively in her garden—in her house—in the parish—?" The questions flashing in first from one point, and then from another. "It always seems strange when a lady living in the country does not care for parish visiting. Our poorer neighbours, you know, Mrs. Adams. And when so much can be done by a word in season—a little advice, a little interest.—Oh no, not gifts. I hope indeed that Frances is not so foolish. Gifts only pauperise, but to exert influence, to advise, to make a worthy use of our superior position, that is another matter. Dear me! So she does not walk much, does not often drive? Then what does she do—? Oh, she reads, does she? Come, if she reads, that is something. Really solid books, no doubt: surely not novels—the pernicious trash that is published now-a-days! You do not mean novels, Mrs. Adams? For an occupation!"

Ursula disclaimed any particular knowledge of Mrs. Bethune's taste in literature. Her friend was fond of reading—in general terms; she had not strong health. No doubt at times she read novels, like other people.

The three ladies shook their heads. "A sad employment, a degenerate employment, for an immortal soul," sighed the younger Miss Lancaster, who wore eyeglasses. And then from generalities the catechism advanced to the particular.

"We came over today," said Mrs. Lancaster, shaking out her laces, "for we saw in the paper that Colonel Bethune is ordered home. Of course," with a keen look at the witness, "Frances is aware?"

Ursula acquiesced in the 'of course.'

"And from himself, I suppose? A letter written direct? Ah," to her daughter, "I thought it was not so bad as people hinted. I thought they must correspond." Then again to the deputy hostess, "We are very interested in Charles, you know, and in Frances for his sake. We are anxious to hear about him, for I fear his illness has been serious. He is really coming straight to England? He is coming here?"

45

The Experiment Begins

Ursula did not know how to evade the rapid questions, and the still more rapid inferences, which assumed before admission. She ceased to wonder at Frances's access of headache, as she strove to reply with some amount of repressive dignity. She knew nothing of Colonel Bethune's plans, except that he had sent all information to his wife. And that he was expected at The Mount.

Again the visitors looked at each other with significant glances, and some nods and tremblings of the graduated bonnets. The senior bonnet was spokeswoman.

"As you are an intimate friend of Frances, Mrs. Adams, you will understand our anxiety. Have you known her long?—Oh, at school together, and did not meet again till last winter. (Of course she knows nothing of what went on in India. That explains it!)" Here the junior bonnets had the aside. Then again to Ursula, with the air of one who of set purpose says little, and withholds, but at the same time indicates, a larger knowledge, "There had been a—a misunderstanding, such will arise at times between young married people," shaking her head. "We are glad, very glad, to know on your authority that Charles has written to his wife, and that he is returning here. Not any tea, I thank you," the servant had just carried in the table to set beside Ursula. "We will not stay longer, as Frances is unable to receive us. I hope her headache will be better. I hope, I really trust, that all may now be well. Any division is so sad, you feel it to be so, I am sure. May I ask for my carriage immediately? The ways of Providence are mysterious. Frances is very much altered, but we have thought it quite a dispensation—where beauty has been a snare, as it was in her case, for the temptation to be removed. Pray give her our best wishes, Mrs. Adams, and our congratulations on her husband's return."

The coveted information had been extracted, and the witness was free to stand down. The three ornate bonnets

46

and the three stiff skirts made a dignified exit, and presently Ursula, standing at the glass door of the hall, watched with intense relief the recession of their carriage down the drive.

V.
THE FOURTH VIGIL

The séance of the second night proved uneventful. Hope was still deferred, and yet Frances continued sanguine. Ursula was required to judge whether she had not already changed somewhat in appearance; there was, Mrs. Bethune declared, at least the sensation of difference. She felt lighter, she affirmed, could move with greater alacrity; and, to her own perception, the rounding of her limbs had become less solid. Ursula could not honestly say she perceived alteration, even when the stout arm was stripped from its sleeve to exhibit, and she was called upon to touch and examine. A white arm, which still preserved the exquisite fineness of skin that had been a personal charm of Frances Wayland's, but on the underside, midway between the wrist and the elbow, there was a curious double scar. "What an odd mark," said Ursula.

"Yes, is it not strange I should have been hurt twice over in the same place, and so many years apart? You remember how I broke the window long ago at school, and what a fuss there was about it. They thought I had cut an artery, and the doctor was called in to stop the bleeding. He stitched the place. See, this is it. It is whiter than the other, but I shall never lose the mark. The red scar beside it is where I hurt myself in India, when I had that fall from my horse and was stunned. I was not cut anywhere else; it was the blow to my head that made the danger. Is it not a strange mark—half white and half red, and like a Roman Two?"

"You were very ill then, were you not?"

"Yes, and for a long time my memory was confused; I could not remember clearly what had gone before. And yet I have to thank that illness for the happiest time in all my life. Oh, I wish it could come over again. It never can while I remain like this. But if I get thin—if my old looks come back to me—!"

She drew the sleeve down over her arm with a sigh, hiding the scar. She seldom spoke of India, and Ursula's curiosity was quickened. "Tell me about it," she said. They were again in the garden, sitting under the cedar tree, for the day had proved unusually warm.

"Well, it came about in this way. There was some kind of disturbance with the frontier tribes, and Charles was sent forward with a detachment. Of course I could not have gone, even if I had been well, there was no question of that, but the illness had made him anxious, and he said I must have a woman friend to stay. So Mrs. Clarkson promised to look after me. I had not known her long, but I liked her. She was older—and clever and lively; she always got a great deal of attention, and she and I were said to be the best dressed women on the station. She was a Canadian by birth, and her husband was away too."

Frances's story was inclined to halt at this point, but presently she went on.

"She made it all so different. She showed me what a fool I had been to devote myself to Charles, and let all the fun of life go by. And how Charles himself would think more of me and like me better if I was admired and run after. And I was—I was! Ursula, you may not believe it, looking at me now, but I was the rage at Bagharaun that winter. Mrs. Clarkson and I were together always, and nobody else had a chance against us—such an effective contrast as we made, she dark and tall, and I little and fair. It was a lovely time. And then to have it spoiled because of that tiresome Prendergast, and because Charles took it into his head to be stupid. If I could choose to live part of my life over again, it would be just those weeks—those months. I often think of them, I dream of them at night—!"

"What, happier than when you were a girl, in love with Major Bethune? Happier than when your engagement was allowed?" Ursula could not help the question, but her friend put it impatiently aside; the vista of those past triumphs seemed to fill up all her mental view.

"I was happy then, of course," she admitted, "but it was a different sort of happiness, and that is all so long ago I hardly remember it now. It is the other that I dream about. As I look back, those weeks seem just perfect: every day with its new interest to carry you on—full of fun and flirtation, dancing and lights and flowers—and whispers in the verandah—and the cool evenings after the heat. Such whispers, Ursula. And the joke it was to talk it over afterwards with Mrs. Clarkson, and hear her story in return. There was no harm in it—no harm at all. I wonder where she is now. I wonder what has become of Prendergast, and all the others. And to think of Charles sending me home in disgrace, to mope my heart out here with Mrs. Romer. No wonder I lost my health. No wonder I got like this!"

Ursula turned away her face with a sharp pang of pity—not for Frances, but for the husband on board the oncoming ship, far away there in the east. Was this the wife on whom his hope was set, who was to meet him with the flowers of June!

"And now he writes me that unreasonable letter," Mrs. Bethune continued pouting, as if in response to the unspoken thought. "It is nonsense. We cannot put the clock back for the years that are gone. He could not really do it, any more than I. That sort of romance was all very well when I was a girl, and ignorant of life. Why pretend to recall it now? He was always stupid about remembering things and going back to them. He will have to understand that nonsense was changed when I began to know. Changed!—I felt like another woman in another life, as if I had been dead before, and only then knew what it was to be alive. Don't look like that, Ursula, I am quite prepared to be a good wife to him, if only we succeed. And I begin to hope we really shall succeed, and I shall be able to fasten the belt about my waist when the seventh evening has come and gone."

That day, the third of the experiment, was Sunday at The Mount and, as they sat under the cedar, the church bells rang unheeded from the valley below. Ursula did not often disregard their summons, but today Frances claimed all her companionship. The lethargy had passed away, leaving Mrs. Bethune restless, uneasy, nervously expectant, counting the hours till the séance. And, oddly enough, as her spirits rose over their undertaking, Ursula's declined. She grew increasingly doubtful of the task to which she was pledged, and distrustful of the issue. When it came to the third vigil, and she sat alone in the twilight listening to those groans behind the curtain, the warning words spoken in London came back to her again and again, and she was almost ready to give back the hoarded notes, and refuse to play her part.

It was very late when Frances came to herself. "Light the candles," she commanded, "light the candles and look at me. There is a difference; I am sure there is a difference. The change has begun." And under the branch of wax-lights hastily kindled, the fair face did look altered, shrunken from the fulness of the cheeks, but at the same time drawn and pale.

"I did not sleep so much tonight," she went on, shuddering with chattering teeth, and clinging to her friend. "I was awake for a little in the middle of the time; I heard the clock strike. I had no power to call out to you and no power to move, except to close one hand about my arm, and it had grown quite small; the bones just covered, that was all. And," shuddering again, "what do you think I saw?"

Ursula was inclined to shudder also, as she waited the information and thought of Salvador. "Not a face, like Mrs. Warden's?"

"Oh no, nothing of that sort; but billows of white stuff all round me, like mist—or very filmy muslin. I seemed to be buried in it up to the neck; and it shone in a light of its own, though the recess was dark. Do you know what I think it was? I believe it was all my superfluous substance drawn away, though it cannot be quite separated as yet, I suppose it is too soon. I believe I was thin for the time, though I am stout again now. And I begin to be sure, Ursula—quite, quite sure we shall succeed."

So upon hope and fear the fourth day dawned. A day of sultry heat, of gathering darkness, of distant thunder, summer lightnings glimmering over the sea from a storm below the horizon. The friends were driven in from the garden by the first drops of falling rain, and before eight o'clock in the evening a regular downpour had set in from the dark sky. The windows of the dining room were open, and sitting at dinner they could hear the rush of its descent on the gravel terrace, and shrubs below. A shaded lamp hung from the ceiling, and the table with its snowy cloth was the centre of a glow of light; a table abundantly spread with sweets and fruits as substitutes for the heavier diet prohibited. Frances beamed with smiles as she stirred her coffee, and Ursula, anxiously watching her, thought those full outlines had undoubtedly diminished, and it might be true after all that a gradual change had begun.

If really it came about, Mrs. Bethune was saying, the change would take everybody by surprise; and because the truth could not be told about it, she would be forced to attribute the alteration to some one or other of the remedies she had tried by turns, and tried in vain.

"Think what an advertisement I shall be to them! I ought to get hundreds out of the proprietors. In one short week; and a doctor's certificate as to my state before and after, the loss of—how many stones! We must invent a telling way to put it, Ursula. And which do you think would give me the biggest premium—the Rasselas Remedy company, or the Finemdown Tablets? I'll put myself up to the highest bidder, and make—oh, far more than the fee I promised you!"

Light laughter over this, light laughter as she pictured the astonishment of friends and neighbours at the change forecasted—the surprise of her dressmaker, who would have to be summoned and charged with fresh orders. She even sent for a fashion-paper, and spread it beside her on the table, calling Ursula to look at one pictured style after another, drawn in the usual way, with impossible wasp-waists and simpering faces. "That would suit me to perfection," she said, "if I am as I used to be. And that—and that! Get a pencil and mark them, that I may not forget." The vanity adverse conditions had smothered for a time, began again to stir. Her pale cheeks flushed, her eyes shone; and, full of dreams of her dresses, and the hope of fastening them once more about a shapely waist, Mrs. Bethune disappeared behind the curtains on the fourth night. The girl who loved Charles Bethune with such sincerity of passion, who waited for him in the June garden long ago, was dead and gone out of Frances world as if she had never been;

buried, fathoms deep under the accretion of a coarser nature, the domination of a shallower soul.

When the breathing Ursula listened for became heavy and regular, she withdrew from the piano to the window-seat as was her wont; feeling her way in the complete darkness of the room, for not a ray of moon or star illuminated it from without. The air was exceedingly oppressive, so, with light touch to avoid noise, she undid the hasp of the window and softly pushed it open, leaning close to the rush of the rain, and drinking in the grateful scent which exhaled from dripping foliage, and thirsty earth. Everywhere else the room was closely shut, the door bolted, the bow window in the recess which formed the cabinet shuttered and barred. Nothing was likely to disturb them from without, as the room was on an upper floor. Nobody could climb up by those wet rose stems, or the ropes of wisteria, to interrupt her vigil. She and Frances Bethune were absolutely alone, except for Powers and Presences not of this world, if such existed—a belief she sought to stifle, though at times it made her tremble.

The hours on this fourth night were long, and went heavily by. She had no inclination to sleep; a certain pressing anxiety, a certain unacknowledged fear, forbade the easy oblivion which might have been hers under the sloping roof at Mrs. Minter's. Darkness, the pouring of the ceaseless rain, the gurgling of full spouts, the dripping of the eaves; no other sound but Frances's breathing, and at long intervals the chiming of the tardy clock. Surely no clock ever before compassed so many minutes in its hour. Eleven—twelve, the hour of ghostly midnight, but no ghosts intruded on her watch. One—two... Two so long past that three would shortly strike; and yet Frances made no sign in her retirement. The new day would be upon them, and find her keeping vigil; she began to speculate whether full daylight would rouse Frances behind her curtains, or whether the house would be astir about them, and she still bound to wait, uncertain what to do.

She conjectured that the trance had ended long since, and her friend had passed into natural sleep, sunk in the comfort of her cushioned chair, and yet she dared not rise to draw the curtains or strike a light; she remembered Salvador's warning, and also the angry blow which struck the floor at her feet in their first trial. Frances was alive, she could hear her regular breathing, though the groans had ceased. Why should her friend be harmed tonight, she argued with herself, when she had remained unhurt before? And yet a conviction was growing upon her that this fourth night had not been like the other nights, but had surely brought about some notable change.

Three at last upon the clock, and out of doors the downpour of the rain relaxed, a fresher air sighed among the trees, the wind that goes before the dawn. The grey light began to spread over the sky, a ghostly glimmer, the familiar aspect of the room became dimly visible. Ursula shivered, her limbs were stiff, her eyes strained by the long effort to penetrate the darkness, she felt herself utterly weary, and out of tune with the new day. Surely the ordeal must now be over, but the curtains which formed the cabinet still hung together unstirred, covering the mystery, if any mystery, dwelt within. She bent forward again to listen to the breathing which assured her Frances still slept, and for the first time noticed a peculiarity which had not struck her earlier.

The regular sound had found an echo, gentler and lighter than itself, but palpably accompanying it: a second breath repeating the other, though slower as well as fainter. Of course it was nothing but an echo, yet it was curious, and she had not noticed it before. Her nerves were strained with the long vigil, she told herself with some self-scorn, holding her own breath to listen, but a shiver crept

The Fourth Vigil

through her veins, chilling the warm pulse of the blood.

It was utterly impossible there could be a second sleeper within those guarded curtains, the recess was quite empty when Frances took her place. She herself had been awake and vigilant, nobody could have tampered with the locked door, and entered while she was unaware. It was impossible, she said again in that inward colloquy—and yet she shuddered, and could have cried aloud in her relief when, some minutes later, Mrs. Bethune stirred at last.

She heard her move in the chair, and stretch herself with a yawn; then came a faint affrighted exclamation, another movement, and then the sound of a fall. What had happened—had Frances fainted? It was her first thought as she sprang up; but before she could reach the curtains they were torn asunder from within, and the white-robed figure rushed out and fell into her arms, panting and trembling, clutching at her with frantic grasp as if for life.

There was hardly any light in the room as yet, for the one uncurtained window did not face the east, but before the possibility of sight, touch was sufficiently indicative. A change had passed upon the form she held. It was no longer the solid and capacious armful, but a creature as slender as herself who clung to her and sobbed on her shoulder. "Ursula! Ursula!" cried the familiar voice, "tell me I am awake and do not dream. Tell me, tell me," quivering with hysterical laughter, "that the burden is gone indeed, and that I am in truth set free!"

VI.
SWORN TO SILENCE

The surprise of their success was scarcely lessened by the measure of expectation which had gone before. Perhaps in her inner mind Ursula never truly believed that such a miracle could be. And Frances's excitement was a further agitation, she clung to her friend in a sort of panic, even in the moment of her joy. "Come away—come away," she sobbed. "I daren't stay here, I am frightened. Come into the bedroom. No, don't touch the curtains, leave everything as it is till after. I feel giddy and faint, and so light—so light! As if I could float away. Will it last, do you think?" And then she repeated again in her wonder, "It is like a dream. Can it be true—can it be true that I am free?"

In the bedroom Ursula drew up the blinds and lit the candles and in that mingling of wax-light and dawn, Frances was able to view herself and to be viewed. Wine had been kept in readiness for an emergency, and presently the hysterical convulsion, the sobbing laughter, passed away, though a degree of bodily weakness still remained. Ursula supported her to stand before the long cheval-glass hung between the pillars of her toilet-table, which reflected her from head to foot, and she pressed with eager hands the loose wrapper to her figure, slight once more, and spanned the compass of her waist. The face which had been so round was now small and shrunken, shadowed on either side by falling hair, but a flush of excitement coloured her cheek, and her eyes were bright with triumph. "Now Charles can come as soon as he likes," she said gleefully. "I can face him, I do not care. And I can have the dresses, we will write for them this very day."

Ursula begged her to lie down. "You must rest, Frances, or you will be ill and then you cannot wear the dresses when they come. See how weak you are, and think how much you have lost. I wonder where it has gone to, what they have done with it. You are only half the size you were last night."

Mrs. Bethune was in bed by this time, looking small as a child under the coverlet, but she turned her face on the pillow with a sharp shudder, and put out her hand again for the wine.

"Were you unconscious all the time?" went on Ursula. "Did you see those waves of white again? And had you any pain?"

"I knew nothing till I woke, and then it was quite dark within the curtains. But I was instantly aware something had happened—that I had changed. I felt—oh, I can't tell you how I felt, all emptied out and light. Then I wanted to get up, but at first I could not," and the shudder came back.

"You were too weak?"

"No, it wasn't that, it seemed as if something heavy was weighing me down—the dead weight of a thing lying across my knees. I am frightened, I don't want to think about it. No, perhaps I had better tell you, only hold my hand."

"Something you felt, but did not see?"

"Yes—yes, I don't know what it was. But it came into my

mind that I must get away from it, must get out to you, or I should go mad with fright. And as I struggled to my feet, the thing slipped down on to the floor. It really fell. I stumbled over it—I think I trod on it—as I rushed out to you."

This was all Mrs. Bethune had to tell of the working of the miracle. She did not care to dwell on that uncanny episode, but at once reverted to delight in her bodily change, and she lay looking at her hands and arms in their new slenderness, while the daylight strengthened, and the sun rose upon the young morning and the rain-washed woods.

"Ursula, I am thinking what I can put on. I cannot lie in bed, you know, till new clothes are made for me and nothing I have will fit. Yes, I know there are the loose gowns, but it would be ridiculous to wear them now. Do you think Truscott will be up yet? I want you to ring for her. There is a trunk upstairs, packed with some of my Indian dresses. I kept them—a few of them—for love of that time I told you of. I could not bear to throw them away, though they are old-fashioned. I have not worn them since, for it was cold weather when I got to England, and before the summer came round again, my shape had altered. Tell Truscott to have the trunk brought down, and we will undo it here."

"Have you made up your mind what you are going to say, how you will account for the sudden change, to Truscott and the others? You see, it is so great, it will astonish them so much." Ursula was putting out the candles, her own face looking altered in the early light, pale and drawn after her vigil. "Don't you think you had better wear the loose gown, at any rate for today, so that the surprise of it may come upon them by degrees?—And before we ring up the servants, or they are likely to be astir, I will go and shut the window in the boudoir, and rearrange the recess, so that it may look as usual."

Mrs. Bethune did not oppose, and Ursula went on her errand. She had not attached importance to Frances's story, but she felt a slight disposition in herself to shudder as she went back into the room. The window was open as they left it, not now upon darkness and rain, but admitting the freshness of the morning, and framed about with fluttering leaves. The silk curtains still hung together, swaying a little in the draught. Ursula took hold of one of them to draw it back.

There was the cushioned chair where Frances had slept in her trance, but what was this, lying on the floor in front of it, white and quiet? Was it—could it be—the Thing which had lain upon her knees?

Ursula barely restrained a cry which must have alarmed the house and only her grasp of the curtain kept her from falling, in the thrill and shock which ran over all the nerves of her body from head to foot. She was not a coward by nature, but here her courage failed. She dropped the folds of silk, and fled to the window, to the comfort of the light and air, looking back over her shoulder, and with one hand pressed hard against the beating of her heart.

The curtains fell together, hiding the new-found terror, and hung as before unmoved except for those stirrings of the air, while she questioned with herself what it was that she had seen.

Nothing terrible in itself, but horribly suggestive, knowing what had gone before. Could Frances's burden have taken human shape in separating from her, and did a body remain, for which they must account, or of which they must dispose? And the house would soon be astir.

Whatever it was, she was bound to face it and acquaint herself with the worst. Not a moment must be given to irresolution, however great the revolt of her humanity from this thing which was out of nature. She forced herself back to the curtain. Materialised shapes were said to be evanescent; Salvador had melted into air, though his living face had confronted her at Miss Sedgeley's. This might be merely a phantom, and would have disappeared when the screen was again withdrawn.

With a desperate effort she flung the curtains aside to right and left, so that full daylight flooded the recess. Alas, it was no transitory apparition. Face downwards at the foot of the chair, one slender arm thrown forward and the other bent under her, lay the naked body of a girl. Not in death, which was her first thought, but in profound sleep. The white shoulder heaved with the expansion of the chest, and when she touched it with a reluctant finger, it was warm and soft with the warmth of living flesh.

This was no lifeless body, hideously suggesting murder, but a naked stranger to be clothed and accounted for. The whole problem narrowed to the need of the moment, spurring her on to action. The servants would be astir in another half hour; the awful tidings must be broken to Frances. Where could a hiding-place be found? And first the stranger must be clothed.

Hurrying to her room she fetched a night dress, and braced her nerves to handle and turn the sleeper, dreading an awakening shriek which must betray them. But that sleep or trance proved deep beyond disturbance. The girl only sighed as the garment was drawn down over her limbs, and fastened at the breast and throat, and again when Ursula, with an exertion of all her strength, lifted the prone weight into a small American chair with rockers which stood in the boudoir. To carry such a burden along the landing to the bedroom would have been impossible; to drag the chair was not difficult; and ten minutes later she drew a breath of intense relief, with the lock of her own door fastened on the outside, and the key in her hand.

But a task equally hard lay before her in returning to Mrs. Bethune. During a hasty rearrangement of the boudoir, she tried to con over some scheme of announcement; but in Frances's presence she stood dumb and white, the power of speech deserting her, so unforeseen and so terrible was the thing she had to tell. Mrs. Bethune was not usually observant of what concerned others, but this was too palpable to be overlooked.

"Good gracious! Ursula what is the matter? You are not going to faint, are you? Take some of the wine—at once." And then, more imperiously, "What is it?"

The difficult words had to be spoken, no tact in communication could make them easier to endure. "I went back to the boudoir," she stammered. "Frances, you must not agitate yourself. Remember, you are not strong."

Mrs. Bethune raised herself on her elbow and looked keenly at the other, there was apprehension in her face rather than surprise. Was she quite in ignorance of what had remained behind?

"You know how altered you are—what a quantity of substance has been withdrawn. We wondered what would be done with it, living matter as it was. I suppose it accounts for what I found."

Those blue eyes looked bright as steel, searching into Ursula's, and the hand which was changed and thin, came with a compelling grip upon her arm. "What?" she said. "Speak!"

"You told me—that something heavy lay on your knees when you woke, and slipped down at your feet and you trod on it. And before, in the trance, I heard a double breathing behind the curtains—yours and another. Frances, when I drew them back I found a body—a fully formed body, sleeping, but alive. A young girl perfectly naked, lying on the floor."

"It is a fraud," Mrs. Bethune cried out, feeling for the words with white lips. "An impudent fraud. Somebody must have got in—to play a trick on us—on me."

"The doors were locked—I was awake and watching. Nobody could have got in, nobody knew what we were doing, it was a secret between us two. There is no fraud, unless I am in the fraud, and you will not think that."

No, she could not think that, looking in Ursula's face. "I suppose it is one of those things they call materialisations," she said slowly, with a shudder of repulsion, "built up out of me. If so, it will only last for a little while. It will dissolve—whatever it is that becomes of them—and disappear."

"It will not dissolve, unless it dissolves back into you, and then you would be large again, as you were before. But I think that will not be possible. Do you remember what Salvador said at the séance—that there could be no putting back in this case, any more than when a child is naturally born. I believe the form will remain. How are we to account for it? What are we to do?"

"And the Thing really seems to be alive? A girl, you say? Is it a child?"

"Alive, but asleep. Not a child, a fully formed woman, slender, but in weight as much as I could lift from the floor."

"You lifted it? Where is it now?"

Ursula hastily recounted what she had done. "I could not leave it for the servants to find, and they will soon be stirring. I took it—her—into my own room and laid her on the bed. And the door is locked. I have the key." Mrs. Bethune sat up in bed, considering, a new and harder expression on her thin face. What with the bodily change in her, and that look of a different mind, Ursula scarcely knew her for the Frances of the day before. As the silence continued, she ventured a fresh suggestion.

"We shall have to think of an excuse to account for her presence here. And some plan for the future, if she lives."

Mrs. Bethune turned that newly-hardened face slowly upon Ursula. "Why should the Creature live?" she said in a whisper. "It is not a human being, it can have no natural life. It cannot have a mind or a soul, only a sort of mock vitality borrowed from me. To kill such a thing could not be murder. They say doctors do away with unnatural births, I don't know whether it is true. In this horrible case of ours," the thrill of a fresh shudder running over her, "there would be equal reason and no more crime. Ursula," leaning out of bed, and grasping the other to draw her close. "If the Creature is asleep, it would not be hard to do. Now, this moment. I would make it worth your while, I would give you money. A wet towel on the face, held till the breathing stops. There need be no violence—or—blood." Perhaps of all the horrors of the night, this was the greatest.

Could it be Frances who spoke? Frances, whose worst faults were a transparent selfishness, an indolent weakness of character, easily led? Oh, if the clock could be put back to the day before; or back over the space of time, so short a time in retrospect, before she coveted the money, and knew the other woman in her vanity would yield. And now money was offered her again, and for what service! The fresh fair early morning brightened outside the window, God's world as it used to be, but with a ghastly difference here within, and in her heart. The horror of it paralysed her like a nightmare, as she looked at her friend's altered face. Mrs. Bethune's body had grown shapely, but what deforming change had passed upon her soul!

Ursula shrank away from the compelling grasp, from the words breathed into her ear. "Frances, how dare you? You would bribe me—to do murder!"

"It would not be murder," returned the other with a frown. "The Creature is unnatural, and should be destroyed."

"It would be taking life, however given. And it would leave us with a dead body to account for, more dangerous and difficult than a live one. The Law will not admit your explanation, remember that. No witness of ours will convince the Law that it was built up out of yours, in the way we must assert, and was therefore yours to destroy. Oh,

Frances, be yourself. You frighten me, turn away from such dreadful thoughts. Let us take counsel together what is to be done."

Mrs. Bethune dropped her eyes in a sort of shamed silence which still was sullen. She said presently, "What do you suggest?"

"Can you pretend—to the servants—that a friend has come on a visit? A friend who arrived unexpectedly, late at night, after the house was shut up. You might say I gave up my room to her, as it was too late to prepare another. And that she is keeping her bed because indisposed. It sounds unlikely, I know, but can you think of anything more probable? We cannot hide the fact that she is here. The pretence of illness will give us time to watch development—to see if there is intelligence, anything beyond bare life. And for the rest, Colonel Bethune will advise you when he comes."

Frances listened with averted face until the mention of her husband's name. Then she flashed an altered look upon Ursula, and her mouth set hard again, the mouth which used to be so soft and ready for smiles. Had she forgotten Colonel Bethune, and his relation to the new difficulty?

"Of course he must be told," Ursula went on.

"And how do you know that he will believe us, any more than the Law?"

"Why—your husband would believe you, Frances. He would know that you told him the truth, however strange the tale."

Perhaps Mrs. Bethune, reviewing her matrimonial experience, did not feel the suggested certainty. She made no direct reply.

"This calamity about the Creature is my own affair, to divulge or to withhold. You understand that, Ursula? I will tell Colonel Bethune, in my own time and way, and until I speak, you must be silent, to him, and to everybody else, without exception. Promise me to be silent."

"You are the right person to tell him; I do not want to say anything. But we cannot foresee what may happen."

"All the same, I want your promise. I should have asked for it in any case, about this change of appearance. I do not want it proclaimed on the housetops, how it came to pass and what I have done. And no one has any right to interfere—between me and Charles."

She watched Ursula narrowly as she spoke, pressing her with insistent will, exacting the words which came reluctantly, a vague apprehension striving to the last to keep them back.

"Very well, I promise."

"You see those books there on the shelf. Give me the one at the end—the last but one—bound in dark leather—"

"Why, Frances, it is a Bible!"

"I know, bring it here. You are a Christian, and you hold a promise sacred. Then you can have no objection to confirm it with an oath. Kiss the book, and swear."

"No, I won't do that, it is not necessary. A promise is enough. I will make it in any terms you like, and I am used to keep my word."

"Well—repeat it after me, and here is the Bible open between us, as a witness of our faith. You have been mixed up in this, without any fault of your own. I don't blame you for what has come of it, and I don't forget what I offered to pay if we succeeded and I got back my figure. Promise never to breathe a word to anyone of what we have done together, you and I. Or of what this Creature truly is, and how she came to be, unless I give you leave, or unless I am dead. Say the words as I say them; promise or oath, it is all one. As you believe in Heaven. Upon your faith, upon your soul. Promise me, Ursula."

VII.
THE BELL RINGS

Frances carried her point, as she had a way of doing, and Ursula was pledged to secrecy. No lips but Mrs. Bethune's might disclose the secret of that June night, and in her heart of hearts she had no least intention of avowing the ugly truth, to her husband or to any other. Her strength and energy returned, stimulated by the wine and the brief rest; and when Truscott knocked at the door some half-hour later, she was up in her loose wrapper, already seated at the toilet table and ready for the service of her maid.

The attitude and the loose robe served for some measure of concealment, still Truscott's amazement was evident. The woman looked gray and aghast, and her hands were unsteady as she combed out the long fair hair, and prepared to arrange it as usual. Frances in the glass had a full view of the maid's face, but she maintained an admirable composure, giving her orders as easily as if concerned with nothing out of the common.

"I shall not require the tray this morning, Truscott."

"No, ma'am?"

"Tell Susan I intend to breakfast downstairs with Mrs.

The Bell Rings

Adams, and we shall both be ready for it early. I think you know my large trunk in the box-room, where I have some dresses put away?"

"Yes, ma'am."

"I want it brought down here, for I am going to look it through. I may be able to make use of some of the things, now I am thinner."

"Yes, ma'am," this time with a gasp.

"I am very much thinner, and I daresay you notice it. That remedy has worked wonders, and more rapidly than the doctors expected. And, Truscott, we have a visitor in the house, come unexpectedly."

"A visitor, ma'am?"

"Yes, and another room must be got ready: the Blue room in the wing. The arrival was late last night, after you were all in bed, so Mrs. Adams was good enough to give up her room to the lady, and to sleep with me."

It was evident that Truscott marvelled greatly as she withdrew. "You were right about the loose gown," said Frances, when the maid finally departed. "I may have to wear it for a day or two, lest people should be too much startled. I thought old Truscott's eyes would have jumped out of her head when she saw me. She has not been here long, and never knew me anything but stout." Her eyes were on the glass as she spoke, smiling at her reflection, and with a hand on either side to mark the changed outline of her shape. "And now, Ursula, I want you to unlock your door, and see what has happened to—to that Creature, and bring me word again."

So Ursula went with her key, sending away a servant knocking with hot water before she ventured to fit it in the lock. She entered cautiously, on shoes of silence, but the mysterious stranger was still asleep, unmoved from the position in which she had been laid down, straight as a corpse upon the bed, with the coverlet drawn up to her chin. Yet nothing but the attitude suggested death, the girl was certainly alive. Ursula drew aside the shade from the window, to admit a fuller light, and this time she held her breath in amazement. Not because of any visible horror, the burden of the mysterious presence was dreadful to these conspirators, but nothing met the eye that was not fair and sweet. She recognised the intruder; there lay the wonder and surprise which seemed again to arrest the beating of her heart. The face on the pillow was a face once dearly loved, and long unseen, lost to her with her girl-friend Fancy Wayland, and never found again in Mrs. Bethune.

She looked, and looked again, and strove to chide herself for a deceptive imagination. The associations of the place must have suggested the idea. The little room, a bower of white dimity and white enamel furniture, with sprays of roses on the walls, had been Fancy Wayland's bedroom, when first her school-friend came as a visitor to The Mount. And it was here Ursula found her, laid with cropped curls on the pillow, in those days of dread and illness, when the one darling daughter of the house was thought to be dying for love of Charles Bethune.

During Frances's married life and years of absence, The Mount saw little change. It had been let furnished to an old couple who were childless, and careful tenants; and now on her return, the chief alterations were in those larger rooms which Mrs. Bethune occupied, and filled full of luxury for herself. She had forgotten all her tenderness for the little white bower, as she forgot many other affections of her earlier life; it served in these days as a third or fourth-rate spare bedroom, and so was good enough for Mrs. Adams when she became an inmate. Now, as Ursula turned to the bed, the face on the pillow, pale and peaceful, was Fancy Wayland's face, the same soft bright hair curled about it in short tendrils. The stranger's lip took on the same half

THE BELL RINGS

piteous curve, till she looked like a child who had sobbed herself to sleep, as Fancy long ago sobbed in her sorrow.

The likeness seemed to grow as Ursula gazed, doubting and dreading to realise the danger of such a duplication. Anyone who had known Mrs. Bethune in her youth, must recognise as her very image this unnatural creature, born from her, not as a child is born, but as Eve was taken out of Adam in the beginning. There were friends in the neighbourhood, friends of long standing like the Lancasters, who could so remember. It was well there were no old servants at The Mount to compare and comment, and make the mystery and the scandal greater still.

And all the while the sleeper slept, undisturbed by Ursula's presence and close scrutiny, moved only by that gentle stirring of the breath, her trance as deep, her suspension as profound, as when she lay white and naked on the floor of the boudoir. Would there never be any quickening to completer life? Would food ever be needed to sustain life, as in the case of common humanity commonly born? Or would the unconscious existence go on unfed, except mysteriously from Frances, for days and weeks, perhaps for months and years, exactly as now, without development or soul?

"Come and look at her," she said later on to Mrs. Bethune. "There is nothing terrible to see." And when she entered the room again, the mistress of The Mount accompanied her, and they stood together by the bed. Frances had been hard to persuade, for all her uneasy curiosity about the stranger, but once at that bedside she stood there, fixed and fascinated, the woman of full age confronting the incarnation of her youth.

The girl slept as before, but, while they watched, a faint colour began to steal into the pale cheek, as if from a stronger stirring of the heart. Yes, the two faces resembled each other, feature by feature, as might two impressions struck from the same die; and yet there was a difference, subtle, significant. The stranger's likeness was to the former rather than the present Frances, for in the loss of bulk, the alteration she so ardently desired, Mrs. Bethune had not reverted to her old appearance except in the mere outline of her form. Her face had regained its former oval, her features were sharpened into delicacy, but the change had aged her as if by the passing of years. The fine skin had slightly withered in shrinking after expansion, and its flower-like texture and tint had disappeared. Ursula looked from one to the other, and thought they might have passed for mother and daughter, so greatly was Frances aged by the transformation of the night, changed also by the expression of an altered mind. Then she became aware that Mrs. Bethune was trembling; her teeth clicked together as she shuddered and caught at Ursula. "Take me away," she said, "take me away!"

The door was locked again upon the incubus, and the conspirators were alone, but Mrs. Bethune's agitation continued. "I will not go near her again," she declared with vehemence. "You will have to see to her, and do what is necessary. She looks like a human being, she is not horrible, but I had the strangest feeling as I stood beside her. It was as if my life were being sucked out of me—into her. I felt as if I should die—!"

"Did you notice the likeness?"

Frances frowned over the question. "She has light hair, I noticed that. I suppose you think she is like the Waylands?"

"She is the very image of what you used to be when you were young—a school-girl at Mrs. Pryer's. I thought you would see it for yourself."

"I hate to think of it—or her. I daresay it is all your fancy. But if we have to give her a name—to the servants—you had better call her Wayland. Say she is Miss Wayland, and my cousin."

The Bell Rings

It was curious in the sequel to remember that Frances herself bestowed the name, and was the first to call her by it. And the need became immediate. The presence of a guest was known already to the household, and wonder doubtless was astir. Visitors were infrequent in these days at The Mount, and this one had arrived at a shut-up house in the middle of the night, had been admitted by Mrs. Bethune herself, contrary to any precedent, and now lay in a locked room, which the usual service was not allowed to enter. There was of course the excuse of indisposition, of fatigue after a journey; but to have left her unnamed would have added to the mystery. The whole situation bristled with difficulty, from Frances's change of shape to the introduction of the stranger. No care or tact could make it appear natural, however great the prudence exercised, comment was bound to follow.

And Frances was not prudent. Her elation over the personal result of the experiment, began to outweigh her horror of the other and more embarrassing consequence. It seemed as if she could shut off the responsibility of that dormant life with the locked door, and stop out reflection by plunging back into her vanities. She wore her loose gown about the house that morning, but, even under its partial disguise, her altered appearance was manifest. Ursula caught the wondering looks of the servants, and noticed that, on one pretext or another, the whole establishment was encountered on the stairs or in the passages. Mrs. Choppington came for her morning interview, and emerged purple and well-nigh speechless, intercepting Ursula in the hall.

"I beg your pardon for remarking it, Mrs. Adams," she said gasping, with one hand on her large side, as if entirely overcome, "but it has given me such a turn to see the mistress, if it really is the mistress?"—the last with an interrogative stare. "Whatever can have come to her to be stout as she was yesterday, as stout as me, though maybe younger, and today all gone to bone, the like of which I never saw. If it has been them vegetarian dishes—which I never did hold with—"

Ursula did her best to smooth over matters. Mrs. Bethune had been undergoing treatment to reduce her size, as Mrs. Choppington knew. It had taken effect suddenly, but she was not ill, and would probably be stronger now than before.

Mrs. Choppington shook her head. The hopeful view was not for her. "Nothing can be good, begging your pardon ma'am, which brings them down that sudden. And the mistress so sharp-like with it, not herself at all. 'Choppington, I leave it to you,' that is what she used to say, 'and it'll be sure to be right.' I don't disguise it give me such a shock, that I don't know however I can stay."

The loose gown was adhered to through the morning, but with afternoon came the opening of her Indian stores, and then nothing could deter Mrs. Bethune from setting off her changed figure with that hoarded finery. The huge travelling-case opened with a waft of sandalwood, a breath of the dear delightful past, or so it seemed to Frances.

Many were the dresses lying in close rank within, and they unfolded little the worse for their long entombment. But altered fashions made them practically useless in Mrs. Bethune's regard, except for present makeshift, and an urgent summons was sent all the same to her modiste. White washing gowns and gauzy silks, the underwear of *35* a hot climate, a wardrobe that would have been wealth to another. Frances turned them all over with vivid interest, trying on one costume after another, each of them bringing to mind some episode of that gay time through which her domestic happiness had suffered shipwreck. Finally she arrayed herself in a gown of changeful tint, with soft blue upper lights "shoaling into green," like that robe of *36*

THE BELL RINGS

old romance displayed to Enid and fastened about the waist of it Colonel Bethune's jewelled girdle. She turned from the glass to Ursula with a smile of delighted triumph, and announced her intention of wearing it for the rest of the day. The gown had once been costly, that was evident, above the common cost of such apparel, and it was as manifestly over-fine for the absence of occasion. But Ursula's objection was based on the imprudence of displaying all the change in her, by showing herself to the household in a gown which fitted to her shape.

"I don't care about that, they must see how much I have altered," turning about to catch a new point of view in a hand mirror. "And the sooner they get accustomed to it the better! Truscott and all of them. My figure is just as it used to be, but I can't think what makes me look so pale. Even my hair seems to have faded. I shall have to send to London for some of that stuff which brightens it. But I can put my complexion right at once, without needing to wait."

This meant the production of rouge and pearl-powder, and certain slight and artistic applications of these pigments to the faded face; effective doubtless, but marking a line of division deeper and wider than ever, between the present Frances and that youthful memory of her which the stranger had recalled. Mrs. Bethune was elated at the success of her operations, and boldly went downstairs. Tea should be served to them in the drawing-room, for after last night she hated to sit in the boudoir. And once in the big saloon, with its old-fashioned console tables and tall mirrors, she fluttered from one to the other, delighting in her own reflection, like a child who has played at dressing-up.

Ursula sat in one of the windows, which on this side of the house commanded the downward slope of the drive, visible at intervals between groups of ornamental shrubs. Presently she caught sight of an ascending figure.

"You don't want to receive visitors, do you, Frances? There is a man—he looks like a gentleman—coming up to the door."

Mrs. Bethune came behind her to look out. "It is Maurice Moore," she said. "He must be staying at Lady Sarah's. Yes, he can come in, it will be fun. He has not seen me for three or four months. I wonder what he will think of the change."

The order was given accordingly, and the visitor entered. A good-looking young fellow, supposed to be reading for an examination, but rather concerned with skimming the cream of life in the way of irresponsible enjoyment. The hostess stood up to receive him, but he paused and made a formal bow, as to a stranger. Frances burst out laughing.

"Don't you know me, Mr. Moore?" she said, a good deal of gratification mixed with her amusement. "Have I altered so very much? Must I introduce myself over again?"

Mr. Moore coloured all over his ingenuous forehead as he came forward, and made what excuse he could to cover the momentary awkwardness. He was short-sighted, he explained, and ladies had a way of transforming themselves when they put on fresh gowns. "You are so splendid today, Mrs. Bethune, that you really must excuse me. People are sometimes dazzled, don't you know, like looking at the sun." But the fact remained, that she had changed beyond recognition, and so did her pleasure in it.

Mr. Moore was presented to Ursula, and then explained his errand. He was the bearer of a message from his aunt, Lady Sarah, about a book-club volume. She desired to retain it a little longer, but promised to send it in at a certain time which he was instructed to specify, if not inconvenient to Mrs. Bethune. Frances gave a ready permission, and was altogether gracious; the book was a dry one, it seemed; one of those solid works advocated by the Lancasters. Lady Sarah was welcome to keep it for the double turn if she wished, for she, Frances, was positive she should die of yawning if she did but look within the covers.

Much more followed in the same flippant style, while tea was brought in and dispensed. Moore was willing to play his part in that airy tossing of the conversational shuttlecock, the idlest pastime imaginable, and Mrs. Bethune was as ready to second him as if she had not a care in the world. He had no real admiration for his hostess, but he saw before him a pretty woman prettily dressed, and it was a sufficiently pleasant occupation for an empty hour, thus to consume her tea and strawberries while tossing back that feathered badinage, together with a spice of hinted homage to give zest to the game.

It was merely a game, at which both were practised players, and neither one nor the other was in the slightest danger of any heart-wound. But it was just this spice for which Frances hungered; her palate long had lacked the flavour, and she gloried in it as the earnest of triumphs yet to come. Probably she had utterly forgotten the incubus of the night; the faint tinkle of a bell, far away in the servants' quarter, informed nobody, not even Ursula. A few minutes passed, and then a maid appeared at the door.

"I beg your pardon, ma'am, but can I speak to you?—The visitor upstairs, Miss Wayland, she has rung her bell. And the door seems somehow to be fastened, for we can't get in to answer it."

VIII.
DIFFICULT QUESTIONS

Mrs. Bethune paled under her rouge, and her light manner suddenly deserted her. "Ursula," she said, as if her voice failed her for more than the appeal and then added hoarsely—"You know about it, will you go?" Maurice Moore was acute enough to notice something had gone wrong, some domestic difficulty was on the tapis, so he negatived that offer of a second cup which had been on the point of acceptance, and presently took himself off, while Mrs. Adams hastened to the upper floor.

As she ascended the stairs the bell rang again, and this time more decidedly. It is not an exaggeration to say the blood ran cold about her heart in a veritable panic of terror, although she forced herself to go on. The summons was alarming and unexpected because so ordinary. A disturbance of vague outcry would have seemed less terrible, but that this being in her newly separated existence, ignorant of necessity as the veriest infant is ignorant, should yet know how to ring a bell and summon a servant, found her altogether unprepared.

Susan was waiting on the landing, and she witnessed

the production of the key from Mrs. Adams's pocket, but this was no moment to delay. The white hangings, which were arranged tent-fashion in a style now obsolete, hid the foot of the bed and its occupant, but a voice spoke from within as Ursula opened the door.

"Polly, is that you? I want my breakfast. I have been asleep a long while, and I am very hungry."

Here was a fresh astonishment; the reaction of the commonplace in the natural girlish voice, the natural demand. She looked back to the servant on the landing to give the order, and then, with desperate self-possession, advanced beyond the curtains into view.

The girl had raised herself on her elbow, her lovely eyes were open and full of intelligence. Evidently she was looking for a different entrance, for when she caught sight of Mrs. Adams's her expression changed—first to surprise, and then to positive delight.

"Ursula, is it you? My dear! Oh, I am so glad. How ever did you get over Mrs. Pryor, to let you come away?"

The eyes were Fancy Wayland's eyes, the voice her voice, the eager embrace was proffered in the old impulsive style. What could Ursula do but yield to it, and feel, if only for the moment and despite herself, that the long ten years were blotted out? The illusion was too perfect as yet, to leave room for wonder and dread before the deepened mystery. She stood again by Fancy Wayland's couch of sickness, the same little white couch, called there by the anxious father's urgent summons. Not then could she question or doubt who this girl could be, who had sprung into existence in the night, and yet called her by her name and talked familiarly of Mrs. Pryor.

"My dear old Ursula! I have been ill, but I shall be better now you have come to me. Did Papa send for you? Do you know it has all come right? He has been kind about Charles—at last!"

ONE OR TWO

What words were these, and how was she to answer them? Yet, as she returned the offered kiss, and suffered the golden head to rest against her shoulder, the heart which had trembled with fear began to warm to the stranger. It was as if she had found again, unaccountably and beyond all expectation, the girl-friend once dearly loved, who had been lost in Mrs. Bethune. She spoke as she might have spoken to the real Fancy, in the time which had gone by.

"Yes, you have been ill. A long, long illness, and now you are getting better you must not excite yourself, or I shall not be able to stay."

"A long illness! And yet it seems only like last night that Papa came in and cried, and said he would write to Charles to come to us, to come home.—So he sent for you as well? Ursula, tell me," the arms closing about her, and the girl's cheek flushing warmly against hers. "Has Charles come yet? Is he in the house?"

Ursula shuddered in her very soul. But to this question she was able truthfully to answer: "No."

"Not yet—not yet," whispered the girl to herself. "A little longer to wait, and to be patient. But he is coming," turning again to Ursula a face radiant with ineffable joy.

"He is coming, with the morning out of the east. I heard somebody say that when I was asleep like a promise. He will soon be here."

A knock: the maid at the door, bringing in the tray before Ursula in her bewilderment could decide for or against admission. But there was nothing Susan might not see in this lovely delicate looking girl sitting up in bed, while Mrs. Adams arranged the pillows for her support. The tray was put on her knees, with its tiny fragrant pot, and thin-sliced bread-and-butter. "Will the lady have anything else," queried the hand-maid, "as she didn't take no dinner?"

"I'll send down if more is wanted," said Ursula hastily, anxious at all risks to dismiss her. Then timidly to

DIFFICULT QUESTIONS

her charge, hardly daring to add the name. "Are you hungry—Fancy?"

The girl did not answer directly. "That is a new servant," she said. "Where is Polly?"

It was many a long year since Ursula had thought of Polly, who used to live at The Mount. She recalled her now as the servant who waited on Fancy in her illness, and was especially her maid.

"Polly is gone," she said. And then added hesitatingly, thinking of the great gulf between the past and present, and not knowing how to explain. "You have been ill a long time, you know. And time brings changes."

"I don't want to think of changes now," said this incarnation of the past, "if they are changes for the worse. I am sorry Polly is gone; I wonder why she left. Perhaps her mother was ill again?—Tonight we will only remember the changes for the better, and reckon them up. I have you, dear Ursula. It was kind of you to come to me, and that is a change on the good side. And Papa has relented about Charles, so there is another. And Charles is coming home, as fast as the ship can bring him, and that is best of all. Then there is another change for the better: I am getting well. Indeed I am not ill at all; I feel quite strong. I am sure I could get up and dress. I don't know why I am in bed."

"You must not be imprudent," said Ursula hastily. "You must stay where you are, at least until tomorrow." And she quailed again before the mountains of uncalculated difficulty. Pelion seemed indeed to be heaped upon Ossa. Here was this new-born creature utterly destitute, even of clothing; Mr. Wayland dead, and Frances Bethune in possession, reigning mistress of the altered house below!

"Oh no," said the girl easily, "I won't be imprudent. But you were always over careful, you dear old Ursula.—And now I want you to tell me all the news at Mrs. Pryor's. Does Mr. Houssaye still take the drilling-class; and has he proposed to Mademoiselle, as we always expected? And is Fraulein as disagreeable as ever? You told me in your last letter that you thought Mrs. Pryor knew of it, and was going to send her away."

Alas, that last letter, dust and ashes ten years since and all the tragedy of her own life acted out and buried in between! The voice which talked in her ear was like a voice out of a grave.—This strange resurrected Fancy, happy and ignorant, was sitting up full in view, and as she chattered on, her hands moved about over the tray to plate and cup. It was impossible not to see that the small left hand had a ring upon it, a pretty ring of clustered blue stones, worn on the wedding-finger. Where had she got such an adornment? With an impulse of curiosity, Ursula captured the little hand and looked at it; she was afraid she remembered that ring as an early love-plight. And yet the real ring must surely be in Frances's possession as the wife. How could it be worn by this duplicated Fancy, who had come naked into the world in the night, and whom she had been forced to clothe?

The warm colour flushed again into Fancy's cheek, as she yielded her hand to Ursula. "Charles gave me that," she said softly. "He gave it me as a keepsake when we were obliged to part. And I wore it night and day about my neck when I could not wear it openly. But last night when Papa consented—(it still seems like last night)—I put it on, for its place is on my finger. And Charles will find it there when he comes. It will be a sign that I am true."

What could be said or done? Ursula was speechless. Meanwhile her friend, girl-like, returned the scrutiny, turning over the hands which had taken hers, and on which there was a gleam of gold. One ring only, but that the unmistakable plain circlet which is so significant a token. Fancy cried out in her surprise.

"Why, Ursula, what is this? You are not married?"

DIFFICULT QUESTIONS

"Yes. For a very little while, and I am now a widow. I am not at Mrs. Pryor's any longer. I told you there had been changes, many changes, but you were right—we will not talk of them tonight. Another time—"

"Married! And I never knew it; you never told me! To somebody you loved, as I love Charles? You have an altered name!"

"My name is Adams, but it makes no difference; I am always Ursula to you. I cannot explain—how it is you did not know. You would not understand unless I told you much—much more, and there is not time this evening."

"Married!" Fancy was repeating in an undertone, as if trying to take the wonder in. "Married! And I never knew. And now a widow, so soon, so soon. Poor, poor Ursula!"— Further questions would have followed, but at this point came interruption. Susan knocked at the door.

"If you please, ma'am, Mrs. Bethune has sent me. She says will you come to her."

Ursula signified assent, and was rising, when Fancy caught her by the wrist.

"I will not be long, dear. Finish your tea. I will come back as soon as I can."

"Who did the woman say had sent for you? Did she say Mrs. Bethune?"

"Yes. Don't keep me: I will come back."

"Wait—one moment. Is it Charles's mother? Did she come because I was ill?"

The question took Ursula by surprise; for such an inquiry as this she was unprepared. What explanation could she give of the latter-day Frances to this incarnation of her youth? The truth must be gently broken if made known, such precaution would only be humanity towards this girl who wore Charles Bethune's ring, whatever the mystery of her origin. —So in her haste and confusion she prevaricated.

"No, not his mother. Quite another person. No one that you know."

Fancy released her, but with the questioning look of one not wholly satisfied.—And from the one interrogator, she passed to another.

It was a singular transition from Fancy Wayland to Frances Bethune; to behold the expanded flower flaunting a hue so diverse from its early promise, when she had just looked upon that promise in the bud. Had Frances been from the first a double personality, Ursula queried and marvelled; were two souls embodied in her organism at birth, a higher and a lower? And in the mystery of the night, had the pure soul separated itself and taken shape, leaving the original form wholly to the evil?—Mrs. Bethune's face darkened with anger over that narrative of the awakening, and the indicative mystery of the intelligence revealed. "If you had done as I bade you," she muttered between her teeth; "if you had smothered the life out of this Thing before it began to rave, it would have been easier for us both—better for you, and better for me. But you would not, so you are responsible for it, no less than I."

She walked the length of the room and back, her chest heaving and anger in her eyes, passing and repassing the mirrors, but this time without a glance of gratified vanity at the shapely figure and the fitting girdle. Then she stopped before Ursula, holding out both hands, and clenching and spreading her fingers.

"I think I might have strength to do it," she said, "even now."

"Frances! Put all such thoughts away. I will not hear them. I will not help you if they are in your mind. And if you act unworthily I will not screen you. Have you thought of the danger? To the law this girl is a separate being, whatever may be your knowledge. Remember, you can never explain. Nobody would ever believe."

The force of this reasoning proved convincing for the second time. For the second time the murderous impulse seemed to die away and presently the fixed face relaxed into a slow smile.

"I know what we can do," she whispered, "and it will be better than the other. If there is any difficulty, we can give out that she is mad."

The smile seemed to Ursula as evil as the anger. "It would be too cruel," she said in hasty opposition. "And besides, you could not prove it. She is quite rational."

"Not prove it? Is there no madness in a fixed delusion about identity? Are not hundreds of people shut up in lunatic asylums for no worse thing than this? What she has said to you would be enough, if she persists in it. I suppose you will hardly dispute that I am I, in spite of all this change that we have brought about?"

"You are the Frances I met in London, that I have known for these last months as Mrs. Bethune. But as surely as you seem to be yourself, she is the Fancy Wayland I once knew, that I was called to by your father all those years ago."

Mrs. Bethune laughed, but the laugh had little mirth in it.

"I am glad at least that you acknowledge I am I. And as you seem to have some tenderness for this unnatural creature—(for whom we are both responsible, as I said before)—you will not mind assuming the charge of her. If she persists in annoying me, an asylum may be necessary; but it will serve the present purpose if I send her out of the way with you. Granted that I am I, it is my plain duty to hold fast to my identity and my place in the world; an impostor claiming these, proves herself either insane or a criminal. I am safe, it seems to me; the danger will be hers, as well as the onus of proof.—I look to you to take her away, the length and breadth of England away from me! To another hemisphere, if you will. You will do it—for money!"

There was a faint sneer about the last remark, but Ursula answered steadily, "I could not do it without money. I am poor, as you know."

Frances moved to her writing-table and sat down, beginning to fill in a slip of lilac paper, which was a blank cheque. To take the girl away! That did indeed seem the best and safest emergence from this horrible entanglement, and neither she nor Mrs. Bethune forecasted any difficulty attending the removal. It would be easy to love this Fancy, so she thought and the care of her might also mean a living—that consideration which she was bound to keep in view. Yes, she would take her away, away from the danger of Frances's hatred, the murderous impulse quick in her now that she was abandoned to the lower soul, away from that threat of the madhouse, which was a danger more tangible still. Strange that she should feel so keen a concern for this non-human projection, which might prove soulless and evanescent, but to her, rational or irrational, it was the girl Fancy of her early affection, whose fate hung in the balance.

Mrs. Bethune returned with her strip of paper.

"Here is fifty pounds. I promised to give it you if our experiment succeeded, and if all went well. It has succeeded physically, to the utmost of my hope, but things are hardly well while that creature remains to trouble us. Take her away, keep her where you please and how you please, so long as she is far from me and mine. And when you have spent the money, I will send you more."

Thus offered, it was the passport of Fancy's freedom; Ursula could not reject it. Did her conscience remind her how she had coveted the offered money, treading in devious ways in pursuit of that small gain. Now a higher motive prompted the taking of the bribe; pity, a desire to protect, a yearning which was almost affection. She folded the thin edges of the paper together, ready for her purse, while Frances Bethune watched.

"When do you wish us to go?"

"So far as the Creature is concerned, I would say, this moment, but I am sorry to part with you, Ursula. There may be difficulties yet before me in which I shall want your help, as you are the only person who knows the truth and understands. You came for a week; stay that time out at least, and perhaps a day or two beyond. We must not part as if we had quarrelled, or it may set people talking. This is the fifth of June, Charles calculated he might be here on the thirteenth. Stay with me till the ninth, by then you will have some plan set in order, and can give notice to Mrs. Minter. I must manage to endure the Creature until then. Will it be necessary for me ever to see her?"

"You must judge whether it will not be safer to treat her as an ordinary guest, even if distasteful and difficult. You do not want the scandal of keeping her a prisoner?"

"No." Mrs. Bethune shrugged her shoulders, as it were involuntarily. "But equally I do not want the scandal of her claim."

"And when she is sent away, she must have clothes to go in; such belongings as would be natural to a person of refinement making her home with me. You will supply these? And the provision will take time."

"You are a woman of business, Ursula, and shrewd over a bargain. But what you ask is not unreasonable. There are a good many things in the India box that will come in for her; those old washing dresses of mine, and some of the linen. I will see that she has what is needful, when you dress her to take her away."

"We must have some clothing ready as soon as tomorrow, to wear while she remains here, for she says she feels well, and wonders that she is kept in bed. She will expect to find her own things—your things, Frances, in all those drawers and cupboards which are standing empty, except for the small luggage I brought in. My heart fails me when I think how I am to make her understand!"

"What does it matter whether she understands or not? If she troubles you with questions, say the first thing that comes into your head, anything to keep her quiet, and get her away. Tell her Papa lost all his money, he did lose a great deal of it and if you want to account for me, say I bought the house and everything in it, with the encumbrance of herself as a fixture. And hint politely that I am tired of my guest, and now she has come to herself I expect her to go away. Tell her I married Charles's twin brother, or his first cousin, if you like it better. And let her think she is going in search of her own Charles, when she sets out with you."

"I mean to tell her the truth so far as I can. It is only right—"

"Right! In a case like this, and to a creature not human? You might as well scruple to excite a false hope in your dog, when you feign to throw him a stone, and hold it back in your hand. The whole thing is horrible—out of nature, and we must fight through it the readiest way, without stopping to pick our steps. Did you not tell me she is expecting Charles? That she believes he is engaged to her, and will come?"

"Exactly as you were expecting him when I left you, years ago."

"And that she even wears a ring, like the one he gave to me?"

"A small ring, with a cluster of blue stones about a diamond. Where is that ring, Frances? You used to wear it."

"I have it upstairs, or I believe I have it. I have not worn it for ages. You see it was a shabby little thing, and he gave me a handsomer one when he came in for that money from his uncle. My fingers have been too large of late to put any rings on, though I have some very good ones, really fine stones. They were all locked away together, and I believe

DIFFICULT QUESTIONS

the blue ring is with them. Now if it has been stolen, will not that look as if she might after all be a real person and a fraud? I will go and see if the drawer is safe, for it is where I keep all my diamonds!"

She went on the impulse of the alarm, and when she and Ursula next encountered, it was on the stairs. Frances held up her hand, which was laden and sparkling with jewels.

"They are all safe, except that ring. Nothing of value has been taken. And I cannot be sure the little blue ring was ever in the drawer with the others; I don't remember when I had it last. It was a trumpery little thing, and I never wear it, so if the Creature likes to have it, she is welcome to it for me!"

IX.

HOSTESS AND GUEST

There was to be no elucidation, even of the mystery of the ring. Ursula laid her tired head on the pillow in the blue room, too weary to question further, while the bewilderment which encompassed them melted into the phantasmagoria of a dream. The separated soul slept doubtless in her white bower, dreaming of her lover and the rose-garden where they were to meet. Frances Bethune slumbered also, rejoicing in release from that encumbering flesh, though it had been drawn away at a cost she could not gauge as yet. Perhaps her dreams were of modes and compliments, and of the gay world for which she yearned; if they concerned the new-formed creature under her roof, which was herself and not herself, and hinted at disaster and peril, the warning was blotted from her mind before the dawn.

So sleep and silence settled down under the roof-tree of The Mount; sleep which visited alike the one who feared, and the two who were confident; and checked, at least for a time, the clack of tongues among the wondering household. It had been rife through the previous day, over the surprising alteration in Mrs. Bethune, and the singular advent of her guest—a young lady ill enough to keep her bed, who arrived in the middle of the night, unheard by anybody in the wing, and without accompaniment of luggage. And surprise was likely soon to spread into a larger circle. Mr. Moore knew nothing of the coming of the stranger, but he had witnessed the change in Frances's appearance; and to whisper such a piece of news to Lady Sarah was tantamount in itself to publication abroad. The whisper left the old lady profoundly curious as well as deeply amazed. She seldom bestirred herself to visit her neighbours, but she would have called on Frances in person had not a severe cold kept her indoors; and it was more than probable that a fresh errand to The Mount would be devised for her nephew in the course of the morrow.

The new-found life in Fancy leapt up to meet her second morning. "I am well," she repeated to Ursula. "I don't know why I am lying here. Cannot I get up at once? Must I really wait for the doctor to give leave?" For this had been suggested as a reason for delay. "It cannot do me any harm to dress and go downstairs, and into the garden. Look how fine it is; and I long for the sun and the air."

So Ursula brought her such garments and appliances as Mrs. Bethune was disposed to allot to her guest, and offered her own assistance—as Polly had gone away. But the toilet was quickly made, Fancy's own fingers were sufficiently deft, and the bright rings of short-cropped hair needed only a brush to set them curling anew about her pretty head. The white morning gown out of the India box might be somewhat flattened with lying by, but it fitted her to perfection—the fit a matter of course, for had it not been made for her counterpart?—and all her fresh young beauty was set off by the simple array, while glad anticipation smiled from eyes and lips.

"What are you looking so grave for, you dear old Ursula?

I am ready to go down."

"Do you remember what I said last night, that there had been changes? And you said we would not talk of them then. You will find a changed house beyond this room. I wanted to tell you—to prepare you, but I have not known how to begin."

Fancy looked over her shoulder, her hand was already on the door.

"Let us go down, and I will see for myself. Then you shall tell me, anything you please. Come!"

She went swiftly out, and Ursula could only follow. Descending the stairs, the broad staircase with its shallow easy steps and substantial balusters, she paused on the middle landing.

"Change number one," she said, and laughed. "Not serious enough to account for your long face. This stair-carpet is not the same, though it does not look new. But oh, why has the picture been sent away? The picture I was so fond of!"

A landscape by a foreign artist hung there formerly, showing to excellent advantage in the upper light. Mr. Wayland had possessed several pictures of value, but they were sold after his death by order of the executors. Ursula could just recollect the Poussin. Now the wall was filled with a trophy of horns and Indian weapons, above a stand of flowers.

"I don't mind about the carpet, though I would like to have chosen the new one. I call this ugly; I hate these mixed colours. But I must ask Papa about my picture—"

Here again Ursula tried to interpose, but the girl with her light swift step went on, down into the hall. A small room on the left, lighted by a French window opening to the floor, had been Mr. Wayland's study. In these days it was quite unused. Fancy tapped at the door, while Ursula stood behind her with a sinking heart. Now at last the tale must be told, the tale she found so hard. And the room Fancy chose to enter promised solitude; it was the one in all the house where they were least likely to be disturbed.

There was of course no answer to the knock. "Papa must have gone out," she said. "That is a pity, for I wanted to surprise him." And then she opened the door.

The shutters were folded back, and the room was rigidly in order, but it was the cold order of disuse. The bureau, which used to stand open at an angle convenient for the light, was closed and pushed away against the wall; the clock on the mantelpiece had stopped. Something in the indicative emptiness struck chill to Fancy's heart, a first apprehension touched her as she stood arrested, while Ursula followed her in and shut the door.

"Papa is not at home? Ursula, you had something to tell me. Is the change—about him?"

She had grown very pale. If to love and to fear proves humanity, this truly was a human soul, entering now upon its heritage of woe.

"Yes. The greatest change of all. He will never suffer or be sorry anymore."

"Dead?—Papa dead!" She put her hand to her heart, and the eyes which had never wept before, filled and ran over with bright drops. Then, through all the difficulty of speech, "When? And why cannot I remember?"

"You are sure you don't remember, Fancy?"

"I did not. But now it seems as if it came to me, like a whisper in my sleep; as if in another world, and some other life, I must have known. Oh, why, why have I been ill? I could do nothing for him. I was only a vexation and a burden. He came to my room and cried, and said that Charles should come. And now I cannot thank him, I shall never be able to thank him. I shall never see him anymore. Oh, my father! Oh, Papa, Papa!"

The words were sobbed out, broken by her weeping,

and it was long before Ursula could soothe her. "This is the great change," she said at last. "But I remember you said changes. Is there—anything more? Is there no message? Am I to stay here till Charles takes me away?"

"It was about that. The house is not yours any longer. It belongs to another person—"

Ursula stopped from sheer inability to speak further, this thing which she had to tell, seemed all at once so cruelly hard.

"It was Papa's own house. Do you mean that he left it away from me?"

"I do not know how to explain. He wished it to be yours, but he had losses, heavy losses in business about the time that you were ill."

"I suppose it had to be sold?" Ursula let her silence pass for assent. "Then who does it belong to now? And why am I here?"

A natural inference, and rational questions. There was a rational mind to be dealt with, as well as a feeling heart. Ursula had placed her in the great armchair where Mr. Wayland used to sit, and, hoping to overcome the passion of her weeping, set wide both leaves of the French window to the air, as the shut-up room felt close. The window opened on the gravel terrace which ran round two sides of the house, a wide terrace with a stone balustrade twined about with creepers; the greenness and the fragrance of the garden lay beyond.

"Who does it belong to now?" Fancy repeated.

"You heard the name yesterday when the servant came for me. It belongs to Mrs. Bethune."

The name had attracted her instantly the night before, but now it seemed to pass without remark. She was leaning forward in her chair, looking out upon the terrace.

Ursula turned to follow the direction of her eyes. There at the opposite side, Frances was standing. She had just

HOSTESS AND GUEST

come up the steps from the lower garden, a slim figure in pale blue, girt about the waist with a crimson sash, bare-headed, with her face full in the light.

Fancy started to her feet, pale and agitated, while Ursula put an arm about her for support. "What is it?" she whispered, a whisper full of dread. "Look, do you see it too? What is it? Is it a ghost?"

Frances moved slowly forward, enjoying the warm air, and swinging her hat by the strings. She was passing along the terrace, before the window, and probably would go by without observing it had been opened. "Is it a ghost?" Strange question for the derived form to put about the real woman! Fancy's eyes were wide with horror, her trembling finger still pointed.

"Hush, hush," said Ursula. "That is Mrs. Bethune."

Did the pointed finger attract Frances? She stopped and shivered, as if suddenly cold, turned, and saw the open window and the figures within, Ursula, and that girl-semblance with the curling hair, which was the incarnation of her youth. It would be necessary some time, sooner or later, for her to come to speech with the obnoxious guest. Now might be as good a time as any other. Overcoming her repugnance by an effort, she moved forward to the window entrance, her face hardening to the pitiless look Ursula had learnt to know.

She came up the two steps, still saying nothing, but staring full at Fancy; while Fancy, white and fascinated, stared back at her. Ursula could only look on dumbly, the situation had passed out of her control. But it was to her that Frances spoke, when at last she broke silence.

"Is this your charge?" she said coldly. "Had you not better explain to her who I am?" Then direct to the Projection, who did not count with its originator as human, who had no claim even to courtesy. "I understand you are Miss Wayland. I suppose you know that I am mistress here? You have been told my name?"

Fancy roused herself to reply to the direct question in the mocking voice, which yet, tone for tone, was the echo of her own.

"I beg your pardon—madam. I am only just aware of it. I would not have intruded on you knowingly. There are many things I have not known, that I am learning for the first time. My father's death—"

"Your father!" muttered angrily, between her teeth. "Well, well, let that pass. But if Ursula is explaining things," she laughed again, in that hard new way of hers, shifting her eyes from one to the other, and then fixing them on the girl, who seemed to shrink under their power. "If Ursula is explaining things, I hope she has made the position plain to you. You are left in my charge, and are bound to do as I say. You are quite without means, except what I supply."

"Madam—!"

"I do not ask for thanks, but I expect to find you obedient. You can have this room to sit in while you remain here. Probably under the peculiar circumstances of—of your bereavement, you will prefer to be alone. Ursula is taking you away next week. A change will be good for you, and welcome to me. I thought it well you should know of the arrangement from me direct. I wish you good morning."

Mrs. Bethune turned and went down the steps, out from the shadow into the sun, which set her crimson ribbons aflame above the blue. She left silence behind her, till Fancy panted out—

"Is it true, Ursula? Ursula, can it be true?"

"Can what be true?" drawing the girl back into her chair, and trying to soothe her.

"That Papa—perhaps he could not help it—left me to depend on her?"

"It was not his fault, Fancy; I can tell you so much, though I cannot tell you why. Oh, my dear, you must take it

HOSTESS AND GUEST

patiently. For the present it cannot be helped, and it is true."

The girl put her hands to her breast, as if struck with physical pain, and sat for awhile silent, her eyes tearless and intent. Then she began to whisper to herself.

"For the present—only for the present; and I must be patient. No, I don't forget that he is coming—with the morning out of the east. When Charles comes for me it will be over, the trouble will be all over, for he will take me away."

And Ursula, listening and understanding, was silent and a coward. She could not bear to break down a last refuge of comfort, and let in the full flood of desolation upon that innocent soul.

So much for the morning of the second day; later on, it had a further noteworthy incident. It was made known to the household that Miss Wayland, being an invalid, would occupy the study during her brief stay at The Mount; and that meals would be served to her there, separately from Mrs. Bethune's table. Frances was at first inclined to demur at any service which brought her guest in touch with the domestics, lest the girl should gossip with or question them, and scandal should creep abroad, the scandal of Fancy's claim to the identity which was her own. But of this she had little to fear. After their interview Fancy became dull and quiet, brooding over her sorrow, and hardly rousing herself to speak, even to Ursula. The small tray of luncheon was barely touched, but she thanked the maid who brought it with a gentle courtesy which belonged to the earlier nature, and Susan was moved to compassion by the sad young figure in the great chair. There was a little sofa in the next room that would be convenient, might she bring it in? She asked of Mrs. Adams. The mistress never used it, and the study was that bare! Permission for this was asked of Frances and obtained, but sundry other small comforts smuggled in, owed their introduction solely to Susan's goodwill: a handy table to set at the elbow of the supposed invalid, and some papers and periodicals for her amusement. "She was the very moral of the mistress," Susan said in an aside to Mrs. Adams, "only she was so young and fresh-like, and looked so sweet." Ursula wondered what would happen if Fancy took up one of the papers and observed the date, but her eye wandered listlessly over the pictured page, and she put it down again, her mind too full of troubled thought for any such diversion.

"She can walk in the garden if she likes, for the short time she is here," said Frances at lunch, with the air of one making a concession. "But she must keep out of my way. And I will not have her go beyond. Heaven knows who she might meet, or what she might say! See to that, Ursula. And any communication between us you must manage for the future. I don't want ever to see her or speak to her again, it gives me too dreadful a sensation," and she too put her hand to her breast, as Fancy had done before. "I am the stronger now, and I can nerve myself to master her. But I think if we were much together, the mastery would be hers and the subjection mine."

Perhaps this feeling, and the effort to overcome it, accounted for her anger and harshness as prompted by instinctive fear. But she seemed able to dismiss apprehension from her mind when the afternoon brought her a visitor. Maurice Moore again. There had been some suggestion of croquet the day before, and now the two adjourned with mallets to a level lawn in the lower garden, while Ursula went back to her charge.

"Come for a turn on the terrace," she said to Fancy. "The air will do you good, and you will not meet anybody. Mrs. Bethune is on the croquet lawn with a friend."

So persuaded the girl went out, clinging to Ursula's arm, and with a light scarf thrown about her. As if governed by their thoughts, she moved like the invalid they feigned her.

All the joyful elasticity of the morning seemed to be gone. She looked about her in silence, up at the house with its plain walls smothered in creepers, and round at the bright garden reflecting back the sunshine like a smile.

"My house—my garden!" she said slowly, "and now not mine anymore. That is the lesson I have to learn. And it was his wish that I should have it always for my home—poor Papa! He wanted Charles to give up the army, and come and live with us here." Then after a while: "You must tell me all about it, Ursula, when I can bear to hear. For today I have heard enough; I can endure no more."

"You remember nothing?"

"It is all chaos, dim, like a forgotten dream, but I feel as if the link might still be there, though it escapes me, as if something—the least touch—might bring it back and make it whole. That happens sometimes with a dream. I must have been very ill."

Another pause while they traversed the length of the gravel, and turned again to face the blue line of distance which was the sea. Fancy's eyes dwelt upon it with yearning, as one who looks outward to a hope, the hope of the hastening ship and of the coming lover, but she did not speak. The next remark was Ursula's, hazarded to probe a mystery which she regarded with curiosity and awe.

"Why were you so frightened this morning when you saw Mrs. Bethune? Why did you ask me if she was a ghost?"

"Did I say a ghost? I was taken by surprise. Of course she could not have been a ghost. That is too foolish. But you will think it quite as foolish, Ursula, if I tell you what was in my mind."

"Tell me."

"I haven't the least reason for what I thought. But it seemed—for the moment—as if I was looking into a mirror, and instead of—of that person who came in and spoke to me—I saw a reflection of myself. Not myself as I am now, but as I might be in the years to come, if I grew old and evil. I suppose it is because I have been ill, and have—forgotten things, that I had such a strange fancy. And then it was like myself speaking to myself, and despising all that used to be in my heart."

"Ursula, I want you!"

That other voice, which was identical in tone with the soft one speaking beside her, came ringing up from the lower garden. Fancy shrank back instantly on hearing it.

"I will go indoors," she said hastily. "I don't want to see her, or for her to find me here."

"Ursula!"

Mrs. Adams replied, looking down over the balustrade, for the second summons was peremptory. Frances was standing on the walk below.

"Send Truscott here to me with my other hat, and a sunshade—oh, and a pair of gloves. I am going to walk down to the village with Mr. Moore, and call on Lady Sarah."

X.
LADY SARAH

Mrs. Bethune departed with her cavalier. The walk was not a long one, hardly more than a mile; Lady Sarah lived but a short distance out of Saltringham on the Braxton Road. Saltringham itself, a small township, lay between The Mount and the sea. Even had Mrs. Romer been at home and at her post of sheepdog, she could hardly have objected to Frances visiting her old friend, escorted by so tame a wolf as the friend's youthful nephew, and it was no part of Ursula's duty to remonstrate or to accompany. She remained behind with Fancy, and coaxed her again into the garden, out on the lawn under the cedar, now that the mistress of the house had taken herself away.

The lawn under the cedar! It was in that very spot that she and Frances sat when they discussed the experiment, and when it still hung doubtfully in the balance, to be or not to be. Did Ursula remember all that filled her mind as she broke the leaf in her hand, divided between Salvador's warning and possession of the money she coveted, which was to be so dearly earned?—Whatever the memory revived by association of place, Mrs. Adams strove to talk lightly of common matters, and to divert her charge. But Fancy was thoughtful and disposed to be silent, which vaguely alarmed her companion. Had she a clue as yet, Ursula wondered, to the passage of time, and had she begun to reckon with amaze the gap of years between her present and her past? What was she, Ursula, to say when that question was formulated and pressed home? And the girl seemed so absolutely rational that sooner or later it must surely come. She strove to prepare herself, plying her knitting-needles and waiting, but when next the silence was broken, it was by a cry of pain.

Fancy was sitting up, with both hands pressed upon her bosom, she gasped breathlessly in the effort to reply to Ursula's inquiry.

"It flutters—flutters here. It is like a string drawing tight. Is this how I was ill before? And—Ursula—with just a little more—my mind would open—I should remember!"

She was greatly agitated, that at least was plain. It seemed as if some seizure, hysteric or otherwise, had become imminent. Ursula hurried to the house for water, and presently supported her back into the study. The crisis was not of long duration; it had passed and she was calm again, when wheels were heard approaching in the drive. There was some bustle of arrival, and then a servant tapped at the door and summoned Mrs. Adams.

"If you please, ma'am, will you come to Mrs. Bethune? She has been taken ill, and brought home in a fly."

Ursula hastened out. Frances had returned, and Maurice Moore and Lady Sarah were both with her in the dining-room. Mr. Moore had assisted in carrying her to the nearest couch, and he was about to leave the room as Ursula entered. Lady Sarah remained to give an account of what had happened. In spite of her cold, which was really a severe one, she had felt it her duty to accompany Frances home.

"She would have done a great deal better to stay with me, and let us send for the doctor to see her there," the old dame said severely, yet with a certain grim enjoyment of the situation. "But we could not get her to consent. She must go back, she said, and she seemed so distressed about it, that Maurice went out and fetched a fly, and came with us on the box—for I did not know what might happen."

"I am very much obliged to you," said Frances from the sofa, "but I am a great deal better now; I am indeed." She did look ill, and was still ghastly pale under her rouge, which showed an unnatural red on either cheek. Truscott was giving her some wine.

The old lady shook her head. "She did not feel well when she was walking down. Maurice says she had to stop more than once for breath, and at last she took his arm. But the attack did not come on till she got into my room. Faintness it seemed to be, and pain about the heart. Well, my dear, I hope you will be persuaded, and will have the doctor and do as he says. I am glad to see you safe back in your own house, and with your own people about you. And now, as Maurice is waiting, it is time I thought of getting back. The fly is at the door."

"You will have tea, Lady Sarah? Oh yes, I beg of you, or I shall be quite distressed, after all the trouble I have given. Ursula, will you see to it, in the drawing-room? Truscott will stay with me."

Lady Sarah was doubtful about the tea; she did truly wish to return, and was conscious of having made a toilet in haste, her bonnet was frankly crooked, and her cloak an old one kept for garden use. But she had a soul which could rise above such disadvantages, and the opportunity of acquiring information was too valuable to be let slip. She allowed herself to be persuaded, and contrived to get rid of

Maurice Moore, who awaited them in the drawing-room. Ursula would be more accessible in a *tête-à-tête*.

"You can tell the fly-man to wait for me," she said to him, "but I'll not detain you. You will like to be walking on, and this good creature, Mrs. Adams, is giving me a cup of tea. Young men don't care for tea, you know," in an aside to Ursula, who stood by amused as much as her anxiety made possible, remembering the day before, and certain evidence that Mr. Moore had found their tea-table attractive. He was quick, however, to take the hint and accept his dismissal, and easily accepted reassurance about Mrs. Bethune.

"Now come and sit down here," said the old dame, when once the door had closed upon him, "I want to have a talk with you. This attack of Frances's, you know, I don't suppose it is serious, but it must be plain to the meanest capacity what has brought it about. Such a change I never saw in any woman; I could hardly believe Maurice when he told me of it yesterday. She must have lost pretty well half her weight, and in a very short time. Whatever the treatment was to bring about such a result, it cannot but be dangerous. And tight-lacing into the bargain, I haven't a doubt!" (The last remark *sotto voce*.) "As you have been staying here, you must know all about it."

This was a terrible old woman, Ursula thought; despairing over her office of teamaker, which exposed her to attack. The Lancaster cross-examination had been nothing to this, for then she was less conscious of a secret to conceal. She did her best to fence off the enemy, without any glaring departure from the truth. Yes, she admitted, it was true she had seen a great deal of Mrs. Bethune in the last few months, and lately she had stayed in the house; but Frances did not care to speak about her medicines, except in general terms, that she was trying a remedy and dieting. Ursula believed it was under the advice of her local doctor, and also of a specialist consulted in London. For a long time the decrease had been gradual, but in the end the change was rapid, and very effectual—as Lady Sarah could see.

"I see it indeed. Call it a change! It is a transformation. But I am not sure that it is wholly for the better. I never did admire bones, or the sort of figures Burne-Jones used to draw. And that's what she has come to now." Lady Sarah had a way of calling a spade a spade, which was sometimes rather galling. "She has got to look a good deal older. And I must say I like young women to leave their complexions alone, and I shan't spare to tell her as much, once she is better. How many pounds has she lost, do you know that? And what was the average in a day?"

Ursula could not tell her, there had been no register on the scales.

"Dear me! I should have thought observations have been kept, if only as a matter of interest. And how many days is it since the rapid effect set in?"

Here was a question which must be answered, other observers would testify, even if she were silent, and Lady Sarah was prepared to probe, and probe again. The change in a single night could not be admitted, so the answer at last shaped itself into, "Four or five days, less than a week."

"Four or five days? You don't say so! It is most extraordinary. And of course illness has followed; think of the depletion of the heart, the strain on all the organs, through such violent means. I should not wonder if it cost her her life. I remember Mary Cumbermere, though hers could not be taken as a parallel case, for it was nothing like so rapid. She was a Lacy, you know, and her grandmother an Alverstoke, and both those families have a way of getting fat. She wanted to keep her figure, which perhaps was natural, and she took some drug or other, an over-strong dose of it, and lost her health completely. She was an invalid for years, an old woman before her time, and I am afraid something of the sort will happen to Frances Bethune. I don't like this attack that she has had today."

Such was the discourse over the tea-table, Ursula longing all the while to cut it short and to escape. The five minutes were doubled and re-doubled before Lady Sarah fastened her shabby cloak, and made preparation to depart, disturbing the old hired horse from his doze between the shafts in the sun. She did feel anxious about Mrs. Bethune's illness, quite apart from Lady Sarah's wisdom, and that supposed similar case of Mary Cumbermere's. But Frances herself made light of it; the giddy sensations which had troubled her, the fluttering and sinking of the heart. She was not used to walking, and had been unwise to attempt the exercise so soon, and after standing over her croquet; she had thought the disagreeable symptoms would pass off, and that it would be wiser to persevere in reaching Lady Sarah's, than to turn and reascend the hill. But the further she went, the worse she became, "and at last I really thought I was dying," she said in conclusion. "I got better very quickly when we were in the carriage driving home. I suppose it was passing through the air."

On Thursday the sixth of June, the dressmaker arrived from town with a stock of patterns and models, and for some two or three hours Mrs. Bethune was perfectly happy, shut up in consultation with her, and oblivious of all other troubles, even the incubus of Fancy's existence. Great was the wonder and admiration over the lady's recovered figure, and profuse the promises made (on behalf of a celebrated modiste who shall be nameless) that, despite all the pressure of the season business, at least one costume should be completed and despatched early in the following week. It was Frances's tribute to her husband's return; if impossible to give him again the heart of their early affection, she could at least receive him in a gown of so late a fashion that it might be considered a prophecy. Surely here was a practical demonstration of welcome far above romance!

On this important day she had not leisure to be visible, even to Maurice Moore, who called to inquire for her from Lady Sarah; there could be no question of croquet or of walks abroad, for the serious business of the hour engrossed her till too late. But after the modiste's delegate had taken her departure, and an interval of refreshment to the inner woman, Mrs. Bethune ordered round her carriage.

"I am going for a drive, Ursula," she said in explanation. "After all we have done today, I really want the air. And I will take you with me, if you can leave the Creature. Will she be quiet, do you think, and not likely to gossip with Susan?"

Poor Fancy! Ursula thought she might be safely left. There had been a discovery the night before, of the absolute bareness of the drawers and cupboards in the little white bower; the loss of all her old possessions, her childish treasures: and this came as a fresh stab upon the deeper wound of the bereavement newly learned. She had been robbed, and was passionately indignant with the robber; all unaware of the strange fusion and division which left her without identity and claim. Ursula made petition to Frances whether it were possible for any of these belongings to be given up, if still they existed, rightly believing her value for them would be small. A few books were found and surrendered, an old-fashioned workbox, and a small locked desk which belonged to that period of her youth. "I don't know what is in the desk," Mrs. Bethune said frankly. "It was left behind here when I married, so there can be nothing in it to signify. I don't mind giving it up to her if it will save a fuss. It is locked as you see, and the key is lost; but perhaps that will not matter. She may not have the wit to wish to look within."

Fancy's wit was sounder than Mrs. Bethune credited, and she did demand the key. Fortunately the lock was slight and common, and a key on Ursula's bunch had served to open it, so she was now engrossed in a first examination of the contents. Mrs. Bethune directed her coachman to the upper road winding among the hills above Saltringham, a favourite drive from the variety of view, commanding the inland valley as well as the sweep of the indented bay. The evening was fine, her spirits high, the horses fresh after a long rest in the stable; but the second mile was barely traversed before they were arrested. Ursula's eyes were on the distant landscape, and thoughts busy with her coming journey and altered plan of life, when she was roused by a smothered exclamation from her companion. Mrs. Bethune had fallen back in her seat and was gasping for breath, her face livid, and both hands pressed above her heart.

"What is the matter, Frances? Are you ill?"

"Stop, stop," the other panted. And, when the carriage was brought to a standstill, "Tell him to turn back, I must go home. Drive quickly."

The colour had vanished even from her lips, and she seemed unable to add a word in explanation. But as the horses were rapidly urged along the uphill road back to The Mount, she drew a long breath of relief, and presently opened her eyes.

"Ursula, what can be the matter with me? It was the same attack, just like yesterday. I felt I should die if I went on. And this time there was no walking—no exertion— nothing to account for it! "

"You are better now?"

"I am getting better. It is passing, the dreadful sensation is passing off, just as it did yesterday when they brought me back. I will have a little wine when I get in, but I shall soon be well."

"Would you like Bolton to turn again, and drive a little farther? He might go very quietly."

But the suggestion did not meet with approval. Mrs. Bethune shut her eyes again and shook her head. "No, no," she said, "I dare not, I am afraid. I will not risk it again, I will go home."

She was well enough to get out of the carriage unsupported when they reached The Mount; and as Truscott was summoned to attend to her, Ursula passed at once into the study where she had left her charge. Their absence had been so brief that she was not surprised to find Fancy still sitting at the table, still to all appearance engaged in examining the little desk. Something found there had perhaps touched a chord of association, and moved her to keener sorrow; for she had sunk forward upon it, her face hidden on her arms, and she was very still. Ursula went forward and laid a hand upon her shoulder; and then, as there was no response, in sudden alarm lifted her head.

It was only a fainting fit. She revived quickly when laid on the sofa, and her dress unfastened in the air, but in the first awestruck moment the fear had been of death. And sitting beside her afterwards Ursula wondered how it would have fared with Frances had her counterpart veritably died. Fancy could give no reason for her seizure; a fluttering about the heart, a pain in all the chest like the drawing of a tightened string, and then she remembered no more. Not serious, and yet coincident in time with Mrs. Bethune's attack, just as was the faintness of the day before.

Of this coincidence, not the former speculation, Ursula ventured to hint to Frances, but Mrs. Bethune would not admit the possibility of a connection between the two. Nor would she consent to see the doctor, she was well again, she said, and it was quite unnecessary, she did not want to send for him at present, as he was sure to ask all manner of awkward questions about her altered appearance, and she hated to be cross-examined. No doubt the rapid change had affected her, as Lady Sarah said, but she had only to be careful for a few more days or weeks, and her full strength would return.

And for the next few days she did take scrupulous care, resting on the sofa in the boudoir, which she no longer desired to avoid, or on the wicker couch in the garden, after her old indolent fashion. Again on this second Sunday nobody went to church. Fancy did not suggest it; she seemed to take no notice of a distinction in the days of the week, any more than she did of the yet undiscovered number of the year. And the fewer people in Saltringham who saw the girl before her departure, the better it would be—so Mrs. Bethune said and thought. That departure, and the journey beyond, was now definitely fixed for the morrow—Monday the 11th.

Mrs. Adams had paid off her landlady, and packed and removed all her possessions to The Mount. Their destination in the first place would be Richmond. Lodgings were engaged where Ursula had resided formerly, and she intended to stay there for some weeks before maturing any further plan. Much would depend on Fancy; whether she proved easy to control, content with the restricted life of limited means. There was also packing and preparation of Fancy's few belongings, such as were granted to be hers; the little desk among them being a treasure beyond price, for did it not contain Charles Bethune's early letters, and portraits of him and of her father? Those few letters, tied with a bit of faded ribbon, the girl would read and ponder over by the hour together, and Ursula could safely venture to leave her happy in their possession, when herself engaged in business which could not be transacted in the study. For her the days were full of occupation. She had no time, or so she told herself, to question whether that happiness over the lover's letters were not in its concession cruel.

Sunday brought a comparative rest, a brief breathing-space before the Monday of departure. "You will be careful of yourself, Frances, will you not?" she said to Mrs. Bethune. "And when your husband comes, I beg, I implore of you to tell him all."

"Of course I will be careful. I have been perfectly well since Thursday, and I don't think I am likely to be troubled anymore." As to the other entreaty Frances would not directly answer, but the mulish expression again disfigured her face, and Ursula felt more that doubtful if from her lips Charles Bethune would ever learn the truth.

This passed at their farewell. The hired fly was at the door, and Mrs. Bethune was shut in her boudoir, for she wished to avoid the sight of Fancy, and the need of exchanging any word with her. The girl was very pale and quiet; whatever she may have felt over this sad unfriended departure from her early home, she did not put it into words, even to Ursula. A veil covered her fair face, her white dress was hidden by a shabby old dust-cloak of Mrs. Bethune's, there was no one to bid her good-bye, or say a parting word of regret, except Susan who had been kind. The last box was hoisted on the fly, the hall door closed, the horse jerked into a trot. Fancy drew up the window on her side, and bent her head, the tears were running down beneath her veil.

A drive of some four miles lay before them, as they were bound for the junction with the main line, there to take up the express. A short bye-line of railway ran down into Saltringham, but it was customary with the dwellers at The Mount to drive direct to Braxton, and save the local change. The hired horse lacked spirit, and, luggage laden, made slow progress up the hills. Ursula looked anxiously at her watch, and more than once put her head out of the window to urge the driver to greater speed; but as they rounded the last curve, a train was seen emerging from the station, puffing white clouds of steam into the still June air.

"Look, Fancy! How provoking! I believe we have lost the express. And the next train is a slow one. We shall not get in till I do not know how late tonight!"

Mrs. Adams was really ruffled, she had a sharp word for the driver, and for the porter who awaited their arrival and barely disguised a grin. The men were hauling down their trunks from the roof of the fly, when the clatter of horses' hoofs advancing at a gallop sounded behind them. "A runaway, ain't it?" queried the youth in velveteens from his lower position on the pavement. The driver on his box stood up and looked along the road, shielding his eyes from the sun.

"Why," he said slowly, "I'm blowed if it isn't the carriage from The Mount. And it looks for all the world as if it was acoming after us!"

XI.
THE DOCTOR IS CALLED IN

The reeking horses were sharply checked, and stood with heaving flanks, they really were Mrs. Bethune's horses, and Bolton, the coachman from The Mount, was on the box. "Are the ladies gone?" he shouted to the driver, and as that worthy answered, Mrs. Adams came forward. Bolton touched his hat.

"If you please, ma'am, will you go back at once, and bring Miss Wayland. I have orders to drive you, and for the luggage to follow on the fly.

"Is anything the matter?"

"Well ma'am, I understood as Mrs. Bethune was taken ill. The order came out very urgent. I was not to spare the horses, but follow and bring you back, and especially Miss Wayland. I didn't think I had a chance, but I did my best, and you having missed the train was just a Providence. I'll turn round this very minute, if you and the young lady will get in."

112

There was nothing for it but to obey the imperative summons; their departure was to be no departure after all. The porter opened the door of the landau, and Bolton again whipped up his horses, though not to the headlong pace of the pursuit. Ursula glanced at Fancy, who had not uttered a word, obeying this order as mechanically as she had acquiesced in her banishment. If really they were recalled on account of Mrs. Bethune's sudden illness, Fancy had experienced no coincident seizure. Just then the girl raised her hands to Frances's cast-off hat, to release and put back her veil, and Ursula had a fuller view of her face.

"You are not feeling faint?"

"No, I am better now. That fluttering in my chest came on again, and the sensation of a string drawn tight—tight— till it was ready to break. I wonder what would happen if it did break. Should I be free?"

A question to which her companion could find no answer. They were not free as it was, and their bondage had just been demonstrated. Ursula was conscious of impatient anger with untoward circumstances, recollecting their delayed start, and the tardy progress of the fly. Five minutes would have made all the difference, and now instead of being dragged back to The Mount at the dictation of Mrs. Bethune's caprice, they would have been on their way to London, speeding on the wings of steam beyond summons or arrest. It was natural to her to love freedom, for it was her only possession; she hated thus to feel her feet caught in the toils.

The Mount again, with gates set open, and curious faces looking from the lodge. The ascent of the steep drive was cut with fresh wheel-tracks, and a single brougham, a typical doctor's carriage, stood at the door. Susan opened to them immediately, and had doubtless been on the watch.

She was ready with voluble answer to Ursula's question, overflowing with the desire to communicate. Mrs.

The Doctor is Called In

Bethune had been taken very ill not long after they started, and all her cry was that they must be followed and brought back—Mrs. Adams and Miss Wayland both, and she was very particular in saying Miss Wayland. And then, as she was getting worse every minute, Truscott took it on herself to send for Dr. Maxworthy. The messenger met him on the hill, which was most fortunate, as he came in at once, and had been with the mistress ever since. Mrs. Bethune was better, she heard Truscott say; Truscott had been up and down waiting on the doctor.

So much on the steps and in the porch. Ursula and Fancy entered the hall just as a gentleman came down the staircase from the upper regions. An elderly man, harsh of feature, and with a pair of very keen but not unkindly eyes looking out from under a grey penthouse of bushy eyebrow. At sight of him Fancy started forward with a cry of joy.

"Dr. Maxworthy! I am glad, glad to see you. I wanted to thank you for your kindness—about Charles."

The quick colour flushed into her cheeks, her eyes shone, the borrowed hat fell back and showed the brightness of her clustered hair; she was a fair vision, even in her shabby cloak. The old doctor took the two small ungloved hands which were stretched out for his.

"My dear young lady—I confess you have the advantage of me."

The happy confidence in her face paled and altered. "Don't you know me, Doctor!—Don't you know me? Not the little girl who stole your spectacles—who used to sit on your knee?"

It was the doctor's turn to look distressed. "My dear," he said again, "you must forgive an old man's memory. But I can be quite sure of one thing, from your likeness to the family. You are related to the Waylands."

Fancy drew back with a gesture of despair; her eyes were full of tears. "What is it that has happened?" she said brokenly. "Why—why is everything so changed? And why cannot I understand?"

The door of the study was set open, close to where they stood, and she fled within as to a refuge, shutting herself in alone.

The doctor made a bow to Mrs. Adams.

"Here at least I can recognize a former acquaintance. May I ask for a word with you? A word in private?"

Already in Ursula's mind the drawing room was associated with her experiences of the witness-box, and the *peine forte et dure*. Was another cross-examination to begin, more terrible than what had gone before? She moved there instinctively, and Maxworthy opened the door for her, shutting it upon Susan in the hall.

"Mrs. Adams, I believe?"

Ursula bowed.

"And formerly Miss Horton. A schoolfriend of Mrs. Bethune's, who used to stay with her before her marriage?—Ay, ay, I thought so; it all comes back to me. It is seldom that I forget a face.—And the young lady with you, who is she?"

"She is Miss Wayland."

"Yes, of course a Wayland, I was sure of it. But what relation to the Waylands here, and when did she know me?—Charles, she said!" in a meditative aside, as if cogitating.

"I do not know the relationship. She has been staying with Mrs. Bethune, and I was to escort her up to London. But we missed our train at the junction, and the carriage was sent to bring us back. I hope Mrs. Bethune—that there is nothing serious—?"

Ursula's voice faltered in her embarrassment, which might very well pass for anxiety. The doctor looked at her.

"I want to speak to you about Mrs. Bethune—to ask you a question. I can hardly pronounce yet about her illness. I must know more fully as to the cause. She was better when I left her, but I am going back. Sit down. You don't look very strong, and perhaps you have been alarmed. I suppose *I* am not alarming?"

It was a sudden thrust, and close upon the truth. Ursula felt half-choked by the beating of her heart, but she was not aware of showing outward tremor. She seated herself as bidden, and Maxworthy drew his chair, doctor fashion, very close to hers. She was full under the fire of those keen eyes. He might have been going to feel her pulse.

He began on the same tack as Lady Sarah. "You have been a great deal with Mrs. Bethune latterly, lodging in Saltringham, staying at The Mount. I come to you to know what she has been doing to herself. It is essential I should be informed."

"You mean about her changed appearance?"

"Yes, of course. You are in her confidence. What has she taken—what has she done?"

Only the first question was possible to answer. Ursula named the remedy which had been prescribed for Frances, adding—"I understood she took it under your advice."

"Ay, ay, I know that. And what else?"

"Nothing—that I am aware of."

The doctor looked at her as she sat before him with hands clasped on her knee, rigidly guarding her self-control. His keen eyes pierced into hers, searching her through and through, and he gave a snort of incredulity and anger.

"Nothing else! And would ye have me believe that yon Rasselas stuff—it is good enough stuff in its way, or I should not have advised it—could have brought about the change I see in her in anything like the time? It is past the power of iodides, or of any drug in the pharmacopœia. God bless my soul! It may be a case of life or death. If she has taken nothing but the Rasselas, what has she done?"

"She tried a vegetarian diet, but perhaps you know that. There is really nothing that I can tell. Is Frances too ill to speak for herself? Why do you ask me?"

"I ask you, for I gave you credit for the sense to know you could best serve your friend by putting me in possession of the truth. On my word of honour, madam, this is serious. You take a grave responsibility if you refuse." Then after a pause, relapsing into the slower speech that was usual with him when not excited.

"I can wait. I will give you time."

He got up from that too close neighbourhood, walked the length of the room to the further recessed window, and stood there looking out. Then he turned and came back, threading his way among the small tables and flower stands with which Frances had crowded the apartment. The chair was taken again, and even drawn an inch or two nearer. "Now?" he said.

Ursula's first attempt to speak died in her throat. She was more successful at a second effort, but her voice sounded strange to herself.

"You are mistaken—in thinking I can help you. I would if I could."

"It takes a woman!" was Maxworthy's comment to himself. "Tell a lie and stick to it, all the world over, though she knows she's lying, and she knows I know it!" Then aloud, and with a wry smile.

"I'll go over it again—what I know, and what I want to know—and perhaps that will help you to see your way. Here is Mrs. Bethune, a young woman—flabby, indolent; vexed over her changed appearance, which is natural. I attend her, prescribe dietary, exercise, Rasselas; but she hasn't the firmness of mind to carry it through, will suck sweets and lie on the sofa, and is always picking up some quack thing from an advertisement, and coming to me to know if it will do her good. She gets a letter to say her husband is coming home, and immediately falls into distress about her figure, Truscott tells me this. She sends for you, and the next morning you go up to London, and are away two days and a night. You are following me? I am correct so far."

Ursula bent her head in acquiescence. Nothing would be gained by denial.

"It is a natural assumption that you, who have been so much at her disposal, went on her errand. You telegraphed to her from town; there was some unexpected delay, and she was very restless and anxious—"

"You are ingenious, Dr. Maxworthy. But I have my own affairs to attend to; I am not solely occupied with Mrs. Bethune's. I went to see an old friend, and was detained in her house by illness. It was she who telegraphed to Frances."

"Wait: I have not finished. You return, and move here from your lodgings. Different orders are given about diet and hours, for which I conclude there was a reason: Mrs. Bethune does not go out as usual, will not see visitors, and you are always closeted together. Five days later comes the change—"

"I repeat, sir, it was not in consequence of anything I gave her."

"Truscott tells me she undressed her the night before, a stout woman with a large body and heavy limbs. The next morning she would hardly accept any assistance, and wore a loose gown; but the change in her was plain to see. She had fallen away to skin and bone—in less than twelve hours, to be as she is now."

A pause, which Ursula did not break. The maid's observation had been fatally precise.

"The change was so sudden, and is so great, that there might well be a doubt of identity. How would you like to be charged with smuggling away the real Mrs. Bethune, and putting this skeleton in her place?—Why, at first I was constrained myself to doubt, I, who have known her all her life! But no, I won't accuse ye of that. 'Tis the same woman, with the same whims and vanities; it is easier to melt the solid flesh, so it seems, than to part a fool from his folly.

And such a nice child as she was; such a pretty little girl! Pity 'tis, that sort of kitten should ever grow into a cat. By the way, she was the child who stole my spectacles, who used to sit on my knee!"

His attention seemed to wander from Ursula, as if in a sudden amaze. "That Miss Wayland is her living image— as she used to be at eighteen. And she said she wanted to thank me about Charles!"

It was impossible he could have found the clue, though he seemed to scent a mystery. He was returning to the charge, when the door opened and brought an interruption—welcome as such to Ursula, though in itself an astonishment.

Frances entered in her dressing-gown, walking feebly like a person risen from a sick bed, but erect and unsupported. She laughed as she came forward, steadying herself with a hand upon the furniture. Her unrouged face looked sallow and shrunken, her hair was hanging loose. She had evidently been too much in haste to study appearances.

"You did not expect to see me, Doctor! I heard you were still here, shut up with Ursula. So I thought I would take you by surprise, and show you I was well again!"

One clause in this speech revealed the motive: "Shut up with Ursula." What did she apprehend might be divulged? She looked keenly at her friend as she spoke, and Ursula made the slightest possible gesture in the negative, not unobserved by Maxworthy. The double action was a complete admission, and he had been right all through. These women held some secret between them which bore upon the case, and which his patient desired to conceal from him. He had failed to wring it out of Ursula, but he did not despair. There was a considerable amount of dogged obstinacy in his nature which might match with theirs, and he had the nose of a sleuthhound for a trail. For this time he thought it better to accept defeat. So he congratulated

THE DOCTOR IS CALLED IN

his patient on her restoration, added some commonplace cautions, and made his adieux.

"I shall soon get another summons, if I am right in my diagnosis. Whatever she has done to herself, it has resulted in serious mischief, and these attacks will be frequent, may even be suddenly fatal." He had got himself out into the hall by this time, and was cramming on his hat; the thought of Fancy and the wonder about her were dissipated for the time, and he had put no question to Mrs. Bethune. "Confound all women," he said between his teeth and almost audibly, as he slammed himself into the single brougham. "I would make a clean sweep of the entire sex if I had my way. Though," with a grim laugh at his own expense, "without them we doctors would live but poorly!"

He was on his way to another lady patient, keenly interested in all the doings of The Mount. As a rule he set his face against the feminine weakness of gossip, but on this occasion he might indulge her.

"Ye'd better go on with the liniment, Lady Sarah. And I'll send you down something fresh for the cough that takes you at night, something a little more soothing. By the way—you are always great on genealogies—do you know much of the Wayland family? Has Mrs. Bethune got any near relatives living, on the father's side?"

To ask such a question was to touch direct on Lady Sarah's chief hobby; if there was one thing she prided herself on above another, it was on always knowing who was who. She settled herself in her chair with an expression of real enjoyment, floating away from the commonplace consideration of doctor's stuffs and physical ills.

"You can hardly call the Waylands a family, my dear doctor. If James Wayland knew his own grandfather, it was as far back as he could go, and I doubt if he was altogether certain, even at that. His father made the money—out of leather; but I'm told he was a respectable tradesman, as trades go. He had just the one son who lived to grow up; the other children died off young. No, Frances has no relatives on the father's side, that I ever heard of. There is Mrs. Romer, of course; but she is her mother's cousin, and a Dorrington. Why do you ask?"

"I'm too busy a man, am I not, to be curious about my neighbours? There is a young girl staying at The Mount, a Miss Wayland, who is the image of our friend Frances as she was ten years ago. I wondered what relation she could be, and if you knew her. I must plead guilty of curiosity—to that extent."

"A young girl like Frances? And named Wayland? When did you see her, Doctor?"

"I happened to call in this morning, and I met her in the hall. She seemed to remember me—spoke of having known me when she was a child; but to the best of my knowledge I never set eyes on her before."

"I was there the other day, and saw Frances, and her friend Mrs. Adams, but nothing was said to me of any other guest. I haven't a notion who she is. She can't be a near relative; and Frances never has had cousins to stay, except the Dorringtons. But Doctor," seeing her chance, and alertly taking it, "you are attending Mrs. Bethune. There never was such a change in anybody as the change in her. And to come so suddenly as it did! I tried to get out of that Mrs. Adams what she had taken, but of course you will know. And do you think it can be safe?"

Dr. Maxworthy got briskly on to his legs, and pulled out a pale watch. Flight is held to be cowardly, but there is such a thing as strategic retreat. "My medicines were quite safe," he said laughing, "and so I believe is Rasselas. Mrs. Bethune assures me she has taken nothing else, and I am bound to believe a lady. Yes, there is a change in her, she has grown quite fashionably slim. I'll send you down the medicine—"

THE DOCTOR IS CALLED IN

"Ay, but I can tell you what you may not know—for she made light of it herself, and did not want anything said. You should have seen her here, on that sofa, only last week. I never was so frightened in my life. I wanted to send for you."

Lady Sarah had caught her victim; the watch slipped back into his pocket unregarded, the man hesitated and was lost: women sometimes have the best of it at such a game as this. Here was a plain duty: to learn all he could about a case which puzzled him; and side-lights sometimes are illuminative. He would not stultify himself by sitting down again, but he stood over her, keenly attentive.

"It was very soon after the—the alteration. At least, so I gathered from what Ursula Adams let out, but she did not seem at liberty to tell—"

Maxworthy smiled to himself. Lady Sarah was right enough there, Ursula Adams was very far from being at liberty.

"My nephew Maurice had been up at The Mount playing croquet; and either he said would she walk down and see me, or else she volunteered it: I forgot which. He knew I wanted to see her, for I had heard she was looking different."

The smile twitched the corners of his mouth, but was not suffered to display itself further.

"So they set out together when the game was over. Now it is downhill all the way, as you know; easy walking, even for an old woman like me; but she had to stop more than once to get her breath, and hold by his arm. And when she came in here her lips were blue, and she cried out in a wild way that she must go back—she would die unless she went back. I made her lie down on that sofa, and wanted her to stay and let me send for you, but she wouldn't hear of it. Maurice fetched a fly, and I went back with her myself— and have had my chest worse ever since. But you should have seen her as she lay there. I thought she was going to

122

faint, but it wasn't a faint. She was like a person convulsed, and there was froth on her lips—"

"Ay!"

"Maurice had pretty well to carry her to the fly when it came, she seemed so far gone. But she revived wonderfully on the way back to The Mount, and when we got to the hall door she had quite come round. Now I don't know if she told you all this herself?"

"She said she had not been well; she did not give particulars."

"That was precisely what happened, and I consider you ought to know it. No such change could come about without a serious risk, to any young creature's constitution. I remember Mary Cumbermere—"

But this anecdote has been told before, and perhaps it was not new to Dr. Maxworthy. No further details were forthcoming about Frances's attack, so he meanly evaded the recital, going forth with a gloomy brow upon his further round. The problem remained with him, and held him uneasy all that day. But when he carried a flat candle up to his room at night, another thought supervened. He recalled two soft hands put confidingly in his, and a young bright face which had grown perplexed and tearful, and taking off his coat and waistcoat, he folded them together with a sigh.

"A pretty creature. I wonder why I don't remember her, when she seemed so certain she knew me. Stole my spectacles, did she? And sat on my knee?"

Maxworthy had a way of talking to himself, in common with other solitary persons, but he did not speak again till the candle was out, and he was pulling a nightcap down about his ears. "Strange," he said, glaring into the darkness as if it figured the blank in his memory. "And she said Charles—!"

XII.

A CONFIDENCE TO MAXWORTHY

It has been said by wise men in the East, that the night brings counsel to a soul in perplexity. But such counsel may suit itself to the open ear, and be the whisper of an angel or a fiend. Frances Bethune woke the following morning with a certain plan of action matured in her brain, and her will ready to put it to the proof.

She sat before the toilet-glass studying her own reflection and the maid's face behind her shoulder, as Truscott combed out the long fair hair already brightened by the application of some cunning dye. The mirror showed her own countenance sharpened and aged, far beyond her years, which were those of woman's early prime. But as she noted the absence of that superfluity of tissue which had inflated the fine-drawn oval into a foolish roundness, her eager eyes read only improvement, and exulted and were blind.

For the alteration was not only of form, there was another and a subtler change in the reflected face. In the eyes and on the mouth was set the signet of a harder soul—a soul rapacious in self-indulgence, ruthless in self-will, a soul that once determined could be cruel and would not spare. Truscott's service had passed in silence, but now the mistress fixed her eyes on the maid's face in the mirror, and roused herself to speak.

"I suppose you know that Colonel Bethune is expected in England immediately. He may be here the day after tomorrow."

"Yes, ma'am. Susan said she had orders to put the best room ready for him."

"I did not intend to have visitors in the house when he arrived, but I changed my mind at the last moment about sending away Miss Wayland."

Silence on the part of the abigail.

"I did not feel fully satisfied about the place to which I was consigning her."

"No, ma'am?"—interrogatively.

"The charge of her is a heavy responsibility to have fallen on me just now, but I am anxious to do my best for her. I hope Mrs. Adams will help us."

Another silence. Truscott had a hairpin in her mouth; but at the same time she was keenly attentive to what might be coming.

"Of course you all know what is the matter with her? Poor girl, it is a great misfortune."

Truscott got rid of the hairpin in time to say "No, ma'am?" again as a question. She was plainly waiting to be informed.

"No? I thought it must have been evident to everybody. She is not in her right mind; she is subject to insane delusions."

"Indeed, ma'am? I haven't seen much of the young lady, but she seems quite the lady, and very gentle and quiet."

"She has never been violent that I know of, here; but of

course she may become so. That is a great anxiety, in a private house, and without a keeper. But it is the nature of her delusion which is the worst annoyance, to me."

Her eyes met Truscott's in the glass, and read, as she expected, aroused interest and curiosity.

"She has always been considered—in our family—the image of what I was as a girl. No doubt that suggested it in the first place. Her craze is an awkward one. She believes herself to be my father's daughter, she thinks The Mount is her property, and cannot understand who I am, and why I am here. Her object all along has been to escape from restraint, and force her way to Saltringham. At last she succeeded, and that was why she arrived so unexpectedly in the night."

A plausible story. Frances paused and waited for comment. "It's very sad," said Truscott, "a very great pity. But I haven't heard of the young lady saying anything—not to any of us."

"I am glad to hear it, I am glad she has been reticent so far. The care of her devolves on me, because the—the old relative on whom she depended is dead. I intend to keep her here for the present."

"I should have thought, ma'am—if I may say it—that the young lady would be better away from The Mount, if the place fosters her delusion."

"I am told not. I am told it is better she should be here, and learn the lesson by degrees that it is another person's property, and that she has no right over it, nor authority in the house. But it is of course an experiment, and I shall have to consult Colonel Bethune."

The last twist of golden hair was settled into place, the last pin fastened. Frances rose from her seat. "Ay, my lady," thought the waiting-maid to herself in inward address, "that poor pretty creature down below may be all you say, or she may not. But, however it is, you would be a wiser woman if you sent her out of the house before the gentle-man comes into it. She's as pretty as a picture in spite of her sorrowful face; and few there be who would look twice at you when she was standing by, for all your fine dresses, and your powders and your dyes!"—But there was no chair of truth to render this speech audible, and, satisfied with the impression she had made, the mistress went downstairs.

Breakfast was over. Ursula and Fancy were together in the study, engrossed over some sort of new-fashioned stitchery, a lesson from the elder to the younger.

Women are said to find in work a species of *nepenthe* and, bending over her needle, the girl looked almost happy. Upon this scene the door opened, and admitted Frances Bethune.

That she should seek Fancy's society was noteworthy and ominous. Hitherto she had kept sedulously apart from the being who inspired her with so much repulsion, the life divided from her life, the animating spirit which had once been as her own. The surprise of both the workers was too great for any common greeting, and Mrs. Bethune offered none. She swept on to a seat which fronted the others across the table scattered with small womanish litter; the morning paper, folded together, was in her hand.

As she sat down she looked full at Fancy, and Fancy returned the hard stare as if evilly fascinated.

"I have come to speak to you, Miss Wayland. There are several matters which, in justice to myself, I wish to explain."

Ursula wondered what was to follow, and listened with quickened apprehension. Mrs. Bethune had professed herself too unwell the day before for any consideration of the future; and instinct told her, her friend was acting without consultation, because in a direction she, Ursula, was certain to oppose.

"I have changed my mind about sending you away, and

A Confidence to Maxworthy

I shall for the present keep you at The Mount. But perhaps you wish to ask why you are at my disposal, and why governed and restricted as you are and must be, whether here or elsewhere?"

Fancy dropped the strip of linen on her lap, and replied with a first assertion of spirit.

"Yes, I do ask that. It will not be for long, as Charles will come for me. But whether the time is long or short, I ought not to depend on you, a stranger. If I have no money, as you say, surely I can earn something; enough to live."

The slow insulting smile widened on Frances's mouth.

"It is always the cry of the inexperienced, that they are willing to earn. But the demand of the market is for trained ability, and what training have you to show? And who will employ a person of defective intellect? You have recovered a measure of reason, it is true; but how about the long interval when you were mindless? And what assurance can you give that the condition will not return?"

There was a stricken horror in the girl's face which was not good to see. Fancy gasped after the voice which deserted her, but the shocked protest she tried to utter was inaudible.

"I will test you. Can you answer a single precise question? Tell me the day of the week—the month—the year?"

"I know I have been ill, but I am sane. You are cruel to doubt it. There has been a blank, but in illness that might happen to anyone."

"Well—answer my question."

"This is Tuesday, you said so just now, Ursula, did you not? I can see the month is summer; I believe it is still June. It was April when I was taken ill."

"It is the twelfth of June. And the year?"

"1887. Did you think I had forgotten?"

For answer Frances unfolded the morning paper which lay under her hand, and pushed it across the table to her

128

victim. There was the heading in all the plainness of print, showing the advance of ten years.

Silence, but silence sufficiently eloquent. Fancy's face changed, conviction succeeding doubt. Then came an utter and piteous dismay.

"You will hardly think me guilty of forging a newspaper, whatever else you may think of me. It is not my fault if circumstances are cruel. Surely it is better for you to face the truth than to live on in delusion. The grave you lament has long been green; the lover you look for exists no longer, in all the world for you. Those blank ten years have blotted out the hopes that once were yours. The chances are that life and its changes would have blotted them equally, had you lived out the interval a sane woman. So you are not very greatly the worse."

Fancy made a shield of both her hands from the hard scrutiny of her torturer's pitiless eyes. Frances went on.

"I am responsible for you, so you need have no anxiety about ways and means. I look upon you as a legacy from— from Mr. Wayland. All you have to do is to remain tranquil and obedient—and let us have no more of this nonsense about an expected lover. Charles Bethune was married years ago; he is a middle-aged man; he has forgotten your existence. Take my advice, a friend's advice I assure you, and think no more of him."

Mrs. Bethune had said her say; she rose and swept out of the room as imperiously as she had entered it, shutting the door behind her on all that helpless woe. It was not long before Ursula followed, to find her in the drawing-room. She was affecting to occupy herself in the rearrangement of her flower-stands, while the warm air breathed heavy with sensuous lily-scents, exhaling in the summer noon.

"Was it necessary, Frances, to be so cruel? You have broken her heart."

"I thought you had come to reproach me; there is a whole

A Confidence to Maxworthy

sermon written in your face. Yes, it was necessary. Only a sharp lesson would be effectual. If live she must, a thorn in my side forever, surely I am justified if I try to blunt the thorn, and render the position endurable. Cruel? It would be cruel if you will to foster her illusions, when my husband will be here in a few days, perhaps as soon as tomorrow."

"Surely you will not keep her at The Mount when Colonel Bethune returns?"

"I did not intend it, and I don't desire it, but, Ursula, do be reasonable, what am I to do? Look at the terrible position I am in. Don't keep your sympathies only for her. It is as if we were two souls and two bodies, with only one life—one vitality—between us. I will not repeat the agony of yesterday. I discovered then, past all doubt, what it was that ailed me. I hate her, I loathe the sight of her, but I must keep her close at hand—of necessity, if I am to go on living. There she is stronger than I, mistress of the life that is mine. I can hold my will over hers, I can keep her out of the position she would claim, I can make her wretched as I did but now, and as I shall again, just as soon as it is necessary. But when we are divided beyond a certain distance, her attraction is greater than mine, and the life is wrenched away from me to be vital in her. That was the matter yesterday, though I could not tell the doctor: that was what happened at Lady Sarah's, and when I went out driving with you. I would not believe it at first, but since yesterday I have known."

"Then what is to be done?"

"Nothing can be done, I suppose, and that is the horror of it, the horror I have to face. Where I go, she must go too. Where I stay, she must stay. If we are torn apart, there is no help for it—I must die. The cousin of weak intellect, to whom I am kind, such is the role marked out by fate for her to fill. And it is absolutely essential she should leave off thinking about Charles."

"Let us go to London, the three of us together, and consult

Miss Sedgeley. She might devise something—Salvador might know. Or let me go and ask, as I went before."

"No, no, remember your oath: we must keep our own counsel. I will have no one told as yet. I may think of some other way of breaking the link," stooping her face into shadow. "Time may help us. A thousand things may happen. If I do send you back to Salvador, it will be as a last resource. Not yet, not now."

"Then what am I to do, Frances? Shall I go to my rooms at Mrs. Minter's. It would be better."

"No, I have thought it all out, you must stay and help me here. You are responsible for this—this horrible misfortune—as much as I. When Charles asks me why you are living with us, I shall say you are my salaried companion, in charge of the Wayland girl. He will be quite satisfied, he will say no more. You know he wished me to have a companion, it was one of the stipulations. And you have come to me in place of my mother's cousin Mrs. Romer, who fell ill."

The study door was heard to open and shut, and a footstep crossed the hall.

"There she is again!"—stamping an impatient foot upon the floor. "For Heaven's sake, go to her, keep her out of my way. Let me forget her while I can. Anything else there is to settle must wait till another time. If you love me, Ursula, go!"

Dr. Maxworthy paid no visit to The Mount that Tuesday, but the day following he thought it incumbent on him again to see after his patient. The single brougham and the good grey horse had served him in the night, summoned out far into the country, so he made his morning round on foot. Approaching in this humble fashion up the curved sweep of the drive, the terrace on the west side of the house came first into view.

This was the terrace on which the study window opened, and opposite those glass doors a solitary small figure in a white gown leaned against the balustrade, looking far away to the blue horizon of the sea. As the doctor caught sight of the mysterious guest, whose address had haunted him through the intervening day, he felt that fortune was throwing in his way a chance not to be passed by. Curiosity would hardly be deemed impertinent, when his acquaintance had been claimed by this young lady, who was ready to weep because he failed to remember her. The conventional summons at the front door, and enquiry for the mistress of the house, might wait a while; he was in no haste. So he turned along the terrace, under windows empty of spectators, and approached the forlorn white figure.

Fancy roused herself at the sound of a footstep, and turned a startled face on the intruder, a face which bore but too plainly the trace of recent tears. Her first impulse after flight was arrested. If this friend of former times could be made to know her, surely from a doctor better than from any other, might she seek counsel in her strait.

Maxworthy raised his hat. "Forgive me for disturbing you, Miss Wayland. My memory was at fault on Monday, an old man's memory, and I come to you to help it out."

"I suppose I am very much changed," she said frankly, putting her hand into his. "And I did not know then, Mrs. Bethune had not told me, why all my friends have forgotten. I should be glad to tell you, to ask you, if I may. Perhaps you will advise me, for my father's sake."

The eyes raised to his overflowed with two large tears, and her breast heaved with a sob. Maxworthy held her hand. That keen old face of his could be kind—even very kind on occasions; and now it looked good to trust, gentle as well as strong.

"I want you to tell me. And if I can advise you, you may count on me. Where can we have our talk?" He glanced round, for the situation was an exposed one; interruption might come at any moment, and he did not intend to be interrupted.

"There is a seat in the arbour. Will that do?"—leading the way thither. "Mrs. Bethune allows me to go in the garden when I do not disturb her," spoken rather bitterly. "I ought not to be ungrateful, but it was my own garden years ago."

The arbour was covered with hanging creepers, which screened it from observation, and the rickety seat within afforded ample room for two. Maxworthy groaned inwardly when he thought of his rheumatism, but he followed the girl and sat down.

"Now, my dear young lady, I am at your service. Something is troubling you: tell me what it is."

"Dr. Maxworthy, what is a girl to do, who finds, on a sudden, that she has lost ten years out of her life? Ten years of utter blank, slept away perhaps, passed she knows not how. What is she to do when she wakes, and her reason comes again? Is her place in the world quite gone?"

"That is not your case, surely?"

"Yesterday morning I believed myself to be eighteen years old, just recovered from an illness measured by days, or perhaps weeks, no more, nor worse, than that. And now they tell me I am twenty-eight, and lost out of life—forgotten by all I ever loved!"

"My dear, to judge by appearances, you are certainly no older than eighteen."

"I was eighteen in 1887, late in March. Is it true—oh, Dr. Maxworthy, can it be true, that ten years have gone by? That woman showed me a newspaper with the date!"

"It is truly 1897. But have you made no mistake?"

"No—no, I have made no mistake." Fancy wrung

133

A Confidence to Maxworthy

her hands together with a gesture of despair, and then repeated: "What am I to do?"

"First you shall answer me some questions; at present I fail to understand. You said I must advise you for your father's sake. Did I know your father?"

She raised her eyes to his in sudden wonder. "Of course you knew him; you knew us all. I can remember you from the time I was a little child."

"My dear, you must tell me in plain terms who you are. I don't dispute a word you say, but it is necessary I should be assured. Who was your father?"

"He was James Wayland, your friend, who bought this house and added to it, and made the garden just as it is now. He was alive when my memory ceases; and now they tell me he is dead. Ursula says so too, it must be true. You know it?"

Yes, Maxworthy remembered well the circumstances of that death. It was one of those scenes and experiences which are not quickly forgotten, even by a man whose profession brings him in common touch with suffering and sorrow. He bowed his head in assent. "And you?" he asked.

"I am his only daughter; Frances Wayland, but they call me Fancy. Oh, surely, Doctor, you remember me? You were so kind to me when I was a little girl. I used to sit on your knee."

"My dear, I remember Frances Wayland, and you are her living image. But there is much that perplexes me. The long interval!"

The sentence broke, for the man was penetrated with profound astonishment over this incredible claim. If in truth this girl was Frances Wayland, who and what could be the woman who reigned as mistress of The Mount, and called Charles Bethune her husband?

"And I am perplexed too. I want you to tell me what happened to me, and how it came to pass. Surely if I fell ill you must have been consulted, you would know. I remember falling ill; I remember that you came to me, and you were kind. You said your medicines were of no use, because I was fretting. Oh, don't you remember?"

"Yes, yes, my dear. I remember."

"And you persuaded Papa about Charles. And Papa came in one evening and cried, and said perhaps he had been too hard, and he never intended to break his little daughter's heart. He said we might be engaged, if I would promise to get well, and he would write to Charles at once, that very night, to come home as soon as ever his colonel would give leave. I was so happy! I cried too, all for joy; and I put on my ring, which was tied on a ribbon round my neck. See, here it is, on my finger now. And then, because I was so tired and weak, I turned round on the pillow and fell fast asleep. O, the sweetest sleep I ever knew!"

"And what came next?"

"Nothing—if you can believe me! I cannot believe myself. Nothing but the blank blotting out of the ten years. I woke a week ago, in my own little white bed where I lay down, and believed it to be the morning after that night. I was quite alone, and then Ursula came, who was my friend at school, who knew all about Charles, and of the difficulty, and why I had been sad. I was not so much surprised at first, because Papa said something about sending for her if Mrs. Pryor would let her off to come."

"And did she tell you? What did she tell you? What did she say?"

"She did not tell me at once; I began to find out, bit by bit, that a long time had gone by. There was a strange servant, instead of my own maid. And I saw the wedding-ring on her finger, and discovered she had been married and was a widow, but even then I was stupid, I did not realise it was more than a few weeks out of that same year. Next morning I would not lie in bed any longer; I insisted on going downstairs, for I was well—strong—the illness was past and gone. Ursula brought me some clothes to dress in; not my own clothes, for everything belonging to me had been taken away. Think of that, Doctor; all the little things I had had from my childhood—the things my own father gave me; surely it was cruel? She wanted to tell me before I left my room, but I was in too great a hurry to listen. I wanted to go down to the study, to my father; but he was gone—the room empty—everything changed. Then Ursula began to tell me that he had died—"

The tears were running over again, but she dashed them away, and strove to speak steadily.

"And presently Mrs. Bethune came—in through the window, from the terrace. I was frightened when I saw her; she terrifies me, she is like my evil genius. Dr. Maxworthy, you know her. Tell me, who is she, and what is she? I know why she is here."

"Tell me first what you know."

"She told me, Ursula told me too; at least she did not deny it." The doctor noticed that Fancy put one hand to her forehead, as if it became an effort to remember.

"Yes, tell me what they said."

"They said, she said; it was she who made me understand, in that clear bitter way of hers, which cuts like an edge of steel. She said my father lost all he had, and died deep in debt, so that everything belonging to him was sold. This house, and all that it contains. And she bought it, charged with the obligation to provide for me, I suppose to keep me here."

There had been much lying in this strange case, or double-dyed delusion, that at least was evident, but there was no question in his mind that Fancy told the truth as she received it. And what could be Mrs. Bethune's motive for such a fabrication?

"She did not tell me then how long a time had passed.

I knew of Ursula's marriage, but somehow I thought Mr. Adams was quite newly dead. It was terrible to find myself dependent, and upon her, but I had still a hope. The hope that Charles was coming back. That he would soon be here to take me away."

Here a sob broke in again, but the doctor was steadily attentive and expectant, and she went on.

"The woman made a plan to send me away with Ursula, and I was glad to go, to be free of her, till Charles should come. We were to have travelled last Monday to Richmond, but we were hardly started away, when she sent to pluck us back. And yesterday she told me all."

"What was the 'all'?"

"About the long blank interval; ten years she said. You say so too. The date is printed on the daily paper so. That I had been all the while unconscious or insane. That my reason had but just come back, when I woke in my own bed where I lay down. Could I have been there for ten years, Dr. Maxworthy? Surely it is not possible?"

"No, no, my dear, I can be sure of that. You were not there."

"She says I have not a penny in the world but what she chooses to give me. And that I cannot earn, for nobody will employ a person afflicted as I have been. And that Charles has given me up and forgotten me, and I must think of him no more. Doctor, you were kind to me when I was little, you and my father were friends. My heart is breaking. Be a friend to me now, and tell me what to do!"

Maxworthy was not of a nature lightly to regard such an appeal. Possibly a phrenologist would have discovered in his cranium an abnormal development of the organs of benevolence and wonder. This girl's pathetic case and her amazing story excited both, though he was resolved to submit the latter to the keenest analysis. This elder doctor was something more than a commonplace practitioner;

he was in his scant leisure a speculative writer on psychology—under a pseudonym, so as not to scare away his patients. In his desk at home lay the unfinished sheets of a work on Double Consciousness and the Suspensions of Trance; and here at his hand was a subject who might prove of incalculable value. And for further motive, setting benevolence aside, he desired to probe to the full Mrs. Bethune's part in this matter, that it was a discreditable one he had no manner of doubt.

She and Ursula, her accomplice, had set themselves to deceive him about the emancipation, they had lied to this girl who was so strangely in their power. Before he had done with them, or they with him, he meant to strip both mysteries of their disguise. He considered himself adept at physiognomy, and he credited Fancy with truth-speaking to the extent of her knowledge. Those eyes, to his thinking, were as full of transparent innocence as they brimmed just now with tears. While it was easy to believe Frances guilty of the sort of deception which hides under a painted face. But the motive was still to seek; and Mrs. Adams presented a problem, for the arch of her head and the clear contour of her brow, would have suggested honesty. These women had plotted against his old friend's daughter, who he believed he held before him; that was the dominant impression, to be further sifted and considered.

He took both her hands in his, and dried her full eyes with his own handkerchief, doing his best to soothe her.

"My dear child—I can promise at least to stand your friend. I must think this over before I can advise you, but if you are in trouble here—in greater trouble, or any sudden need, send for me, or come to me. You remember where the old man lives? The same little house that Fancy Wayland knew. And I believe you are Fancy Wayland."

"I know it! With the mulberry-tree in the back garden, and the bowling-green, and the birds I used to feed. And those high wires to keep the cats out, because you did not like cats!"

"I see you have not forgotten. Now Fancy, listen to me. I don't think your suspension (whatever its nature) goes so far back as you suppose, though you have lost memory from that date. My former knowledge of you shows that to be impossible. But there came a later time when—when I was no longer familiar with your daily life, and when some shock, mental or physical, may have thrown you into the condition you indicate. I think your memory may come back."

"Yes, Ursula said so too. And I feel sometimes as if I almost remembered—later things. As if it wanted only a touch, and the blank would pass away."

"Exactly. I believe your memory will return and render plain what now perplexes, what greatly perplexes even me. I ask you to trust me. I will not tell you yet. I will not prompt you yet, though the time may come when I shall think well to do both. I will not even answer the question you put to me about your hostess here, who is my patient; I am on my way to see her now, perhaps I cannot certainly answer it even to myself. I ask you to trust me. Be patient, be submissive, do not lose heart. I must know more before I can safely act, even for your protection. But I can tell you this, my dear, henceforward your father's daughter shall be as my own child. And now, time presses. I must go, but certainly I will return."

They both rose, she with a detaining hand upon his sleeve.

"You are good. You give me new life. I will trust you. I will be patient. But oh, Doctor, do you think they have told me truly about Charles? Must we be lost to each other? Has he indeed forgotten me?"

The doctor looked at her, with a pause and arrest of recollection running over his nerves like a physical shock.

A Confidence to Maxworthy

He had forgotten the husband. Charles Bethune on his way home was almost at the door. He at least should know which was the woman he married: this girl who lingered over his name as if it were the echo of a passionate charm, or the painted creature who called herself Mrs. Bethune, and reigned as mistress at The Mount. And if Frances were indeed an impostor, how was it she had dared to introduce the real wife under her roof at a juncture such as this?

"My dear—I cannot reply to your question. I can only ask you to wait. To be frank with you, I do not know. But I mean to know very shortly. You shall not be kept in suspense an unnecessary moment."

The windows again were without witness. Could the denizens of The Mount be under a spell of enchantment on this momentous day? He walked round to the porch, but before he could enter, running feet behind him came quickly up the drive. The messenger was in urgent haste, and had just caught sight of his quarry, not this morning was it fated for Dr. Maxworthy to interview Mrs. Bethune. He was called to an accident case, a divided artery, and imminent danger; and the summons found him again the ready surgeon, alert and practical, speculations and suspicions put aside. He clapped his hand to the pocket which carried his instrument case, and a moment later, Fancy and Frances alike forgotten, his long strides outstripped the lad who brought the message, hastening in the direction of the town.

XIII.

IN THE ROSE GARDEN

While Maxworthy and Fancy sat in the arbour and cemented their alliance, Mrs. Bethune, all unconscious of increasing danger, descended from those upper regions where she was accustomed to pass the morning, and betook herself to her favourite nook under the cedars. Here the rug was spread as usual for her feet, and the wicker couch was set out with its cushions. Ursula also was in attendance. Her new duties as companion included secretarial work so it appeared; and on this particular morning there were several letters Mrs. Bethune wished to dictate—one of them being a sharp remonstrance to her dressmaker, who had failed to send the promised gown. Ursula carried out writing materials, but Frances was not disposed immediately to concern herself with business. The morning's letters were in her lap, and with them a small registered packet which bore a jeweller's label. This was the first to receive attention.

"I'm glad it has come in time," she said, smiling. "It might have been awkward if Charles had returned, and found me with no wedding-ring to wear."

IN THE ROSE GARDEN

"No wedding-ring?"

"Why, when my hand altered so much, of course it did not fit; it was nearly as big as a curtain-hoop. So I sent it, and the little old one I was married with, to have it made the proper size."

"Why did you not wear the original ring when your finger was small again? That would have been simpler."

"Oh, but I like a broad ring, such as is the fashion now. That little old one is so commonplace; a cottage-woman's would be just the same. Here it is, you see; and here is the thick one, which looks a great deal better. But I have had the names engraved inside, and the date with them, copied from the other. I want something to remind me of the date, for do you know—it is curious—my memory of that time seems to have grown so faint and far away. Last night I got out Charles's photograph and looked at it—the one he had taken in India, for, try as I would, I could not recall his face. He is a good-looking man, but I cannot get up any interest in him. I wish he was not coming home."

This was surely a strange avowal for the wife. Ursula listened in surprise, though, in these later times, she had never credited Mrs. Bethune with any strong affection for her husband. Frances began to justify herself.

"He is so particular about the things I do; and he is certain to be jealous, as he was before. If only he had stayed away! I might have had a good time now I am thin again—even shackled to the Creature. We could have gone to London for what is left of the season and to Cowes for the yachting—and have kept her in the background, only near enough for safety. I want to be happy again. Surely I have a right to be happy, and get some fun out of life like other women—not always to be shut up here!"

She had slipped the broad ring on her finger and was looking at it, while the other lay neglected among the papers in her lap. The self-revelation might have been yet more full, but it was doomed to interruption. A servant came down the steps to this sheltered lawn, tray in hand, on which a significant brown envelope lay displayed.

There is always something about these brown envelopes which arrests attention, even of recent times when they are frequent. Frances tore hers open with eagerness. "Now I do hope this is from Aldegonde," she said, and then her countenance changed.

"Ursula—Charles is in England! He is coming today."

"You thought it might be as soon as today, did you not?"

"This is the earliest day he mentioned as possible, but I did not expect it would really be so soon." There was complaint in her tone, no joy to meet the news. The telegram dropped from her hand. Ursula caught it up and read it aloud.

"'London, 10:30. I am spending an hour at Mary's. Shall then come on at once. Hope to be with you about six.'— Who is Mary?"

"His sister, Mary Bethune. She is older than he is, and a sort of Protestant nun, given over to good works, a stupid person, but he is very fond of her. By six! That means the 5:15 train at the junction. And oh, how tiresome it is I have not got my dress."

"You look very well in those you are wearing. And men seldom know anything about the fashion."

"He may remember I had them in India. A gown four years old! It is enough to stamp any woman as a dowdy, and first impressions count for much.—Ursula, I won't write to Aldegonde, I'll telegraph that it is urgent. And Bolton must be ready to take the carriage to Braxton, to meet Charles's train!"

She sprang up full of energy, grasping the papers on her lap, but forgetful of the little golden circle once endeared. It slipped to the ground unnoticed by either of the women, and, falling edgewise, rolled beyond the rug, finding shelter in some tufted grass about the roots of the tree.

From this time forward Ursula had scant leisure to think of Fancy, none to question her about the employment of her morning. Even had the girl been ready with any confidence about the old doctor's kindness, no one was at hand to receive it. Frances was moved to some excitement over the homecoming, despite her avowal of indifference; and she kept the newly styled companion fully employed over her preparations, and capricious changes of arrangement. The whole of her available wardrobe was displayed by Truscott, and Ursula was expected to assist in the examination and choice. "You can attend to the Creature by-and-by," Mrs. Bethune whispered. "As soon as Charles arrives, you can go to her and keep her out of the way." The elaborate toilet, the final tinting of complexion, was but just complete when the carriage was heard returning. It proved, however, to be empty when Bolton drew up to the door, except for a wooden box upon the seat.

"If you please, ma'am, the Colonel wasn't there, and as there isn't another train till half-past nine, I thought I'd best come back. The stationmaster put in a parcel, which he said was for The Mount."

The dress at last from Aldegonde's, and the satisfaction of this arrival effaced all disappointment in the other failure. The box was ordered to her room, and Ursula must accompany her there to see the gown put on. It would help to pass the time, as Charles could not arrive till late.

"You are sure he would travel by the 5:15?" said Mrs. Adams doubtfully. "The telegram said six."

"That meant for arriving here. Oh yes, quite certain. It is the best train in the day, we always use it. Mary must have kept him talking. And a good thing too, for now I have my dress."

Ursula seemed hardly satisfied. "It is not possible, is it, that he would come on by the other line?"

"Possible perhaps, but most unlikely. Allonby is only a wayside station, and no conveyance to be had. He would have to walk over the hills."

"But if he missed the direct route, might he not take that instead of waiting?"

"He might, but I don't think it. He would not be in such a romantic hurry. He will wait for the 9:30, and come down comfortably to Braxton, and I'll send word to Mrs. Choppington to have a supper ready. Come upstairs, Ursula; I can't wait any longer. We must have that box opened, and see what Aldegonde has sent."

It is often the unexpected which happens; and the romance with which Mrs. Bethune did not credit her husband, had actually determined his choice of route. While his wife hastened upstairs to inspect her gown, he was already on his way from Allonby by the path traversing the hills. After the confinement of travel and burning tropical heats, that wide stretch of upland, green with early summer, the soft air, the cool sky with its blue half-veiled in cloud, were all a refreshment and delight. A shower had lately fallen, and he breathed the odour of damp earth and springing herbage, and left the track for the pleasure of treading beside it on the short turf of the downs. English grass, for long a stranger to his foot.

The old country was dear to the exile. If his wife's welcome was in store for him, it would be dearer still. Had the letter he wrote her from India, almost from his sick bed, touched the hoped-for chord? Would her heart indeed turn back to him, back to its old allegiance, and all the coldness of division and distance be done away? Much in the past had wounded his love and hurt his pride; but all should be forgotten and forgiven to the Frances Wayland of old, when he held his wife in his arms, believing in the affection she had once professed. In London he felt vaguely disappointed. It was true he had bidden her await him here, and he could not expect to be met, but she might have written to him to Mary's car, so he thought. One word to await his landing would have told him all he yearned to know. And Mary had heard nothing, so she said, and except from the newspapers did not know of her brother's expected return.

But again the absence of any word might be taken as hopeful. He was at least unforbidden. Surely when they met, when he held her hands in his and could look in her eyes, the ice of their long estrangement might be trusted to melt away. Far off in exile, in health and working days, and still more in illness and danger and the weary weakness of convalescence, he had longed for the Fancy of the past, the maiden he wooed, the girl-wife he had won, to whom he once was all in all. And at last he grew to believe, or to half believe, that his very longing must of necessity recall her and recreate her—back from vanity and coldness and change, out of all the dismal deterioration of soul he had witnessed aforetime, till love was lost in a burning flame of wrath and wrong, and honour alone remained, an honour hardly saved.

He asked himself again as he walked, how did he fail towards this wife of his, for the hope and promise of their union to make such early shipwreck? Was it want of patience on his part, lack of those outward forms of tenderness which familiarity is apt to lay aside? Had he made too sure of her affection, trusted overmuch that she would be certain of his, as a wife ought to be certain, not needing the constant assurance of the lover? Had there been fault of his as well as fault of hers?—Or was it all due to the physical change of her illness, the influence of a vile woman, the accident of his absence during those weeks of border fighting, when he was forced to leave her under Mrs. Clarkson's care?

The physical change of her illness! There the line of demarcation cut sharply across their lives. With that sudden peril, the blow which stunned her and held her unconscious, the Fancy of his love died utterly; and when the bodily life, which for a while hung in the balance, revived and was restored, there almost seemed to be a different animation. A new Frances came into being, of whom he had afterwards most bitter knowledge. The caprices and exactions with which she tried him in the beginning, were thought only the peevish temper of a sick woman, but then, hard upon her recovery, there followed the disastrous association with Mrs. Clarkson. He had sometimes been tempted to wonder whether the angel in her was killed by that blow and long suspension of conscious life, leaving only a baser soul. And now, in his homecoming, it was the angel that he yearned for, the old Fancy with whom he hoped to join hands in reconciliation, and begin life anew.

Would she remember, he wondered, the occasion of the father's relenting when he came back to her before?— Would she divine how, to repeat it in all its circumstances, he had travelled to Allonby instead of Braxton, walking over the hill-path to The Mount? Would she come down in her white dress to the rose-garden, as he asked her in the letter—would she meet him there, as she met him all those years ago? The Indian Frances, who had graduated in Mrs. Clarkson's school, would be ready to scoff at such romance when the hero of it was only a husband; but Fancy his lost angel, Fancy his early love, would understand and be tender to the recollection and the wish. Which was he fated to meet, he asked himself, walking rapidly forward with The Mount almost in view; and the doubt took him by the throat, man as he was, with a choke of strong emotion that might have been a woman's.

IN THE ROSE GARDEN

The familiar road was gained, the gate came into view, the side-gate of the garden, no flaming sword debarred him from his Paradise, but what were Paradise without an Eve? The sheltered dell which Mr. Wayland had beautified, lay beyond the close-ranked shrubberies; and now, as in that former June, the banks were bright with blossoming roses and sweet with the very breath of summer. And surely the cry of his heart had found its answer; for there was the girlish figure gowned in white, descending the steps from the upper garden. Not in haste, as if aware of one who waited, but lingering here and there, bending to inhale the fragrance, lifting a drooped flower into view with delicate touch that did not break or mar. This was the angel Fancy, the Fancy of his love—so he told himself with beating heart as he watched her, dwelling on her simple dress, and noting her uncovered hair, worn as he remembered it of old, still short from the doctor's scissors, and clustering in curls about the little head. He moved forward, holding out his arms, whether he spoke her name he could not tell. Perhaps it was only the advancing step which caught her ear. She turned—looked—and the sad young face was at once transfigured with the white radiance and wonder of an overwhelming joy.

His arms held her once more. Her lips met his full in the kiss he longed for, and so silenced speech—the broken words of thankfulness and love. In that first recovery he could only hold her, he grudged even to put her apart for the joy of sight. But soon it became possible to speak—to hear.

It was his name she was sobbing out in breathless appeal. "Charles, Charles! You have not forgotten me! You love me still, after all these years?"

"My darling!" The question seemed to need no answer but the closer kiss. "You expected me? You had my wire this morning?"

"No, I had nothing—I heard nothing. I was trying to be resigned, to believe it was all over, and that I should never see you anymore."

"Fancy, what put such a thought into your mind? Surely you knew—you could not doubt I loved you through it all? At least you knew I was coming back. You had my letter?"

"I had no letter, but I thought I knew. I thought I could be sure, till she told me all those dreadful things, and broke my heart."

"No letter! Is it possible it did not reach you? And she? Who told you? Who do you mean? Don't cry, my dearest. We are going to begin again, a new life, you and I together, and forget the old, as if it had never been."

"I hoped for that. It was my own hope. Charles, hold me safe. Tell me it is true. That you are come for me indeed, and that you will take me away?"

"Yes, yes. As soon as ever you like. Tomorrow, if you will."

"Tomorrow?" she said, drawing back and looking at him. "But could we be married as soon as tomorrow?"

It was now his turn to look at her. "Married?" he said in astonishment. "We have been separated it is true, but there was nothing to break our marriage. Why need we be married over again?"

He had no clue to the doubt and distress in her face. "Is it possible?" she was saying, more to herself than him. "Have I been married, and can I have forgotten it? Was that what Dr. Maxworthy meant when he talked to me only this morning?" Then she looked at her hand. "If I had been married, even if I had forgotten it, I should wear a ring."

He took the small hand in his, still holding her with that clasp about her waist. There was the blue betrothal ring still in its place, but the marriage-circlet, fitted on years before in haste and mourning, was no longer to be seen.

"I don't know where the ring has gone to, but most certainly I put it on, as surely as I gave you the other which

In the Rose Garden

you wear. Fancy, if you love me, what do you mean by forgetting? Make me understand."

The distress in her eyes overflowed into tears, which she hid upon his breast. "Don't you know?" she said. "Must I tell you? Oh, I hoped you knew it, and that you had come back to me in spite of all."

What could she mean? A chill shadow of apprehension passed over that perfect joy. "Tell me," he said with peremptory tenderness. "Do not keep me in suspense."

"They say—she says—that I have lost my memory. That there had been a blank of years and years till I woke the other day, a week ago. I had not forgotten you—I had not forgotten our love. Never think that, my dear, my dear—!"

She lifted up her face and he kissed it, though in doubt. It was much that she clung to him in her trouble, and he found it sweet to console.

"But I fancied Papa had just given his consent; all else was a blank to me. I fancied it was the morning after that night, when I was so ill, you know; and he came to me and cried, and said we might be married. I believed he had sent for you—"

Her voice broke again, and failed her. Was this all, he thought as he held her in his arms; and if so—if he truly understood—was it not the fulfilment of his hope and dream? That all the pain, the disappointment, should be blotted out, and that she should be as the girl again, his bride. But how had it come about, and why had there been nobody to send him word?

"I can remember all that happened when I was quite young, but nothing nearer than that night, until I woke the other day. And now will it change your thought of me, that I am not like other people? That there has been this blank?"

His assurance met the question before it was half spoken. She was his wife, he said, his dearest wife.

"Can I be your wife if I have forgotten? And there is

another thing, I have no money, I am poor." Then another thought seemed to strike her with wonderment. "But if I am indeed your wife, how is it I am here, depending upon *her*?"

She drew back anxious-eyed, looking in his face for reply.

"Why, Fancy!—Poverty is comparative, but my wife would not be poor, even if she had no means but mine. You are not so rich as was once expected, because Mr. Wayland had losses; but you are not dependent upon anybody. Who do you mean by *her*?"

A strong shudder thrilled through her as she answered, sinking her voice to a whisper. "She is like a ghost—she frightens me, she told me all those cruel things. The woman who bought this house after my father died, who says she keeps me here for charity. Mrs. Bethune."

"My darling—" the former alarm returning, could there be aberration of mind, as well as this strange oblivion? "What can you mean? You are Mrs. Bethune."

She shook her head. "There is another, as you will see. I suppose you will have to see her, before you take me away. A cruel woman, with hard eyes. The house belongs to her. She was sending me away on Monday, because she would not be troubled with me any longer. I was to live at Richmond with Ursula. I used to tell you about Ursula, who was my friend at school. We had actually started, we were at the station, when she changed her mind at the last, and sent for us to come back. Charles, if I had gone, would you ever have found me? You would have come here to look for me, and I should have been away, and—oh, she is hard, hard! She would never have told. She said I had lost you forever, and I must not think of you again. She said there was no such person anymore, in all the world for me. It broke my heart—"

"Don't cry, my Fancy. See, here I am. I exist, do I

not?"—smiling at her in the midst of his own perplexity. "But who could have treated you like that, and told you such lies? Mrs. Bethune! Who on earth is the woman, and what can be her motive?"

"It is strange she should have your name. I did not think of it before. You will find her there, at the house. And Ursula seems in some odd way to depend on her as well; she rules everybody. I cannot account for her, I cannot even guess. But Dr. Maxworthy knows her. You remember Dr. Maxworthy?"

"The old doctor who was your father's crony, and who took our side about the engagement. He has been attending you?" It flashed through Bethune's mind that here was something tangible at last; a commonsense person who would throw light on Fancy's delusion. "You are his patient?"

"I saw him this morning. No, he is not attending me. I told him my story, and he was very kind, but he seemed puzzled. He promised to stand my friend, and help to protect me from her."

"Do you mean that this woman, this Mrs. Bethune, is at The Mount now? That if we go on to the house, I shall find her there?"

"Yes, yes," with the same shudder. "But you will not go?"

"I must, my darling. I must see who this is that makes my wife unhappy in her home, and puts her out of her place. You need not be afraid of her, or of anyone now I am with you. Come!"

He put his arm around her waist again, and led her up the steps, but the fear he deprecated still remained. She clung to him, and he could see she had grown very pale.

The windows of Frances's upper rooms looked upon the garden, the bedroom as well as the boudoir. The fitting on of the new gown had proved a lengthy affair; some small matter of adjustment was not to the wearer's mind, and Truscott was called into requisition with needle and thread, to alter, and alter again. All this made delay; but at last Mrs. Bethune was arrayed to her mind, and able to withdraw a fixed attention from the mirror, and bestow it on less important affairs. Truscott was dismissed, but for a while she still stepped to and fro before that long swing-glass of hers, a small reflecting mirror in her hand, contemplating the back view of bodice and sweep of skirt. Finally she laid it down, and turned to the window.

"The room is very close, don't you think so, Ursula? I will put up the sash before we go down."

She pushed up the window and leaned out, breathing the cool air. Then she drew back abruptly, changing colour under her rouge. "Look!" she said, seizing her companion's arm and pulling her forward. "Look there!"

Two figures were ascending the grassy slope to the foot of the steps. One tall, upright, soldierly, with a cheek browned by foreign suns, and hair just touched with grey; the other a girl in white, the projection of Frances's experiment, the incarnation of her youth. The stranger's arm was round his companion's shoulders, her face was raised, as if in eager confidence. Mrs. Adams's exclamation died unuttered; small need was there for any question, the situation was too plain.

It is possible to be jealous without love; to be angry at an invaded right, though the right has been unprized. Both passions found in Frances an expression so fatal that Ursula was stricken with alarm, and checked her as she turned to the door.

"Frances! What are you going to do?"

IN THE ROSE GARDEN

"To ask him how he dares! Has he come back to insult me?"

"Don't you see it is a mistake? He has taken her for you. And surely it is not wonderful. She is what you were once."

"A mistake I will set right. Don't hold me; let me go." Her hands clenched beside her, her teeth clicked together. She looked like a Fury incarnate.

"For your own sake, be gentle. Have mercy on the girl. And oh, Frances, I entreat you, be open with your husband. Tell him all."

The remonstrance was hardly heard. Mrs. Bethune vanished through the door. Ursula heard a rush of feet on the stairs, and turned back to the open window, but it did not command the point of meeting. And so, with apprehension at her heart, she followed to the garden.

XIV.
TWO WIVES

This enemy of Fancy's had made herself profoundly feared, so much at least was plain to Colonel Bethune. He strove to rally and reassure her as they approached the house; but the sweet tint of her joy paled and whitened, and she spoke only in a whisper. Once she stopped and held him back as if in panic. "She will part us," she said, "I know it. She will send me away where you will never find me anymore. Oh, don't go; don't go!"

But wiser counsels prevailed, and they ascended the steps, and gained the upper terrace. And there, as Fate had decreed, the three met face to face.

Colonel Bethune was a bold man, the habit of perilous adventure had steeled his nerve, he had been trained in a school which develops heroes. Had he returned to this safe England to quail before a woman? He did not want for courage, but his heart stood still within him as he looked. Here was the survival of his sorrow, his pain, his disillusioning, as surely as the girl beside him was the survival of his joy. What could the division mean? What evil witchcraft had set in his path, older, decked out by fashion, false of face, the very Frances, Mrs. Clarkson's pupil, who in those Indian years had brought misery on herself and him? She came on swiftly, thrusting herself between them, pushing Fancy aside. "Charles," she said, "Charles! Don't you know me? I am your wife."

He looked at her sternly and hardly, for all that sinking of the heart. "No," he said, and lied as he said it, but where was a place for truth? His love, his Fancy of the rose-garden, came first to his arms, and he could own no other—the frail white girl who shrank back with a heart-sick cry, and seemed to flutter away broken like a shot bird before that anger and that claim.

"No," he repeated, "no. My wife is here." But he held out an empty hand to the white dream. Fancy was in the grasp of another woman who came hurriedly from the house, and held her arm, urging her away. And when he would have followed, Frances came between them, commanding, restraining him; mistress of the situation for the one crucial moment, while he stood paralysed. He looked at her again, fascinated by repulsion: she was speaking, words cut through with sobs, shaken with passion. He did not know her, he would not hear her, he would only know the other; and yet she was horribly like his wife—aged beyond the years of their separation, which after all were few—painted, deteriorated, the evil in her grown like a rank weed to be weed only, and no flower.

"I cannot understand you," he said, brutally in his strait. "I don't know you. I must have proof."

She caught up the word with a cry. "Proof—proof!" she said, "he asks for proof, when I am his wife! Have you forgotten already how you married me and took me away? Proof that I was Frances Wayland, and you made me Frances Bethune? Is that indeed your demand? Well, I can give it you to the full. I suppose you are conspiring with that idiot girl, my cousin. Fool! To be taken in by her so soon. Is it to insult me that you have come home?"

That idiot girl! Fancy had disappeared into the house, and here again was the woman who led her away. A slender woman in a black gown, who dared to interrupt the torrent of passionate speech which flooded ears and sense. "Frances, I implore you," she began.

Mrs. Bethune turned frantically on Ursula. "He does not know me," she cried, "he says he does not know me!" The sobs choked in her throat, mixed with frenzied laughter rising to a scream; and then she fell down at Bethune's feet twisted in convulsion, and with froth gathering on her lips.

"What have you done?" said Ursula, alarm quickening indignation. "She is ill—in danger. If you have any humanity left, help me to carry her in. We must have the doctor instantly, or she will die."

This was no moment for repudiation. Wife or no wife, his aid was claimed for a fellow creature in sore need. Frances seemed quite unconscious, and was livid under her rouge; she moaned and writhed feebly as he carried her, the light small figure in his arms, into the house, up the broad shallow stairs to her own chamber, Ursula directing, and laid her under the lace canopy of the bed. The bell was rung for Truscott; there was a hurrying hither and thither in alarm, for remedies, and to summon Dr. Maxworthy. But ere he withdrew, Bethune spoke out to Ursula. Except in name, the two were strangers, but the slender woman in black appeared to be in authority. "I do not know this person," he repeated. "I do not recognize her claim on me. But this is my wife's house, and therefore mine. I await explanation, and I shall be found below."

He went down to the dining-room, and sat alone there in a confusion and horror of mind that at first made only solitude endurable. To deny—to repudiate; there lay his sole hope, but what if this horrible thing should be proved true? And where was Fancy; his white Fancy of the rose-garden? He had seen her enter the house, but she did not come to him; where and in what durance was she held? He got up after a while and crossed the hall, opening one by one the doors of the deserted sitting-rooms. He glanced up the staircase, but did not venture again upon the unknown regions of the bedroom floor. Frances's chamber was open as the servants hurried in and out, and her moans were audible below; it seemed as if they barred the way like a prohibition, and he could not continue the search. The long minutes went by. A brougham drove up. Dr. Maxworthy arrived, and hurried to the sick room; not then could Bethune intercept him with his questions. There was nothing for it but to wait.

Wheels again upon the gravel, a station fly, and his servant who had followed with the luggage on the other line. Bethune went out to speak to him before there could be any summons at the bell, and sent him away to find quarters at the Saltringham inn. Later on, as he stood looking moodily from the window over the wide landscape which began to brown with twilight, a maid came in to light the lamps and lay the cloth; meals are accounted necessary to poor humanity, even in the enactment of a tragedy.

"I beg your pardon, sir, for being late. Mrs. Adams hopes you will take something, and is sorry it was forgotten earlier."

Mrs. Adams! So she was the woman in the black gown, who took command of the situation and directed the servants. He was doubtful how to frame his enquiry without giving the sick woman the title she had claimed.

"How is—your mistress?"

"I believe she is better, sir, but the doctor is not satisfied, and he won't leave her yet. He is coming down for dinner by-and-by, but you are asked not to wait, as he may still be detained."

The swift ordering of the table went forward. Place was set for two persons, and a covered dish brought in. "Dinner is served, sir."

Bethune hesitated. He felt strongly disinclined to sit down to any meal under that roof while the circumstances were so extraordinary, but his hope lay in waiting for the doctor. And Fancy, if a guest here, might she not be present also?

"Are neither of the ladies coming in?"

"No, sir. Mrs. Adams is engaged with the mistress, and Miss Wayland never dines at table."

Miss Wayland! So that was what they called her. She had taken back her maiden name with her maiden nature. Of necessity, doubtless, when the other title was assumed by the usurper.

"Where is Miss Wayland?"

"She has gone up to bed, sir. She commonly goes early. Susan has taken her some bread and milk, it is all she ever has for supper."

While this information was imparting, a quick tread came downstairs and Dr. Maxworthy entered.

"Glad to see you, Colonel Bethune. A long time now since we have met. Mrs. Adams told me I should find you below, and I want to have a talk with you."

The doctor naturally took the guest's chair at the side, and Bethune felt obliged, for all his hesitations, to do the honours of that table. When both were helped to the viands, Maxworthy said with his customary abruptness, "We can wait on ourselves I think; and my time is limited." And then as the servant withdrew, not impossibly curious, "I want to speak to you about your wife."

"And I no less. But your communication shall take first rank. What I have to say can wait."

"First about my patient upstairs, Mrs. Bethune—"

"Ah—you mark a distinction. You know there is a doubt!"

"There has been a doubt in my mind since this morning. I do not suppose there is any in yours. There are two women

Two Wives

under this roof, both claiming to be James Wayland's daughter. But only one of them carries it further, and styles herself Mrs. Bethune."

"And that is the patient upstairs. Well," pushing away his untasted plate, "what of her?"

"I feel bound to tell you her health is in a very unsatisfactory condition—due to her own fault or folly, as I believe, though I can give you no particulars. Just now her life hung on a thread; but she has rallied, and will recover—for the time. But if the attack recurs, it may be even suddenly fatal."

"You tell me this—and expect me to be interested?"

"I tell you because it is my duty when you are called her husband. Is it true the seizure was brought on by agitation, because you failed to recognise her?"—looking very keenly at his interlocutor across the division of the table.

"Doctor—you said there was another, and under this very roof, I repeat your words. I have but just landed from India, invalided home. I walked over the hills from Allonby. I had asked my wife to meet me in the rose-garden; there was a reason for it of old remembrance. She was there—the girl I married, the wife I loved. I never doubted my good fortune."

"She knew you?"

"At once, there was no uncertainty, no hesitation. But when we came to talk, she told me strange things. Of a blank of memory—of dispossession here, in the house which should be her own. Of a woman who played the tyrant, and who called herself Mrs. Bethune."

"Ay, ay?"

"We walked up to the house together, and the woman, your patient, came to meet us. She—assumed injury, inferred a claim on me—the claim her name would indicate. I asked for proof. She fell into a fury, and then into this fit. I cannot think myself to blame. Now I have not married two wives."

160

"Of course not."

"What does Fancy mean by a blank of memory? You are the doctor here, you would attend her if anything went wrong. Has there been illness—a period of insanity—and why have I not known? And who is this other woman who calls herself Mrs. Bethune?"

"God bless my soul, are you in the dark too? I have looked to you to clear up all the mystery. Surely you must know which of the two is your wife?"

"Doctor, I married an angel. I suppose it is in the nature of marriage to dispel illusions, but my angel kept her wings. She had been four years my wife when she was thrown from her horse—out there in India, and a serious illness followed."

"The wings came off, I suppose. Well, it is a way they have. What sort of illness?"

"Concussion of the brain. She lay between life and death for weeks, totally unconscious."

"Ah!"

"And when she came to herself, she was like another person, not my Frances, but a stranger. We did not get on well; and at last we agreed to separate for a time, and she came home."

"Could there have been an actual substitution, in that illness?"

"I never thought of it. I don't see how. No. She was the same in body. It was like the animation of a different soul. A very much lower soul."

"Go on: I understand you."

"My hope in my homecoming was to find again the wife that alteration lost to me; and I believe I have found her. The woman who calls herself Mrs. Bethune is horribly like the survival of what came after, but with all the evil intensified."

"And yet, it is not a question of which you would choose,

but of positive identity."

"That is the awful part of it. But if Mrs. Bethune is my wife, how do you account for Fancy—for her recognition of me, her love for me, her recollection of the past? The other woman called her 'my idiot cousin.' I appeal to your knowledge of them both. Who is she supposed to be?"

"I'll tell you what I know of her and, frankly, my opinion inclines to believe her Wayland's daughter and your wife. But there is one very curious difficulty. I wonder it has not occurred to you."

"What difficulty?"

"She looks like a girl of eighteen; it is hard to believe her a day older. And on the other hand, Mrs. Bethune (as she calls herself) has the air of a patched-up forty, mutton dressed lamb fashion. And your wife should be eight and twenty, in the very prime of womanhood, but yet no girl. But if she is right in her account of herself—I am talking of Fancy; if there has been any long suspension of consciousness, such as she believes—that would account for the youthful look. I am almost sure of it. I have made a study of those suspensions; and while in them the wheels go round without friction, don't you see? It is the wear and tear of life that makes us old."

"You say she gave you an account of herself?"

"Since you married her and took her away—if she is the real Frances Wayland—I have seen her only twice; on Monday for the first time, and again this morning. She came to The Mount a week ago, secretly in the middle of the night, the servants say so, and I conclude they know. On Monday I was called to Mrs. Bethune, who was ill with the sort of seizure she has had today, but not such a bad attack. As I came down from her, I met this girl and Mrs. Adams in the hall. Fancy came forward at once, as if to an old friend, but I could not recognize her, and I am afraid I showed it. She was disappointed and shrank bank, and her eyes—they are pretty eyes—filled with tears as if she were going to cry about it. I am rather a soft-hearted old fellow, and I could not get the look of her face or the tone of her voice out of my head. It haunted me, for I was sure I knew it, and yet I could not put a name to her, as the country people say. I never thought—how could I think?—that she was James Wayland's daughter. This morning I caught sight of her out there on the terrace, and got a chance to speak to her alone. It seems she woke up in her own room the other day, and thought it was ten years ago, that her engagement to you was just allowed, and her father still alive. Possibly a return to familiar surroundings may have restored her reason after suspension. Such cases are on record. She knows nothing about the interval, but I have hope her memory may come back and help us. She was in great distress when I saw her, for Mrs. Bethune had enlightened her, not very gently, and told her some manifest lies."

"As to the property? Yes, I gathered that."

"And she asked me to help her and stand her friend. I promised, and I mean to keep my word. And the truest service I can render, will be to find the right thread out all this snarl. Strange things have happened here of late, which raised my curiosity before ever I knew of Fancy. Mrs. Bethune is an unaccountable woman."

"Unaccountable indeed!"

"But now tell me something on your side. Have you been in regular correspondence with your wife during your separation? Or was there any long period during which you knew nothing and heard nothing, and her way of life was unknown to you?"

"I had letters at long intervals; stiff, cold letters, with as little information in them as might be about herself or her surroundings. But, as I told you, we parted in anger, and I supposed I could expect no more. I knew, or I thought I knew, that she was living with her old cousin Mrs. Romer, first in the south of France, and afterwards when this house was vacant for her, here."

"Mrs. Romer is going through a 'cure' at Buxton, but she survives and can be interrogated. Were the letters all in your wife's writing?"

"I believe they were; it never occurred to me to doubt. I did not preserve them. They were not such as a man cares to receive."

"Handwriting can be imitated, so that is not conclusive. Well, as you know, this place was let to the Wades, and Mrs. Bethune did not return here till their lease expired. She was out of health, and I was called in—as I believed to my little friend of former years, the girl who was the light of Wayland's eyes, who set her young heart on marrying you."

"And was she the same?"

"I was constrained to believe her Frances Wayland, as she was in Frances Wayland's place, and called herself by your name. But she might well have been a stranger. There was a change in her, a change of which, I was given to understand, you were ignorant. The woman who came back here as Wayland's heiress and your wife, had grown hugely fat, and was altered beyond recognition."

"She is thin enough now. I carried her into the house, and she seemed to weigh no more than a child."

"Ay, and on that further metamorphosis hangs my tale. But at the time I speak of, she was shapeless in person and bloated in face, and yet a young woman to look at, which made the pity of it all the greater. She wanted to consult me about treatment, and cried over her lost figure; told me her diseased condition—for the putting on of adipose tissue is a disease, and a serious one—had set in eighteen months before, and had made rapid advance. I sent her to a specialist in town; indeed she paid him several visits. There was hope for her—I thought, and he confirmed me—if she would adhere to rule: diet, exercise, and so on.

But for all her lamentation, she had no more firmness than a wet rag. She was thoroughly indolent and thoroughly self-indulgent, and had got it fixed in her empty head that some quack dodge or other might be found, which would put her right by magic."

"Well, you and the specialist succeeded, to judge by appearances. Or was it the quack dodge?"

"It was the quack dodge, more shame to me and my diplomas! But for the life of me I can't think what it can have been, and she will not tell. Nothing that I gave her could have worked such a change in anything like the time. Why, it happened in a few hours, in the course of a single night, and she was a changed creature to look at—thin as a lath, as you see her now. And she is close as wax about it, and stands me out it was my own medicines, which is a flat impossibility."

Maxworthy was too much ruffled to continue any pretence of dinner. He got up and took his stand on the rug. The enigma of Frances's proceedings had touched him on a tender point, the professional acumen which was his greatest pride.

"I am pretty sure Mrs. Adams, that friend of hers who used to be a friend to the real Fancy, is in her confidence, and could lay bare the whole conspiracy if she would, and about your wife into the bargain. There was a great sensation when the news came that you were expected home earlier, as you know, than was expected. Mrs. Adams took a hurried journey to town, and no doubt brought the drug back with her, whatever it was. I'd give half I'm worth to find out, and to experiment with it in a guarded way. It would make any man's fortune. But given as they gave it, suddenly, violently, no wonder there is organic injury. She has just thrown away her life."

"You think she will not recover?"

"She may linger, but she will never have a day's health

again. There has been excessive strain upon the heart, and failure is sure to follow—perhaps in one of these seizures, which are pseudo-epileptic. Think of the result attained: pretty well half the substance of the whole body burnt up by the vital heat, or rendered fluidic and drained away. I tell you she turned the scale at over fifteen stone, and now I doubt if she weighs eight. Talk about latter-day miracles, here is one for you with a vengeance."

"It seems to me there are two pretenders in the field against my wife: the fat Mrs. Bethune who has disappeared, and the thin Mrs. Bethune who remains. Surely they cannot be identical!"

"I was tempted myself to doubt it, but they are identical. There was a scar on the forearm, a very singular scar, and that remains. I took an opportunity to look for it. And, more indicative than all, the personality is the same. The alteration you were sensible of in India did not occur."

"You think we could get at the root of the mystery, the double mystery, if we put the screw on Mrs. Adams?"

"I think it is our best chance. I can frighten her with Mrs. Bethune's danger. Hint that she will be held responsible in case of death, for having administered the drug. And when thoroughly alarmed on that count, we can charge her also with the plot against your wife. For I believe she introduced Fancy into the house, as she was instrumental afterwards in taking her away. The motive for it is inexplicable, so far as I can guess, and so is Mrs. Bethune's in sending for them back when once set off upon their journey. Why should she risk discovery by having Fancy here at all, when she knew you were expected home?"

"Then, Doctor, what must be our action? I am willing to be guided by your counsel."

"We cannot do anything tonight, I take it. Mrs. Bethune's state forbids it, and the other woman cannot leave her. Any fresh agitation may be fatal, and we must not forget humanity. Tomorrow I propose to question them—apart, not together. And I look for your help in this."

"You may be quite sure I will give it."

"They must satisfy us, satisfy you, the husband, who the girl is that they call Fancy Wayland. We must be put in possession of her previous history, and referred to credible witnesses; and if they assert her to be of weak intellect, they must say who has so pronounced, and who has been in charge of her hitherto. All such particulars must be closely sifted. She cannot have dropped from the skies; there must be continuous history of some kind, in her case as well as in Mrs. Bethune's. That is the chief point of attack, though with Mrs. Adams I shall work in the other charge about the drug."

"And now for my own course, pending this—I am going to the hotel."

"I think you are wise. Though you are expected to remain here, and a guest-chamber has been made ready."

Colonel Bethune got up to stand beside him on the rug.

"Look here, Doctor. Will you stay and occupy it? Cannot you make a professional pretext out of the patient's state? The fact is, I hate to leave my wife without a protector, under the same roof as these women who are her enemies, and yet I cannot remove her without scandal. I must avoid that, for her sake, till all is proved and known. She bears her maiden name, she does not remember her marriage, and I am here supposed to be the husband of that woman upstairs. If Mrs. Bethune, as she calls herself, would only die, it would simplify matters enormously. I would marry Fancy over again—"

"Stop, stop; you are running on too fast."

"If I stay here tonight, and without open protest, I may appear to admit that woman's claim on me. I will not do it. Doctor, will you stay instead?"

"Since you wish it, I will stay, but the girl is safe enough.

They dare not hurt her, they cannot spirit her away. Come back early in the morning, when I must leave to go on my round and for the rest you may make your mind easy. I remain in charge."

XV.
THE LOST RING

No full measure of night's oblivion visited Colonel Bethune at the Saltringham hotel and there were sleepless pillows also at The Mount. Ursula kept watch in Frances's room, sitting up in a deep chair wheeled beside the bed. Medicines had to be dropped and given in the small hours, and some spoonsful of light nourishment, for the patient was very weak. Early in the night she lay in an exhausted doze, but, later on, Ursula noticed that her eyes were always open, and her face had lost the repose of sleep. When the first light began to look into the room, she raised herself on her elbow, speaking in a whisper.

"I want you to do something for me. No—I don't need to take anything, and I could speak louder if I chose, but I do not wish to be overheard. I intend to remain the invalid for a day or two, and keep my room. It seems to be expected, and will be useful, for I can keep that man and his questions at arm's length—better so. Ursula, I am in a dreadful strait."

It was Mrs. Adams's conviction also and had been the subject of her cogitations through the wakeful night. The strait was a strait indeed.

"I see only one way out of it, indeed, Frances, and that is perfect frankness. Tell your husband the truth; then at least your conscience will be clear. Begin at the beginning. Tell him your motive, and how the suggestion came, as well as the consequence of what we did, unforeseen by either of us in its development and confusion. Leave him to act for the best."

"It would kill me to tell him. It would kill me for anyone to know that—that Creature—is flesh of my flesh, separated from my substance, as I suppose she must have been. And who could believe such a story? Would you, if told of another?"

"Let me tell him, if confession is more than you can bear. Nothing can be gained by deceit. I believe the truth will carry conviction, as it should. What else can explain the position in which we are placed? Give me leave to tell."

"No—no. Remember your oath. It may come to that, but I have one more expedient—to try first." Her eyes shifted from Ursula's, and she turned her face to the pillow and was silent, plucking at the coverlet with restless fingers.

"What expedient?"

The question seemed to rouse her, and renew a purpose drifting away.

"I will not confess, till we have asked Salvador whether there is any hope or help. Ask him if this thing can be undone, even if it should leave me as before. Or if that link of vitality can be broken, so that I may send the Creature away, and keep her far from me where she will trouble us no more. That is what I want to know."

"Am I to write and ask?"

"No, you must not write. I want you to go, now, immediately. Is it not nearly time for that first train from Saltringham to the Junction? Go softly across to your own room, and get what you need and let yourself out at the side door. Nobody must know, lest you should be hindered, kept and questioned. The doctor and Charles are here, both bursting with curiosity I doubt not. We cannot tell what may happen, once it is day."

"I am to go to London?"

"Did I not say so?"—her restless impatience growing with the manifest reluctance of the other. "Go straight to Miss Sedgeley. I suppose you must tell her, under seal of secrecy, but I am never likely to have anything to do with her again, so I do not care. She is an old woman; she will soon die.—Get her to have in the medium, so that you may speak to Salvador. He has got us into this scrape with his horrible counsel. He is bound to get us out of it again, and there must be a possible way. If his evil magic could bring such a thing about, surely it can also undo—"

"He said not, if you remember. He said it would be irrevocable."

"Never mind what he said before. Ask him—beg of him. Tell him the trouble I am in. You will know how to put it—only go, go!"

"I will go on one condition. Frances, you must promise me, if Salvador cannot help us, that you will tell your husband. Promise me you will tell him tomorrow, or let me tell him, as soon as I get back. Then I will do your errand, though it will be of no use. I am sure of that before I set out."

"I will see about it.—Well, well, if you must have it, I promise. Provided Salvador can suggest nothing, provided the situation is unchanged.—You will only just have time. Look at the clock."

"I am going immediately. Will you ring, or shall I call Truscott to come to you?"

"You are not to call anybody," spoken with peremptory emphasis. "The house is not to be disturbed; no one must suspect you are leaving till you are safely away. If I want Truscott I will ring for her; see, the bell is close to my hand.

And now—go."

Mrs. Adams obeyed, and for a while Frances lay motionless, listening with guarded breath till she heard the light footstep pass her door again, and in descending creak upon a faulty stair. Then the side door opened and softly closed. Her messenger had set out.

When time enough had elapsed to make Ursula's departure certain, the patient sat up, still listening. Then, with stealthy movement on her own part, she slipped out of bed, and crossed the room bare-footed to a cupboard set high up in the corner of the wall. When opened, it disclosed an array of pots and phials, cosmetics for the most part, or such drugs as are innocuous. But quite at the back was a bottle of different appearance, carefully closed with glass stopper, as if the contents were volatile. Frances took this from its place of concealment, and looked about for her wrapper.

Hurriedly arraying herself, and choosing a large handkerchief from a drawer, she turned at last to the door.

The strength of her purpose had kept her real weakness in subjection, but a genuine disablement remained from the convulsion of the evening before, and was about to assert itself. The light faded out of her eyes, and instead of finding the handle, she fell forward blindly against the door, and there leaned, panting and helpless, afraid to move further lest consciousness should wholly desert her. It seemed an age before the feeble heart regained its power; then, dazed and trembling and drawing difficult breath, she crawled back to her bed, first bestowing the bottle in a fresh hiding-place easier of access.

It was a white pinched face laid now upon the pillow, with that warning shadow of blueness plain to see about the mouth; a face which looked as if this world and its concerns would soon be unimportant, unless indeed some device of Salvador's could restore to the fount of life all the vital essence which had been drained away to fill full the cup of another existence. Yet the woman's heart was hot within her, raging with baffled passion over her impotence and failure. She had never hated the Projection, the duplicate Fancy who was young and fair, as she hated her now, when memory showed her at Charles Bethune's side, and with his arm about her waist. "If I could but pull myself together, for one little half hour," she was saying in a wordless self-commune, clenching her nails into the palm. "It might have been over by now, all over, and her power to harm me at an end. Another day is an added danger; still I have one chance left. Ursula cannot return till tomorrow, and there are all these hours to grow strong in. I have tonight. I have tonight!"

Colonel Bethune was punctual to his appointment, and released the doctor, coming early to The Mount. Maxworthy shook his head when asked about his patient. "Not at all satisfactory," he said. "There appears to be great weakness, though the pulse is certainly steadier. Just now she seemed hardly able to rouse herself to attend to me. I am afraid our questions must wait. But one is answered already, to my mind, if not to yours. There is no doubt Mrs. Adams is guilty. She has taken herself off."
"Not really gone?"

"Clean gone. She let herself out of the house before the servants were astir, and she must have got away by the early train from Saltringham. She thinks the game is up, and the reckoning about to follow. Mrs. Bethune says she expects her back tomorrow, but we shall see."

"And with her goes our best chance of finding out the truth!"

"Some part of it perhaps, but I do not lose hope. Mrs. Bethune may come to confession now her accomplice has deserted her. I'll be back again later on, and then I will have a word with her. Now I must be off upon my round."

So Bethune was left at The Mount, on guard as he considered. The servant looked curiously at him when he asked for Miss Wayland, and did not seem disposed to further meeting; she professed to be unaware of Fancy's whereabouts, as she did not happen to be in the study. Was the woman acting under direction, or was it the natural thought that he was remiss in neglecting his supposed wife, upstairs in her sick room? The situation, complicated by the sudden illness of the imposter, proved appallingly difficult; but with regard to Fancy he had already determined what to do. Mary should give her an asylum in the Anglican convent of hers, till the right had been established and made clear. The convent was accustomed to take in paying guests for temporary retreat. And there under his sister's care Fancy might be sheltered and happy, safe from her enemies, pledged to a future husband, as in those days to which her memory reverted, oblivious of all the pain and sorrow that had come between.

He had already sent an urgent telegraphic summons to Sister Mary Cordelia, which he knew she would not disobey. He would meet her at Braxton by the last train and tell his story, and on the morrow she and Fancy should depart together for London. And now it was necessary Fancy should be informed, and should consent to go. Pending the servant's search for her, he wandered into the drawing-room, where Frances's lilies bloomed in their stands, and the air was oppressive, heavy with perfume, though the windows stood open to the sun.

Something in the air of the room stirred a chord of association, and smote him again with horrible misgiving, as on the previous day in the garden, when he met Frances face to face. What if this woman should be proved his wife, the link between them one he could not break; what if the girl who met him among the roses and gave him kiss for kiss, had touched his life only for the moment, and was fated to fade away from him like a dream unrealised? In that brief yesterday he held in his arms his utmost hope, attained and perfected: could it be doomed to evade him evermore? The married Frances of India had loved these cloying scents, the breath of them brought to mind the bungalow where she had reigned. Here, littered about the many tables, were toys and trinkets of hers which he remembered. He knew the embroideries draped upon the wall, the rug he was treading underfoot; her personality informed the whole. These things might well have been filched from his wife by the imposter who had stolen place and name; but the sight of them now was like a stab—the danger and the doubt seemed nearer and more real, while the hope became remote. He turned back from the threshold with a shudder. In some other place he and his love might meet, he might take Fancy in his arms and kiss her with the kisses that belonged to former years, but here it was impossible for him to deceive himself, and believe her as he desired, his very wife.

Fancy had risen early, and wandered into the garden. All night long she lived again through the meeting of the afternoon, the echo of her lover's words lingered in her ear, and she turned her face and blushed to the pillow at the sweetness of his recollected kiss. The sun of her life had risen, and the clouds and darkness which gathered thick about her would soon be dissipated by its beams. She understood in a vague way that Frances was still in opposition, but hope brightened with the morning; now that Charles had found her, the crooked would be made straight, and all the confusion plain. The rose-garden was a first attraction, but after a while she tired of its solitude, and wandered on by devious paths of Mr. Wayland's planning and planting, till she came beneath the spreading cedars where Frances commonly sat.

On this one morning she felt free to wander. Mrs. Bethune was ill and keeping her room, so Susan informed her, and as Ursula had gone away—without any farewell to her, at which she wondered—there was no companionship to seek. The couch and the carpet were not set out today for the mistress, but a rustic seat girt the cedar round about, and from under a screen of thick-shelving branches could be seen the far prospect of the sea. The seat, the spot, were endeared by associations of her youth, her childhood even, which seemed near at hand as only yesterday. Had she truly grown old as they said, and had so much happened to her in those blank years, only to be wiped out as a sponge is passed over a slate? Sometimes she fancied she could almost remember other and later events—dimly, like an escaped dream, as if it wanted but a touch to make it plain. And her lover spoke even of marriage. Was it possible she could have been married, and not know?

Thinking thus, and intent upon her thought, she pushed the pebbles to and fro under a restless foot, her eyes bent on the ground. One rounder than its fellows escaped the pressure, and jerked away into the tufted grass. With mechanical attention her glance followed it, she saw the gleam of gold, and stopped to look more nearly.

The little ring Frances despised as fit only for a cottage-woman's finger, lay on Fancy's palm to be regarded and wondered over. Was this the needed touch? Her memory, blind and imperfect, began to stir. A ring! And might it not be hers, which Charles said he had given, and she had lost, though she knew it not? Her lips parted with quick breath, the colour dyed her cheek and again left it pale, fluttering with the flutter of her heart. And at this moment steps came up behind her, over the gravel and the grass.

"Look," she said, turning to him. "Look what I have found!"

He took the hand in his, with the marriage ring on the palm, held out for him to see. How fair she was, and as Maxworthy said, how young! Hers was that early charm of womanhood, which in the first bloom of its unfolding preserves much of the child. She was just as he remembered at the time of their betrothal and who would credit her with the intervening years of wifehood, which to her memory were a blank? Again his heart sank as he thought of that other, unaccountably in possession, who might stand between him and his desire. He was more intent on her than on what she was displaying.

"A ring, Fancy? Is it yours?"

"Do you think it can be mine? You said—yesterday—that, although I had forgotten, you once put on my finger—a ring like this."

The significance of the little circle and its recovery flashed upon him. "Where did you find it?" he asked.

"There, in the grass under the tree. I think it would fit me, but—can it be mine?"

He took it up, and looked within. It was worn with use, but the engraving was still legible which marked it with the date of marriage, and with the two names, his and hers; an inscription cut within it by his order all those years ago. There could be no doubt, however lost, and now so strangely restored. "Read this," he said, "and then you will be sure."

"'Charles—Frances.' And a date." She looked at him with again that fluttering colour, and eyes that just met his and swiftly fell. "It is my name, and yours," she answered timidly.

"It is the proof of what I told you. Let me put it on your finger as I did before. See, I take off this other, only for a moment, that it may pass on first, as it should. Fancy, look at it. Does it not seem familiar? Oh, my love, now it is on your hand again, have you no memory now?"

She trembled at the entreaty in his voice. She dared not look him in the face. A wave of agitation heaved her breast and made speech difficult, but the instinct of obedience spurred her to the effort. She would at least tell him what she could.

"Nothing that is clear. But when I look at it, here on my finger, something rises that is like a dream of shadows. Was there an empty church, very early in the morning? And had I a black dress on, not like a bride at all? And did something fall down at the back and make a noise, just when the clergyman said 'whom God hath joined together?'"

"My darling, yes. Thank God, you do remember, you are mine. We were married hastily, after your father died, that I might take you away. And you did wear the black gown, and I remember the noise. Some bench fell over. If I could but take you away with me now, as I did then!"

The temptation was strong upon him. Why should he wait for his sister's coming, for the long delay of legal process to expose the conspiracy, when the false pretension might by some quibble triumph, and result in life-long division? The evil of a nine days' scandal, a passing breath on her fair name, what was it weighed against the greater evil and danger that they might in the end lose each other and be held apart? It was hard to hold to right and prudence; but was it not his plain duty to think for her, to be wise for her? The self-indulgence of such hasty action might jeopardise her place in the world, and play the enemy's game.

"If I could but take you away, as I did on our marriage morning!" He almost groaned as he kissed the fair face laid upon his breast. "My dearest, when we met yesterday I thought no other; and now I am compelled to wait, even to send you from me. The woman there who is ill; I cannot explain, but things have been very wrong here in my absence. You have been supplanted and ill-used, and I am bound to see you righted. Your knight must fight your battles before he claims his guerdon. Do you understand?"

"You are sending me away—alone?"

"I cannot let you remain at The Mount with this woman calling herself mistress, and I cannot pull her out of her sick-bed. I want to place you in safety; while you stay I dare not attack. I have sent for Mary. You remember Mary?"

"I know who you mean. Your sister."

"She lives in a sort of nunnery and works among the poor; she has the kindest heart in the world. She will love you and take care of you till all the trouble is over, and all the wrong put right. I have sent her a message to come to me, and I want you to go back with her tomorrow. Will you do this for my sake, Fancy my wife?"

"I will do all you wish. But will it be for long? What if I forget again! You will come to me?"

"Certainly I will come. And the love of you and the thought of you will be in my heart every moment of every hour. They will be longer hours to me than to you, of that be sure. Now, listen: Mary will bring a carriage for you, here to the house, early tomorrow. There is to be nothing secret, nothing clandestine, about your going away, but I do not want you to say a word beforehand about a possible departure. Have ready all you care to bring away. Then at the last, if there is opposition, I shall proclaim who you are, and maintain your right to take your freedom, and go at my sister's invitation, as her guest. But I do not think the woman will dare."

The girl shuddered in his arms, as she had shuddered the day before. "I hope I shall not see her. I am afraid of her.

She is terrible. Who is she, Charles, and what has been the wrong? Why does my father's house belong to her? Do you know?"

And he, man as he was, was fain to shudder also, thinking of what reply he might be forced to give. The doubt and danger rose up dark before him, the riddle of the confused identity, the fear which smote him when he thought of Frances.

He answered "No." And then, because of the necessity there is for doublet and hose to show itself courageous, he added more cheerfully, "Not yet. But I mean to know, and so does Maxworthy; and between us we shall make it plain."

XVI.
A LATE CONFESSION

Very little could be elicited from Mrs. Bethune, and that little was not encouraging. She kept her bed the whole day, and lay there in a condition of complete prostration hardly able to speak above a whisper. Maxworthy was sharp enough to suspect some clever feigning; but the mischief the stethoscope revealed was too acutely serious, for him to embark at once upon the course he meditated. It was quite possible she desired to gain time, though he knew not to what end, unless to facilitate Mrs. Adams's escape. For the rest, she seemed in no way agitated by his questions, doubtless she expected them. The young visitor was a cousin of her own, a girl of weak intellect. Colonel Bethune could have all particulars as soon as she was well enough to give them. She had nothing, she said, to conceal. The cousin's name was Wayland; and the delusion which led this younger Frances to personate herself had been annoying, but she had never supposed it of consequence, or that anybody could be deceived; the girl was hardly more than a child.

It was plain the struggle must be deferred until the

morrow. To get Fancy away into safe keeping, and without exposure or scandal, was the object first to be attained. And so the day wore to an end. Bethune met his sister by the late train at Braxton, and took her to the Saltrington hotel, where the two sat up late in their comfortless private sitting-room, discussing the situation, which to the gentle nun seemed an amazing one indeed. Maxworthy agreed to remain through this second night at The Mount, with a view to Fancy's protection rather than his patient's danger; and on paying a late visit to the sick-room, Mrs. Bethune declared herself better, and seemed unreasonably irritated by his fiat that a night watch should be kept. It was quite unnecessary she said, even with asperity, she did not want Truscott; she could never rest when anyone was near her in the room. She should sleep much better if left alone, and she could ring if she wanted anything. But the doctor was absolute; Truscott was not much of a nurse perhaps, but she was better than nobody; for this one night at least, Truscott must sit up. He would get somebody more efficient, if Mrs. Bethune preferred it, on the morrow.

Perhaps Frances saw the wisdom of submission, for she said no more, and this second night began after the pattern of the former one, but with the maid in Ursula's place in the great chair. The window was set open behind the curtains, the night-lamp flickered and threw strange shadows on the wall; and the mistress of The Mount lay watching them with wide open eyes, sleeping not at all. Truscott was attentive and vigilant; the medicines, the ordered nourishment, were all at hand, but about two o'clock the patient expressed a wish for something else.

"I would like a cup of tea, Truscott. I am so thirsty; and I think if I had it I could sleep. The doctor said I might have tea, provided I did not take it strong. Make a little pot and bring it up; and a cup for yourself as well, as you are watching. I hate to take anything alone."

An unusual sentiment for Mrs. Bethune, and an unusual piece of consideration. The maid obeyed her and brought up the tray, and the two cups were poured out on the small bedside table. When both were ready, the mistress bethought her of a Shetland shawl which lay in the wardrobe; she felt chilly, she said, when she sat up in bed. And as Truscott crossed the room in search of it, and had her back turned opening drawers, Mrs. Bethune leant over and dropped something from her hand into the further teacup—not her own.

It did not hinder Truscott's consumption of the beverage. But when stationed again in the watcher's chair, the light doze she thought she might permit herself now the mistress had settled down, deepened into downright slumber audibly enjoyed. When the first nasal sounds became apparent, Frances drew down the covering with which her own face had been screened, and watched her companion with a curious smile—the self—surrender of the attitude, the dropped-back head, the open nostrils and mouth. Then with careful movement on her own part, she slipped out of bed on the side furthest from the chair, sought that hidden bottle and, without daring to seek for slippers or wrapping-gown, in her night-dress and barefoot, crept softly from the room.

A few steps along the gallery brought her to the white bower, where lay the other self who had become her rival and her enemy. Not till she touched the door, did it occur to her that her victim might have fastened herself in, but the misgiving was hardly felt ere it opened under her hand. Wholly unsuspicious of evil, the girl had not sought even the slight protection of the bolt. The window was open, the room was in deep twilight, the darkness of a summer night which is not absolute. The bed-foot was screened by the tent curtain and behind it Frances waited and listened, till reassured by the soft even breath, just heard from within.

That very room had sheltered Frances Wayland's childhood and innocence, but no such recollection had power over Mrs. Bethune. The past was dead for her since the purer soul withdrew, leaving only the evil. A terrible embarrassment had closed about her, and under its pressure she knew no relenting; the girl must die. This unnatural existence could not be counted as humanity, nor its extinction be the same as murder; it belonged neither to earth nor heaven, and she the begetter had a right to crush it into nothingness if she could find the power. That the stroke which divided the borrowed life, might by the same act sever her own, she did not think at all.

It would, she imagined, be possible to simulate a death from apoplexy, or some such natural cause; and how could she be suspected, if known to be helpless in her bed? She loosened the stopper in her bottle, and crept round beside the sleeper, crouching low; she could dimly see the fair head on the pillow, dark in contrast to the faintly shimmering whiteness above it and around.

No ill-timed headache detained Ursula in London on this second visit, and the return train deposited her at Braxton at two in the afternoon. The branch communication with Saltringham would entail a delay of half an hour; so, pledged as she was to haste, she secured an open fly to drive out to The Mount. The air and the quiet would be welcome after the heat and harass of her journey; a fruitless journey, for no expedient had been suggested for relief. Her old friend received her with every kindness, but wonder and concern over the story she came to tell; the sempstress-medium was bidden for the evening as before, and the scene of three weeks earlier repeated itself in all its leading details. Again the floating torso, wrapped in drapery and dimly lighted, formed over the table in that oppressive darkness; again the swarthy face, Jewish in character, resembling the medium as a brother may resemble a sister, turned full before her, and opened a pair of bright penetrating eyes which seemed to search into her soul. This time she found courage to address it, and speak out her reproach. "We did as you directed," she said, "and terrible harm has followed. There are two bodies and two souls instead of one. Which is the true Frances? What is the link between them? Can it be undone? Can the link be broken?"

The open eyes regarded her with the steady intelligence of one who hears and understands; and then the face floated away, the light paled and vanished, and the medium was entranced as before.

"You were warned," the voice spoke solemnly in answer. "You were told of a possibility, but you were warned. The urgency and the prompting were not mine."

"What was the use of so vague a warning?" continued Ursula. "Why did you not tell me plainly it meant division into a double life, and that misery and confusion would follow? We thought only of dissipated bulk."

The solemn voice went on. "I could not tell you what I did not foreknow. It might have been dissipation and no more, had the woman been one only. And what is, is well. The true soul has gone forth in the fresh embodiment; and the lower animation will not endure, it has had its day and its desire. Be content: there can be no undoing."

A pause followed, and Ursula repeated, "What is the link? Can the link be broken?" though she scarcely expected further speech.

"There is but one life betwixt the two. That is the link. It will continue only for a time. And when it breaks, the true soul will go free."

A Late Confession

"Is that all? Can nothing be done? Have you no message?"

"If I sent a message, it would be of no avail; you will return too late. Shall I tell you what I see reflected as in a mirror; an action present or to come, I know not which, for the time-limit is not shown. I see the Two which were One, and can be One no more. And the hand of the lower is lifted against the higher, but not to prevail. And the Link breaks, so that the higher can go free. It is shadowed as present or to come, but when you return it will be past."

A dark saying, hard to understand. Ursula pondered over it as she drove. One thing was certain; the help Frances craved could not be given, and the confession to the husband must be made, whether credited or no. Had the true soul indeed gone forth, while yet personality remained? It was beyond comprehension, she told herself; she dared not take it in. And if the Oracle spoke truly, which was the wife? The hired conveyance reached the brow of the hill, the driver quickened his pace, and so passed rapidly a similar equipage, on its way to the station. Ursula in her abstraction hardly noticed the occupants. The lady next her wore a conventual dress, and, bending forward in hood and veil, screened the figure beyond, a girl lying back in the carriage as if faint or ill. The man sitting opposite she did not observe at all. Had she seen the second face there would have been instant recognition, as also of Colonel Bethune; Sister Mary Cordelia was unknown to her. Bethune on his part did not notice the open fly, nor the anxious-eyed woman it conveyed, her black dress dusty with travel. Both he and Mary were intent upon their charge, setting out on her journey this time unopposed; and the three had started for London by the time Ursula reached The Mount. The gate was open, the hall door stood wide, an air of something unusual hung about the house, at least to her excited imagination. Salvador's words were again in her ear, "You will return too late."

186

She paid and dismissed the driver; and as she entered, Susan came into the hall, looking startled and distressed.

"Oh, ma'am, they thought you were not coming back. Such dreadful things have happened. My mistress is dying."

"What has been the matter? Is it another attack? Is the doctor here?"

"Yes, ma'am, I think it is the same sort of attack. But it came on in the night, and in Miss Wayland's room. And Truscott says the mistress tried to do something dreadful to the young lady, and might have killed her. Miss Wayland was ill too, but she is better, and they have taken her away."

"Away? Where?"

"I don't know, ma'am, but she has only just gone. She went with a lady like a nun, who is the Colonel's sister; and the Colonel went too—in an open fly. He was dreadfully upset, but he did not go near the mistress."

"Is the doctor with Mrs. Bethune?"

"Yes, ma'am, Dr. Maxworthy is with her, but he says there is nothing he can do. She is quite unconscious, and is sinking fast."

Ursula stayed only to throw off her outdoor things, and went straight to Frances's room, entering softly. Dr. Maxworthy looked up, expecting Truscott.

"Mrs. Adams—you!"

"I have just returned. Can I do anything? Is it really so serious?"

Here was the chance which had slipped through his fingers, suddenly, presented again, the chance of penetrating the mystery, of unmasking the conspiracy, of which he was persuaded this confederate had full knowledge. He stood up on one side of the bed, as Ursula came to the other; the dying woman lay between them.

"You are the last person I expected to see. I thought you had made good your escape."

"My escape!" repeated in amazement, and with the

A LATE CONFESSION

sensation, if not the physical manifestation of recoil. "From what?"

"From the consequences of—this," signing at the white fixed face. "Yes, there is one thing you can do. Put me in possession of the facts, before it is too late. What has she taken? What did you bring her from London when you came before? While there is life there is hope: I may save her yet. You lied to me once. Now I must have the truth."

He was too imperatively in earnest to soften manner or words. The time was ripe for confession; it must follow this demand. And then, standing as at the bar of judgment, Ursula felt the full weight of her difficulty. She had to confess what was incomprehensible, incredible, save to the instructed; and the instructed would be few. Ninety-five people out of any ordinary hundred would scoff at her story, and meet it with utter disbelief. Would this elderly doctor, with his air of rough unfriendliness, of keen suspicion, prove the ninety-sixth who might believe? Her grey steady gaze fronted his, and he, the physiognomist, thought again that she looked strangely unlike a woman who would lie.

"I will tell you all I know. I begged Frances to speak out from the first, but she would not. Yesterday morning she promised me to confess all to her husband if I failed to help her in London. I have failed; and surely the secrecy I swore to her may be broken now!"

"I repeat what I said before. You are bound to speak, it is her only chance of life."

"You ask me what she has taken. I remember you put the question once before, and I replied to it. She has taken nothing. It is what she has done, and what I helped her to do."

"Go on: tell me all."

"I daresay you know nothing and believe nothing about such things as mediums, and sitting in circle, and communications, and the building up of forms—?"

"I know something of it. I know it may be playing with edged tools if handled by the ignorant. What I believe is beside the question."

"I met Frances at a séance in a friend's house, after a separation of years. And when she was in distress about her altered figure, I repeated to her—as I now know, unwisely—a remark the medium made to me about her bulk. That if she 'sat' as they call it, it might be drawn away and dissipated, leaving her slender as she was before. She caught at the notion, and when she sent me to London the first time, it was to inquire of this same medium how the sitting should be managed, and what she was to do."

"And I suppose the medium offered her services, and stipulated for an ample fee?"

"No. Frances wanted her to come to The Mount, but she refused. And the advice it seemed was not hers; she knew nothing about it. It came from a spirit who spoke through her—"

"Ay; they all say that."

"The spirit told us what to do. We were to sit in the boudoir at night, Frances and I, with a curtain drawn between us in the dark, and wait for what might come. The expected effect was that her bulk would disappear. I do not think she quite believed in it, I did not either. But it seemed simple and harmless, and we resolved to try."

"On your honour, was this all?"

"That was all. She was told to bathe before sitting, and to abstain from flesh-meats and from wine, but there was nothing to be taken. The change came on the fourth night—"

"Was it complete at once?"

"Entirely, as you see her now. She spoke of feeling lighter at the earlier sittings, but there was no alteration in appearance. She came from behind the curtain on the fourth night a different creature, wild with delight over the change. Oh, if that had been all!"

"How do you mean?"

"No harm would have been done; nothing but good. And we meant no other; neither she nor I. Of the astounding consequence we had no suspicion—no slightest thought!"

She stopped abruptly, for the remembered scene was plain and vivid before her—the shock again curdled through her blood, as when she drew the curtain, and found the separated figure lying behind it. But her hearer still regarded her with keen expectation and attention, and she was bound to go on.

"I took her to lie down here, for she was weak, and gave her wine; we were instructed so. Then I went back to set the boudoir in order, lest the servants should suspect anything unusual. It was beginning to be light in the morning, we had sat all through that night."

Another pause to master her voice, for it grew hoarse and failed her.

"It was my business to put back the curtain, behind which Frances had been placed. She said something heavy seemed to slip down off her knees when she came to herself and got up. And there, lying on the floor, was the form of a young girl; breathing—alive—!"

"You don't mean the girl who was here? You don't mean Fancy?"

"Yes. I found her there; and that is all we know of her, or can tell. She was naked, and in a deep sleep, lying on her face. There were two bodies where one had been before: two souls, and yet the same. That was what had happened. Then came the question, what were we to do? How could we account for her; who would believe us if the truth were told?"

"It would have been better to tell the truth."

"It was Frances's secret, not mine. And in the first embarrassment she made me swear to keep her counsel;

before I had time to think; before we knew that the girl would prove a real thing with a mind and heart, and not only the breathing form she was at first."

"What did you do with her?"

"I was a guest here, sleeping in the white bedroom—a room which has never been altered since Frances was young, it used in those days to be hers. I put a nightdress on her, and laid her in my own bed; and Frances pretended to the household that a guest had arrived unexpectedly, late at night. We said she was tired and must not be disturbed; and we locked the door and took away the key."

"And she woke a rational being, the Fancy of ten years ago, and thought her engagement was just allowed, and her father was still alive. Is that what you mean to say?"

"Yes. I don't know how you know?"

"I know it from herself. She told me; she spoke of her trouble over what she believed to be the blank of memory. So it was a lie about the cousin of weak intellect?"

"A lie, but not of my devising. What was Frances to do? There was her old self again, in love with Charles Bethune, broken-hearted about her father. The very girl she used to be, as I who knew her know. And yet here was still Frances in her altered body; Frances as the added years had made her—older, harder, grown quite away from all tenderness for the past. Think of the position! You have the whole truth now, whether you believe or disbelieve. I am thankful the responsibility of action is yours and not mine. I am thankful you know all, though the knowledge cannot avail to save her as you thought. Must she die?"

"I can do no more. Her heart is worn out; the strain on it has been over-great, the attacks have followed over quickly. Perhaps it is as well. Trouble will follow if she lives. Do you know what happened in the night?"

"Susan began to tell me—but I was in haste; I did not understand."

"I found her in the girl's room, and without doubt she had attempted murder. A sudden madness we must call it. Better she should go."

A quiver of movement passed over the figure in the bed, which caught the doctor's eye, and his finger sought the pulse. Ursula listened to him with caught breath, and horrified realisation of the tragedy barely prevented. He looked up at her again, the wrist still held, and saw her speechless.

"The responsibility has become mine, as you said just now. And all authority here. I assume it in full till Colonel Bethune returns."

"You wish me to leave the house? I was Frances's guest, and she is dying. Let me stay till all is over, and I will trouble you no more."

"Not so. I ask you to stay here at our disposal. I ask you to be silent as to the mystery, till Colonel Bethune resolves how he will act. Pledge me your word for this."

"I freely give it. Dr. Maxworthy, you have asked for my word. About this other matter—do you believe me?"

How was it possible to answer? The reply was never spoken, for interruption came. The woman on the bed opened her eyes, in a last effort before the vital flame sank in the socket. She looked at the two who fought their duel above her—at Maxworthy who had forced to light her secret, at Ursula who had revealed it, first at one and then at the other, whether consciously or not they could not tell. Her friend bent down to her, and there was a movement of the lips, as if attempting speech, but without sound of words. A last sharp shudder followed, a grey shadow on the face, and the eyes fixed, still open. The end had come.

An hour later Dr. Maxworthy dispatched the following wire to town, addressing Colonel Bethune. "Come at once to 2 Cliff Road—urgent—I want you. Your wife is dead."

XVII.
"WENN DU DAS HERZ HAST—"

Number two, Cliff Road, was an old-fashioned house of time-worn red brick, shouldered on either side by pert modern villas, but preserving the privacy of its own walled garden. The French window of Dr. Maxworthy's bachelor parlour opened at the back on a smooth bowling-green of perfect turf, set round with thick shrubberies and some half dozen forest trees. A paradise for birds, who had the boldness of privileged guests, the great-grand descendants of those fed by Frances in her childhood, twittered in the branches and looked for a daily dole; while the high iron standards and wire netting still surmounted the walls, their defence against the prowling cat. To this parlour in the early morning of the following day, was shown a traveller by the night train, Colonel Bethune.

He had hardly time for impatience, before the doctor came in from his consulting-room to bid him welcome. "You have been prompt, and that is well. Can I give you breakfast?"

"I breakfasted at the hotel. I went there to wash and change. Your wire said 'urgent,' and I took it literally. So

"Wenn Du Das Herz Hast—"

the woman is dead. But why did you call her my wife?"

Dr. Maxworthy looked him full in the face from under his bushy eyebrows; the speculative scientist fronting the man of action. The problem had kept him wakeful in the night watches, querying how this impatient young soldier would brook the tale he had to tell. Young he called him, for to his greater age, Bethune's middle level of life seemed to belong to youth.

"Because I have reason to believe her identical with the Frances Wayland you married, so far as touches corporeity. Hear me out with patience, and remember death divorces, and has swept the main difficulty out of your path. What you could have done had she lived, God knows!"

"I will tell you what I should have done—and I thought we were agreed upon it. I should have charged her with conspiracy and attempted murder, and maintained Fancy's claim. I cannot put her in the dock as she has escaped me by dying, but I have still to reestablish Fancy."

"Sit down quietly, and hear me. It is a position in which we must walk warily, above all for Fancy's sake. How did you leave her?"

"Still weak—tired with travelling, but reviving every hour; happy I think, with Mary."

"Good, so far." Maxworthy in his own mind had questioned whether the derived life would persist, now the source of it was cold. That doubt at least was answered.

"Now, look here. Ursula Adams has come back. She is at The Mount on parole. I have her full confession, given over the deathbed, when 'the woman' as you call her, might still have revived to give her the lie. I had a further talk with her last night, and I wrote out a statement, which she has signed. She is pledged to an absolute silence if we require it, and if you agree with me in thinking it best—in Fancy's interest and your own. I want you to read this over; there are several sheets, as you see, for it is a full account of all

ONE OR TWO

that took place. I will leave you to yourself, for I have got some patients waiting, but by the time you come to the end, I shall be free. We can then discuss what must be done."

The sheets were closely written, but the Doctor's hand was fairly legible. Ursula's signature stood at the end. As Bethune glanced over them, his face changed, then he turned back to the first page, and began to read with close attention.

Nearly an hour went by before Maxworthy returned. The papers lay on the table, and Bethune was pacing the room, his face pale under the sunburn. It seemed difficult at first even to speak.

"Doctor," he said, "you don't mean to say you believe this?"

"I believe Mrs. Adams has told truth so far as she knows it. I commit myself to nothing beyond. I grant you the thing is extraordinary—beyond parallel. But I have studied experiments which lead in this direction, which may be taken as stepping-stones, though they go only part of the way."

"Is it not simpler to conclude she is screening herself, and the conspiracy we thought we knew of only yesterday—behind a lie, which on the face of it this seems to be?"

"If she had chosen to lie, she would have thought of something more probable. Strange as this is, it fits the whole position, Frances's altered bulk, the girl's sudden appearance, her partial memory, her presence here when you were about to return—which would have been fatal to a contemplated fraud—her manifest youth, astounding when we thought of her as eight and twenty and your wife. Mrs. Adams says Frances's identity with the woman lying dead up yonder, can be proved step by step throughout. Mrs. Romer is old and ill, but she still has her wits about her. She joined Frances as soon as she landed from India, and lived with her in France as well as here, and in both places

195

"Wenn Du Das Herz Hast—"

they had friends. Mrs. Romer is a woman of unblemished character, and a near relation of your wife's. She would have nothing to gain in putting forward an impostor. You cannot think of her as privy to any plot which would dispossess the true Frances, and establish a stranger in her place."

"She is above a bribe, and therefore to be trusted, is that what you would say? And this Mrs. Adams, on whose word you rely, was bribed, on her own showing!"

"Frances offered her money, it is true; but it was no large sum, and I think she had earned it. She was at your wife's beck and call for months, as an unpaid companion. And in trying the experiment they did, neither of them intended any harm, or fraud upon you."

"Doctor, don't you see how intolerable this is to me? To have the woman I love made out an unnatural creature—with no human birth, or place in existence—an *Ignis fatuus*, who may fade out of life as mysteriously as she has entered it and leave me wedded to a dream! How can I believe? I would rather fight to the last!"

"I was afraid you might take it so. Make the fullest enquiry, test the thing from every point; there I am entirely with you. But set up no open scandal till you find you have ground to go upon, or it will hamper your action after. If you cannot disprove the Frances who lived with Mrs. Romer and was mistress at The Mount, and still wish to marry Fancy, all your friends will pity you as the victim of an adventuress, and will turn their backs on her. She at least is innocent."

"I would stake my life upon it; and, Maxworthy, I love her. But—marriage! If she is what this damnable story would make out, can marriage be thought of? Suppose there were children, suppose in the years to come they asked me who was their mother? And yet if I forsake her, what will become of her?"

The old doctor looked away from his questioner, out at the green lawn and the fenced garden; perhaps he saw again a little child feeding his birds, with the sunshine on her hair. The fingers of one hand tapped a devil's tattoo on the table, with him a rare sign of disturbance; but he spoke quietly enough, a dry statement to the point.

"I will see to that. My home is open to her; she shall be my daughter by adoption, if she may not be reckoned as Wayland's. I loved her when she was a child. She will need nothing at your hands. But she may break her heart."

"You say you loved her as a child! But the contention of this story is that she has had no childhood. That she is just—built up, as I understand it, out of the substance of another body, and animated by half a soul. If you believe Mrs. Adams—as I never can and never will—how do you reconcile the two?"

"You ask for my theory? It is an imperfect one. I do not expect it to satisfy you. I cannot fully say it satisfies myself. Experiment has proved the existence in some exceptional natures of a double personality, as if a twin birth of soul had been incarnated in one body through lack of material. Let us call them A. and B.—A. is dominant at first, and we know nothing of B. till some accidental shock subverses the system. A. goes under and B. comes to the surface, and confounds the onlookers, who give A. credit for sudden madness. Sometimes B. has been sufficiently awake to share A.'s knowledge and A.'s past, and only manifests a changed disposition and nature; in other cases the B. phase is totally ignorant, and has to be taught to read and cipher like a child. A. may be a saint and B. a sinner, and all that would have turned A. sick with disgust, B. will revel in. (I am not romancing, my friend. Don't think it. I can give you chapter and verse for all I say.) I should contend this was the case with your wife. A. the primal soul, was—is—the child I knew, the girl you loved. Did you not tell me yourself

"Wenn Du Das Herz Hast—"

that Frances changed utterly after an illness in India, an illness brought on by sudden shock, a fall from her horse, brain concussion and long insensibility? She came to herself another person, though the same in body. I quote your very words. Your home was wrecked, your happiness blighted, by the change in her."

"That is true, I grant you. But—"

"Wait and hear me. A. had gone under. B. had come to the surface. Not a malignant B., but heartless and frivolous. B. with a knowledge of A.'s past, but no tenderness for it, and little affection for anybody but herself. A. slumbers dormant, and would have slumbered till the end of life, but that it occurs to B. to try the experiment you know of, hoping to have her substance melted away from her by spiritual manipulation."

"There again you go beyond me into the incredible. Can such a thing be done?"

"I can bear no personal witness, but there is a fair amount of testimony, enough to hang half Saltringham, to the withdrawal of substance from the medium—the alteration of weight upon the scales, and that without vital injury, during the building up of temporary forms. I know nothing about permanent change; but I do not see why it might not be rendered permanent, when the initial difficulty of displacement has been overcome. But to return. B. sits in an improvised cabinet, the process goes forward; the veil of the body is rent, and the superfluous tissue drawn away. But here comes in the unexpected, for the dormant soul is projected also. It has been supposed that every soul is in itself a centre of vital energy, attractive and creative. The fluidic substance, instead of dissipating, gathers to a fresh embodiment. A. and B., separate entities from the beginning, are henceforth separate persons, as, but for an accident of nature, they should have been born. There is my theory. A. is the woman you loved and wedded in the body she shared with B. Where is the horror and the objection to marrying her over again in the body she now has of her own? It is social and fictitious, not radical and natural, so far as I can see."

The haggard-eyed man looked in silence at this expounder of marvels. The explanation sounded plausible, it had a ring of possible truth.

"Mind, I do not urge you. I would not lift a finger to push you two together, with a danger of after regret. Better the child should break her heart now, than live your wife burdened with bitter knowledge. She will be safe with me."

"My little Fancy." There was the choke of a sob in Bethune's voice. "In my arms this time yesterday; loving me; looking for me. If I could only be certain. If it were possible to know!"

How would the struggle end, what would be the far-reaching consequences to both these lives? *"Wenn du das Herz hast,"* Rohtraut's stipulation, might have been spoken also to him. "If thou hast manhood sufficient to dare and do, put out thine hand and take; not otherwise."

Bethune was left alone a second time, for one of the frequent calls which break in upon a doctor's leisure summoned Maxworthy away. He strolled out bare-headed in the quiet garden, treading soft turf under foot, lingering under the shade of trees still delicate with early summer. The little innocent figure which used to frequent that garden, could not be visible to him as to the old doctor's memory; but something of its influence may have lingered, pleading Fancy's cause not ineffectually to a willing heart. He could not understand, he would not believe, but he could dare. That was the result of his musings: anything rather than to lose her. And having dared, there should be no misgiving, no shadow between them. He had set his hand to the plough, and there should be no looking back.

He carried a clearer brow into the house when his host

returned. "Doctor," he said, "I have made up my mind. Fancy shall be my wife."

Neither of these men were prone to express emotion in word or gesture. But the elder put out his hand to the younger, and the close clasp was eloquent on both sides, not only of approval, but of assurance given and received.

"I am not going to take anything for granted. If I can restore her to her place in the world, I will make a fight for it yet. But, should it prove impracticable to reinstate her, I will marry her over again, and she shall have every honour I can give. I mean to follow your advice, and raise no scandal till the case is plain. I intend to see Mrs. Romer, to question this Mrs. Adams; most likely I shall cross over to France, where my wife first made her home. Meanwhile Fancy shall stay with Mary; I would let her come here to you, but it is wiser for the present to keep her away from Saltringham. If I fail, her fortune will be lost to her. Nothing remains but my life-interest, as no doubt you know."

"You have that under her settlement?"

"Yes, and failing issue, she had power to appoint beyond. She made no will in India; if *the woman at The Mount* made none, it will go to her next of kin."

"And be scrambled for among a host of collaterals. Poor James Wayland; he would have been sorry. But loss of money is the lightest evil; you will have gained, I take it, in the truer riches. I wish you God speed, my son, upon your quest, whether you succeed in it or no."

The summer had passed beyond its prime, into those dry heats of August which mark its decadence and age. London grew insupportable, and Sister Mary Cordelia on her holiday carried Fancy to a cool retreat high up the river, among shorn meadows and leafy ways. It was only a farmhouse lodging, but it seemed a Paradise after bricks and mortar, the glare of pavements and the dust of traffic. Some boarded-out children from the slums went with them, and furnished occupation; and there Fancy waited for the lover or the husband who was pledged surely to return. Perhaps Sister Mary knew more than she chose to say; for as the days went on, some secret preparations were in progress, a note of expectation was in the air. And one August evening she took care to leave Fancy alone in the parlour they shared together, at a certain hour when the down train was due at the wayside station, and a pedestrian might reach them by the path across the fields. The sun had just dipped under; but where Fancy sat at work, the western window was still flooded with light reflected from a glowing sky. A firm strong step long unheard came striding through the house; the door opened.

If sometimes to himself he had questioned her reality, he could not doubt it now that her arms were about his neck, her sweet eyes looking into his. She was true woman, real as Eve, externalised out of his substance in a deep sleep, was to her husband Adam. What mattered the mystery which hung, a cloud undissipated, upon the past; from henceforth love should be lord of all. His love, his wife, Bethune called her as he kissed her. Never to part again after the morrow, if she was content to have it so.

He had one arm about her waist, and held her hand in his—the hand with the thin gold circle on the wedding finger, and the cluster of blue stones still worn above. "I shall put on a new ring tomorrow morning," he said, "and we will drop the old one in the river, because everything begins afresh from now. Fancy, will you trust me, will you forgive me? Your knight has been worsted, and yet he claims his guerdon. Just one word about the past, and then we will both forget it—drop it in the river with the ring. I

"Wenn Du Das Herz Hast—"

had to leave that woman in her grave with the right she claimed. I found to tear it off her would avail nothing, and might do far-reaching harm. Are you satisfied, my wife, that it should be so, even to your loss? To believe I acted for the best, having your interests at heart?"

She put up her face to his in mute assurance. Hers was the simple trust, the reliance of a child; he should judge for her. She was abundantly content.

"And because of this it seems better—necessary—that there should be a fresh marriage to legalise our union. You suggested it yourself—in the garden, where we met."

"Yes," she whispered, "but then I had forgotten."

"And now, my darling, you remember?"

"Just that; hardly more than I did. And a very little, dimly, about India. Like a dream; I might have dreamt it all."

"But although you remember, we both remember, there must be a fresh marriage; there are reasons why. I have arranged everything; very early tomorrow at the church here. Dr. Maxworthy is with me at the inn, and he will give you away."

"Dear Dr. Maxworthy; he was always kind."

"He loves you, but that is not wonderful. I could not think it wonderful, could I? But I have something to ask of you, from him. I think you will consent. Knowing we both wish it, both he and I."

"I will consent. Why should you doubt it"—drawing apart to look at him, for a faint uneasiness had crept into his tone, and his face was serious. How would she take what he was going to say? Would she have misgivings, and probe for the reason why?

"He told you once you should be as a daughter to him, now your own father is dead; do you remember? He wishes you really to regard him as your father, your adopted father, from now henceforward. And he wants you to take his name, and be married in it. We thought you would consent, and the license has been made out so."

He unfolded a paper from his pocket, and showed her the names. It was a special permission for the union of two persons, both of age: Charles Bethune and Frances Wayland Maxworthy.

"There, my dearest, you see and you sanction it? Tell me so in plain terms, that I may take word to him—to the old man who loves you. It will only be for this one night. You will have my name again tomorrow."

The strangeness of the request might be realised hereafter; she thought little of it now. It passed as a whim of the old doctor, who was her father's friend. What chiefly impressed her was that her lover-husband should ask her consent with that quiver in his voice.

"Yes," she said. "For tonight I will be Frances Maxworthy."

"For tonight; only for tonight. From tomorrow, and for ever after, you shall be Fancy Bethune."

He lifted the fair face, the face which met him in the rose-garden, and sealed the pledge once more upon her lips with a kiss.

The seasons succeed each other and pass away; and Mother Earth, vital with perpetual youth, spins round the vast track of her orbit regardless of her dust of human atoms, and their lives and fates. That summer faded and dropped into the past, and so did the nine days' wonder over Bethune's second marriage. The Lady Sarahs and the Miss Lancasters of the neighbourhood—and perhaps of wider neighbourhoods—wagged their heads over confidential cups of tea, and discussed it after their manner. "So indecently soon," that was the prevailing comment. "And a girl he cannot have known anything of, if it is true he met her for the first time at The Mount on his return. A poor

"Wenn Du Das Herz Hast—"

relation of Frances Wayland's; and you know, my dear, the Waylands were a very low lot. Frances's good blood was on the mother's side. Dr. Maxworthy adopted her, and I daresay there was a reason; a bar sinister somewhere that is not talked about. She used to be called Wayland, but she was married in his name, didn't you see the announcement? Oh, there was quite a stir about it in Saltringham. Adopted daughter of Dr. Maxworthy; and I expect she will get his money. Not that the doctor is a rich man, but he must have laid by something, and the house he lives in is his own."

And then a further voice. "I would have given Charles Bethune credit for better sense; he is not like a young man to be infatuated with a pretty face. But they say there is no fool like an old fool! You remember Truscott, poor Frances's maid? She has gone to live at Copestone; and Augusta tells me she hears from her that this Maxworthy girl is half-witted. Very pretty of course, and all that, but hardly more than an idiot. She was at The Mount with her for a fortnight, so of course she ought to know; and, what is more, she had it from poor Frances herself."

"I don't know whether Truscott mentioned it, but—" Here the speaker's voice was carefully lowered, and the four chairs drew nearer together. "I heard it on the best authority. There was something curious about the way in which Frances died. She had been very much excited over her husband's return; and soon after he came back she fell down in a fit, and never got over it. You know they were not on good terms. Of course Dr. Maxworthy certified to the cause of death, but perhaps he had this marriage in his eye, even then."

"I don't think anything of that; Frances was subject to fits. She was taken with one in my house before Charles Bethune came home," it was not Lady Sarah who put in her word. "She had been taking strong medicines to reduce her figure. That was what was the matter. It was just her vanity which killed her, neither more nor less."

"Then you heard no whisper that she was jealous of the Maxworthy girl, and that she tried to smother her or strangle her in the night? Frances did her best to send her away when Colonel Bethune was expected, but the girl insisted on coming back. Oh, it was all hushed up, I am quite aware, and Mary Bethune took her away into Retreat before poor Frances died; but there was something in it, beyond a doubt. You don't get smoke of that kind without fire. And now The Mount is let, on a long lease I understand, and the newly married pair have gone abroad. Perhaps we may meet them at Florence. It is very awkward, you know, for Charles Bethune is a connection; but we can hardly be expected to notice her!"

It is not known whether the Bethunes and the Lancasters did encounter at Florence; but another meeting took place on the wedding journey, a tour prolonged over that winter into the early spring.

The short afternoon was drawing to a close, the throng on the terrace had already thinned; the hotel windows began to shine from within, and lights to twinkle in the town below. An elderly lady, returning from a promenade in her bath chair, was apparently a person of consequence, for she had an escort of three persons, her own man and own maid, and a lady-companion in addition. The own man and own maid helped the infirm invalid up the steps into the hotel; the companion looked at her watch.

"I will stay out, I think, for another half hour, if you are not likely to want me. My head aches, and is better in the air."

The excuse was admitted, the three figures disappeared

"Wenn Du Das Herz Hast—"

under the portico, and Mrs. Adams, for it was she, turned back to the terrace.

It appeared to be solitude she wanted, and not exercise. She wrapped her arms in her mantle—for the air, so mild at mid-day, was apt to grow sharp about sundown—and stood leaning against the parapet, lost in thought, or watching the passersby under the lights. They were growing fewer, when a fresh couple turned into view. The outlines of these new figures struck her as familiar, even at a distance. He was tall, with a soldiers upright carriage; he seemed intent on his companion, who was slight and small in figure, while she looked up at him, smiling as she spoke. There was an air of happy confidence, of frank enjoyment, about them both, evident to the most casual observer, it caught and fixed the attention of the lonely woman who watched. They came nearer, walking quickly; and now the delicate face was plain to see, fair as a flower above its setting of dark fur.

As they passed behind her, she heard the girl exclaim to her companion: "Charles, did you see that woman? She looked just like Ursula. Can it be Ursula—Here! I should like to go back—"

And then the man's objection: "No, no; impossible. And see how late it is! I want to get you in."

The couple turned to the hotel. But perhaps Colonel Bethune did not think it so impossible as he professed to do. After a brief interval he emerged from under the portico, and approached the figure in the mantle. Ursula had not moved.

He lifted his hat. "Mrs. Adams, I believe?"

"Yes. I knew you at once." And then, with some latent reproach, "You would not let her speak to me."

"I thought it better not. From no ill feeling, believe me. But there are some things I would have my wife forget. I do not want her to put questions, and she might question you.

I would rather you did not meet."

"I promised silence, and I have kept my promise and will keep it. But you are within your rights; we will be strangers henceforward. I need not ask if she is well and happy, I saw her face."

"She is well, happy also; and it is that happiness I fear to disturb." Ursula turned towards the hotel, and he walked beside her. "You are staying—here?" He indicated the hotel before them; they were almost at the steps.

"Only for one more night. You need not be afraid. We leave early tomorrow, and we have private rooms. I am travelling with Lady Stallington, as her companion. We go on to Nice. She moves from place to place, and is well nowhere, and never will be. But there is always hope."

The tone was bitterer than the words; and Bethune, seeing her face in the illumination of the hall as they entered, thought she looked like one who failed to find the hope of which she spoke. He felt an impulse of pity, but it was only a faint one; men seldom have ruth for a woman who has crossed either their affection or their will. And this woman had been intimately concerned with an episode which displeased him in the past; and instead of helping him to disprove and blot it out, had baffled him by adhering simply to the truth. It not unfrequently happens that plain truth is incredible, and any specious substituted falsehood is easier of belief. So pity was nipped in the bud, and only courtesy remained; such frigid courtesy as may subsist between foe and foe who meet after a passage at arms. The world might continue to be a hard world for Mrs. Adams; it was no business of his or of Fancy's to render her path smoother to her feet. He lifted his hat again with a formal gesture of farewell; and the two turned apart in the lighted vestibule, never more to stand face to face till the secrets of all hearts shall be made known.

THE END

VISUAL GLOSSARY

Mandylion Press revives overlooked nineteenth-century novels. This act of resuscitation is enhanced by placing Mandylion novels in their full visual, material, and affective context. The following Visual Glossary expands upon the text in the form of image references.

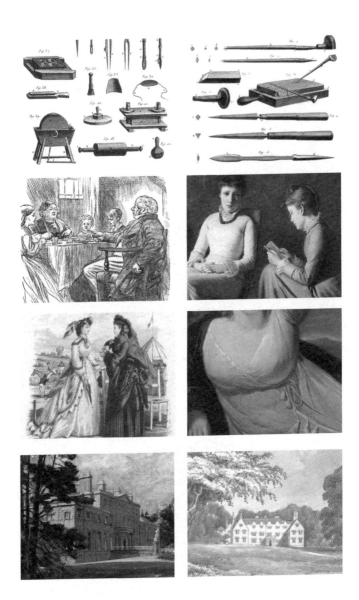

01
Wood Engraving, *The Encyclopedia of Diderot & d'Alembert*, 1765

02
Intaglio Engraving, *The Encyclopedia of Diderot & d'Alembert*, 1765

03
"Mr. Caudle Dines at Home, Cold Mutton!" in *Mrs. Caudle's Curtain Lectures*, Douglas William Jerrold, 1866

04
Two Friends, Oliver Ingraham Lay, 1877

05
Fashion Plate, *Le Moniteur de la Mode*, 1871

06
Henri-Pierre Danloux, late 18th century

07
Malvern Hall, Warwickshire, John Constable, 1820-21

08
Oakley Hall, Henry Edridge, 1860

TOO FAT!!
DR. GORDON'S
Elegant Pills
Cure STOUTNESS rapidly and certainly. State height, weight, and send 2s. 9d., 4s. 6d., or 11s.

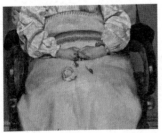

09
Love's Melancholy, Constant Mayer, 1866

10
Havering Bower, Essex (A View of a Country Mansion), artist unknown, 1819

11
West Lodge, East Berghold, John Constable, 1813-16

12
Too Fat! Dr. Gordon's Elegant Pills

13
Figuroids Obesity Cure, 1908, courtesy of Wellcome Collection

14
Untitled, Félix Vallotton (1865-1925)

15
Sick Girl, Christian Krohn, 1880-81

16
Picking Flowers, Auguste Renoir, 1875

17
Five Pound Banknote, 1952

18
*Line of Hansom Cabs at
the Temple Underground
Station*, 1899

19
Plate from *Phenomena
of Materialisation* (1923),
photograph from 1911

20
Plate from *Phenomena
of Materialisation* (1923),
photograph from 1911

21
Plate from *Phenomena
of Materialisation* (1923),
photograph from 1911

22
*Hydropathy; or, the cold
water cure, as practised
by Vincent Priessnitz,
at Graefenberg, Silesia,
Austria*, R.T Claridge, 1842,
courtesy of Wellcome
Collection

23
The Somnambulist,
John Everett Millais, 1871

24
*Drawing Room of The Grand
Hotel*, Tramore Co., 1905

25
Woman Wearing a Bonnet,
Frances Benjamin
Johnston, 1900

26
*A gloved hand making
surgical stitches,* 20th
century

27
*British men and women in
India during the Raj,* artist
unknown, before 1947

28
Fashion Plate, 1897

29
Fashion Plate, 1896-1897

30
How They Met Themselves,
Dante Gabriel Rosetti, 1896

31
A Lady's Dressing Table,
from *Chippendale
Drawings, Vol. II,* Thomas
Chippendale, 1761

32
Sleep, Odilon Redon, 1898

33
Rocking Chair, Hudson and
Brooks, ca. 1823

34
In Bed, Edouard Vuillard,
1891

35
Negligee, 1902

36
Enid, Julia Margaret
Cameron, 1874

37
And Enid Sang, Julia
Margaret Cameron, 1874

38
Geraint and Enid ride away,
Gustave Doré, 1868

39
*Talcum powder, household
salve, face creams, hair
pomade, and face powder
manufactured by the C.L.
Hamilton Co.*, 1921

40
Woman at Her Toilette,
Berthe Morisot, 1875-80

41
The Ring, John White
Alexander, 1911

42
*Below, I saw the vaporous
contours of a human form*,
Odilon Redon, 1896

43
Coronet Corset Ad in *Ladies
Home Journal*, October 1900

44
*Attaque Hystéro-Épileptique
Arc De Cercle*, Jean-Martin
Charcot, 1880

45
*The Radcliffe Asylum,
Headington, Oxford*, J.
Fisher, 1840

46
A Lady's Writing Table, from
*Chippendale Drawings, Vol.
II*, Thomas Chippendale,
1761

47
The Long Engagement,
Arthur Hughes, 1859

48
Dressing Gown, ca. 1885

49
Landscape with Three Monks, Nicolas Poussin, before 1690

50
Mantel Clock, Firm of John and Myles Brockbanks, ca. 1791-1806

51
Haunting, Odilon Redon, 1893-4

52
Croquet, James Tissot, 1878

53
Corset ca. 1900

54
King Death on the Stage. Tight Lacing!, 19th century

55
Psyche's Wedding, Edward Burne-Jones, 1895

56
At the Milliner's, Edgar Degas, 1881

226

57
At the Milliner's, Edgar
Degas, 1882

58
*Miniature portrait of Henri
de Rohan, probably Louis
Charles Philippe Henri
Gérard, comte of Rohan-
Chabot*, Mlle Voullemier,
1840

59
Doctor and Patient, artist
unknown, 18th century

60
La Sylphe, ca. 1900

61
Night Cap, early 19th
century

62
Lotus Hair Color Treatment,
19th century

63
*The phrenologist Bernard
Hollander illustrating with
his own head his system of
cranial measurements,* ca.
1902

64
*Illustrated London
Newspaper* from June 12,
1897

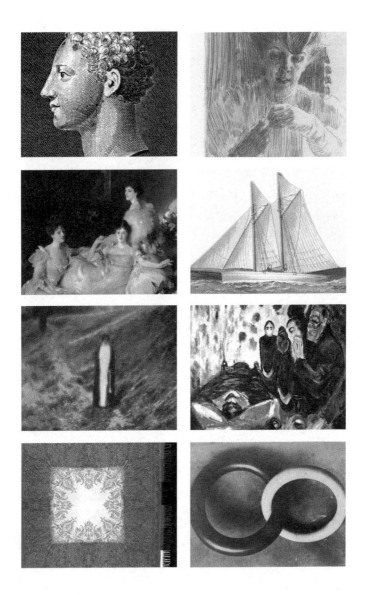

65

Heads demonstrating points of physiognomy, in *Essays on Physiognomy,* Lavater, 1797

66

A Ring, Anders Zorn, 1906

67

The Wyndham Sisters, John Singer Sargent, 1899

68

Schooner Yacht, from the Types of Vessels series (N139) issued by Duke Sons & Co. to promote Honest Long Cut Tobacco, 1889

69

Robed Figure on the Path, George H. Seeley in *Camera Work,* July 1906

70

By the Deathbed (Fever) I, Edvard Munch, 1915

71

Shawl (probably Scottish), 1840-60

72

Passage of Matter Through Matter, Charles Williams, 1878

MANDYLION Press

All of our authors are dead!

1

Other Things Being Equal by Emma Wolf (1865-1932) invites you into the scandalous lives of post-Gold Rush San Francisco's Jewish elite. In this forgotten treasure of a novel, Ruth Levice is a daddy's girl. That is, until she meets a handsome gentile doctor who turns her world upside down...

2

The Gadfly by Ethel Lilian Voynich (1864-1960) delights with this story of Italy's Risorgimento starring a mysterious satirist, a hard-working lady-radical, and a Catholic cardinal with a BIG secret... Millions of copies sold in the Soviet Union and the People's Republic of China!

3

The Morgesons by Elizabeth Stoddard (1823-1902) is an arresting bildungsroman about a weird girl and her even weirder sister growing up in New England. Adored by men, hated by women, and feared by their parents—Cassandra and Veronica Morgeson break the mold.

4

One or Two by H.D. Everett (1851-1923) wins the title of freakiest nineteenth-century novel you've never heard of. Frances Bethune is desperate to lose weight before her husband's return from India—in just two weeks! A slenderizing séance has fatal consequences.

@mandylionpress
www.mandylionpress.com

Mandylion Press

Mandylion Press was founded on New Year's Eve 2022 by Madeline Porsella and Mabel Capability Taylor, who met while studying chairs in graduate school. Mandylion is an independent press that unearths lost literary gems written by women and weirdos in the (very) long nineteenth century. Based between New York City, Connecticut and the fourth dimension, Mandylion Press pairs special stories with inviting introductions producing totally cute books of historical merit.

@mandylionpress • www.mandylionpress.com

Mandylion Press
c/o Mabel Taylor
P.O. Box 84
Cold Spring, New York
10516